SEWN WITH JOY

This Large Print Book carries the
Seal of Approval of N.A.V.H.

SEWN WITH JOY

TRICIA GOYER AND SHERRY GORE

THORNDIKE PRESS

A part of Gale, Cengage Learning

GALE
CENGAGE Learning·

Farmington Hills, Mich • San Francisco • New York • Waterville, Maine
Meriden, Conn • Mason, Ohio • Chicago

GALE
CENGAGE Learning·

LIBRARY OF CONGRESS CATALOGING-IN-PUBLICATION DATA

Names: Goyer, Tricia, author. | Gore, Sherry, 1965- author.
Title: Sewn with joy / by Tricia Goyer and Sherry Gore.
Description: Large Print edition. | Waterville, Maine : Thorndike Press, 2016. |
    Series: The Pinecraft Pie Shop ; #3 | Series: Thorndike Press large print Christian
    romance
Identifiers: LCCN 2016035014| ISBN 9781410494979 (hardcover) | ISBN 1410494977
    (hardcover)
Subjects: LCSH: Amish--Fiction. | Large type books. | GSAFD: Love stories. |
    Christian fiction.
Classification: LCC PS3607.O94 S49 2016b | DDC 813/.6—dc23
LC record available at https://lccn.loc.gov/2016035014

Published in 2016 by arrangement with Harvest House Publishers

Printed in Mexico
1 2 3 4 5 6 7 20 19 18 17 16

To my new daughters
Arianna, Lauren, Jordan, and Florentina
God has planted you in our lives,
and I'm thankful!

— TRICIA —

ONE

Pray not to have easy lives;
pray to have stronger backs.

AMISH PROVERB

Joy Miller gingerly folded one white curtain panel and slipped it into a large paper bag. "I finished these up, Elizabeth. I thought I'd head over to Jeanette Slagel's house and hang them for her. She might want to have them up for tomorrow's sewing frolic."

The sound of a car's horn interrupted the otherwise peaceful scene outside the window of Pinecraft Fabric and Quilts, owned by her older friend Elizabeth and set in the quaint Amish community of Pinecraft within the city limits of Sarasota, Florida. Joy's hands smoothed the white cotton fabric of another panel before slipping in into the bag on top of the first.

A yawn attempted to overtake her, and Joy took another sip of her coffee. She'd

7

stayed up late sewing while the hum of her machine lulled *Dat, Mem,* and two of her four sisters to sleep. Still living at home, her oldest sister, Lovina, managed her pie shop, and her younger sister Faith worked at Yoder's Restaurant and painted landscapes at every opportunity.

Their youngest sister, Grace, who wrote for the *Budget,* still lived at home as well, but she was currently visiting a cousin in Ohio who had just had her first baby. And Hope, her second-oldest sister, was living in Kentucky with her fiancé Jonas's sister. She was also planning her wedding — which reminded Joy that once these curtains were hung, she would have to start on wedding dresses next, for both Hope and Lovina. And then she had to get working on the order of aprons and dish towels for her sister's pie shop, Me, Myself, and Pie.

Would she be the next to be married? Joy released a soft breath. She hoped so.

The double wedding was to be held in Hope's garden at Christmas, just two months away. Joy couldn't think of anything lovelier. Well, except for the fact that someday it might be *her* wedding she was sewing for. Matthew Slagel's handsome face filled her mind. *Is he the one?*

A small smile turned her lips upward as

she thought of Matthew's light hair, his face tan from working in the Florida sun. Mostly she thought of his blue, blue eyes whose color changed according to his mood: light blue when he smiled and a darker greenish-blue when he had work worries on his mind. Her favorite was when they were more of a sea-foam green. They lightened and softened whenever she sat and talked with him, as if his soul were a warm ocean inviting her in.

Elizabeth Bieler leaned heavily on her cane as she exited the back storage room. "I'd say you got those curtains done in record time, and a fine job too." Elizabeth slid onto the stool behind the sales counter. "I just wonder what got into the bishop's wife. It's as if she had a bee in her bonnet, ordering new curtains for the whole house." Elizabeth glanced up at Joy. The older woman's light-colored eyes twinkled with mischief, and Joy guessed her next words. "Of course, I heard it was her son who thought new curtains would be a lovely birthday present for her. That wouldn't have anything to do with his interest in one beautiful and talented seamstress, would it?"

Heat filled Joy's cheeks. "Oh, Elizabeth, I'm sure it had everything to do with it."

"So I guessed right, *ja?*" Elizabeth chuckled. "I can see by the way your face just turned as red as a crab." She settled herself onto the stool at the front counter and grinned. "I don't know. Maybe you're even an official couple now," she said with a teasing tone.

Joy finished putting the third panel into the bag and then placed her hands on her hips. Behind her the air-conditioning unit buzzed, causing cool air to blow over the colorful bolts of red, green, blue, and yellow fabric. Since she'd moved to Pinecraft, Florida, two years ago with her parents and sisters, this small store had become her favorite place, and seventy-year-old Elizabeth her special friend. She tilted her head toward the older lady and chuckled.

"How did you guess?"

Elizabeth's face registered surprise. "You are? I didn't think . . . I mean, I never thought Matthew Slagel would find someone who met his high standards." Her white hair was tucked neatly into her *kapp,* and her face was a map of wrinkles. Of course, Elizabeth didn't call them wrinkles — she called them smile lines. And at Joy's confession, Elizabeth's smile was wider than Joy had ever seen.

"How could you *not* know this is where

things were heading, Elizabeth? You know how much I've been talking about him. You know how often he's stopped by the store in the last few months." Joy lowered her voice. "Then three weeks ago he talked to my *dat*. He just wanted to know if he could call once in a while, but there hasn't been a day since that we haven't spent time together. And last night he made his intentions known."

His intentions to spend as much time with her as possible. His intentions that they'd marry, perhaps next year. "I've nearly been floating, and I can't stop smiling."

"Well, I'll be." Elizabeth placed a hand on her cheek. "And it makes sense. I've never seen such a devout young Amish woman. No wonder he's chosen you. The way you act, think, dress, care . . . I'm sure his parents are pleased. Everyone expects so much from the bishop's family, you know. And to think that my prayers were being answered unbeknownst to me. And the Lord let me live to see it."

"Your prayers?"

Elizabeth's face softened. Her eyes widened and in the inner corners Joy saw a hint of tears.

"Dear Joy, I pray about many things. You know that. God put it on my heart to pray

11

for that building Lovina now owns. I prayed for the pie shop even before the warehouse came up for sale. I prayed for a garden too, even before Hope had a glimmer of an idea that she could make anything grow in the hot Florida sun. And you, my dear, are like the daughter I never had. Of course I've been praying for your future husband. I started within the first weeks you worked here. I'll continue to pray for you." Elizabeth nodded eagerly and closed her eyes. "I'll pray for you, that you will become the woman you need to be in marriage. I'll pray that Matthew will discover God's true purposes for his life too." Elizabeth opened her eyes, and they sparkled with conviction.

Sunlight stretched its fingers through the store and slanted on the counter where Elizabeth sat. The woman's face glowed, and Joy was certain she had a direct line to God. Joy hoped she'd be as devout someday. She wanted a faith that couldn't be shaken and a love for others that couldn't be challenged. Mostly, she wanted to trust God as Elizabeth did. She wanted to learn to pray about everything, knowing God's answers were always best.

I'll pray for you. The words penetrated Joy. Elizabeth spoke the truth. "I'll pray for you" weren't words the older woman spoke lightly. If the Amish woman said it, then she meant it.

"*Danke* for praying. *Danke* for caring." Joy offered a soft hug. "My whole life I've wanted this one life more than anything — to be a wife, to have many kids, to sew for them." She touched her neck with the tips of her fingers and turned to meet her friend's gaze. "Does that sound silly, Elizabeth, just to want to live an Amish life? I mean, Lovina longed for a pie shop. Hope finds her calling in a garden. Yet I just want to have a family, a home, and a buggy, and to live the way my family members have been living for generations."

"Well, there's nothing wrong with that . . ." As Elizabeth's voice trailed off, her brow furrowed and the grooves in her forehead deepened. She opened her mouth as if to speak and then closed it again, pressing her lips into a tight, thin line.

"What's wrong, Elizabeth?"

"Oh, it's nothing really."

"*Ja*, there is something wrong. I've been working for you for a long time — there's *ne* fooling me."

"Joy, I know your family is so thankful that you have never thought about leaving the Amish life — that it is your dream. But, well, out of all those desires you listed, you never mentioned God. Not once."

Joy's mouth opened slightly. She dropped her gaze and looked away. A tight ball formed in her throat. She attempted to swallow it away, but it wouldn't budge. "That's a given."

Elizabeth's gaze penetrated deep, but the older woman didn't say a word. Elizabeth didn't continue, didn't press. Instead, she rose and leaned heavily on her cane. She shuffled to the front of the store to finish the new window display she had started yesterday. It didn't matter that it was easier for Joy to set things up — Elizabeth always insisted on taking care of the front window. She wanted the first view of her store to be just right. Picking up a spool of dark orange tulle, Elizabeth released a heavy sigh.

"I best get going before . . ." Joy tried to think of an excuse for not continuing the conversation, but she knew Elizabeth would see through it. She decided to speak the truth. "If I want to see Matthew during his lunch break, I don't have much time."

"You better hurry then," Elizabeth called, disappointment clear in her tone.

The bag was heavy in Joy's hand as she hurried out, and a strange weight settled on her heart. She tried to swallow her emotions to keep tears from springing up, and her thoughts skittered from anger to a deep knowing that Elizabeth told the truth. How could Elizabeth's one comment cause such a reaction?

I do care about God . . . I do. The words pounded, matching her quickened steps. God was why she was Amish. Why she dressed this way, lived this lifestyle. Wasn't He? Her whole life as an Amish woman was meant to model devotion to God in heaven.

Yet even as she tried to convince herself, the lump of emotion expanded in her throat. The truth was, with Matthew Slagel's attention, she'd thought little of God lately. She lived her life for Him as she always had, but she'd not given much time to Bible reading and prayer. The wonder and holiness of God hadn't crossed her thoughts. But that was to be expected, right? The newness of any romantic relationship was all-consuming. And surely God understood. He brought Matthew into her life. Surely staying true to her Amish beliefs with someone who cared strongly about the same was God's plan for her.

Wasn't it?

Sewing Enhances One's Character

Outside of the practical advantage of being able to use the needle, the mental training through hand and eye has proved to have a permanent effect on the character. The training of the hand makes it dexterous in other employments. Habits of thrift, cleanliness, patience and accuracy are inculcated, economy taught, and the inventive faculty developed . . .

An enthusiastic and progressive teacher can, through sewing, make freer and more capable beings of her pupils and help round out their characters.*

* Mary Schenck Woolman, *A Sewing Course for Teachers* (Washington, DC: Frederik A. Fernald, 1893), 3.

TWO

Associate yourself with people of good
quality, for it's better to be alone than in
bad company.

AMISH PROVERB

The sun beat down on Matthew Slagel's
hat, shoulders, and back as he framed the
new bedroom being added on to one of the
quaint cottages in Pinecraft. It was warm
today — a warmth that didn't seem right in
late October. Still, the heat was nothing like
it was in the summer. On summer days the
humidity made it hard to breathe, hard to
work.

He'd been doing construction in the three
years since he'd moved back to Pinecraft to
be close to his parents. His only respite during the summer months was retreating into
the small workshop he'd set up in their
garage. With the cool air of the air-
conditioning blowing on him, he often lost

17

himself in the wood, in the grains and designs. It was a clean-smelling work, and the sounds of his tools were his music. In his workshop he moved at a slow pace, with no worries about construction deadlines, work crews, or deliveries. He had found his greatest peace within the workshop until recently, when something — or rather someone — drew his attention away.

Matthew smiled at the changes in the last few months. Smiled at the emotions he didn't think he'd ever feel. A love was growing deep for a woman, and for the first time in his life something mattered more than his workshop. It was unexpected. It was wonderful.

He glanced at his watch. A hint of excitement urged him to hurry, but he held himself in check. Joy said she'd try to meet him during his lunch break at his parents' house. She was delivering his mother's new curtains, and they'd have time to see each other, to chat. It hadn't been hard to talk his *mem* into new curtains — a gift from him for her birthday. He'd urged her to order what she wanted and he'd cover the bill. It was a good excuse for Joy to spend more time with his mother — time both women seemed to appreciate.

With sure fingers, Matthew placed one

last nail against the two-by-four, sank it with one hit, and then stepped back, figuring this was as good a place as any to stop. He took a deep breath. The aromas of ocean breezes, citrus, and the gardenia bush on the side of the house were welcoming.

On the other corner of the addition, Abraham John still pounded nails in a steady beat. Abraham whistled one of the gospel songs he'd heard on Birky Street the other evening, and Matthew hated to interrupt his friend's work.

Matthew dropped his hammer into the top of his toolbox and strode toward his coworker. "I'm heading out. You should get yourself some lunch."

"Yep. I will. Just want to finish this header."

Matthew moved toward the framed section that would soon hold a door. Abraham's eyes followed him.

"You have an extra hop in your step today, if I say so myself. Off in a hurry too." Abraham was Matthew's age — late twenties — and was also still single. But unlike Matthew, Abraham sometimes acted more *Englisch* than Amish, heading down to Siesta Key Beach to play beach volleyball and flirt with the *Englisch* girls. Abraham had a mischievous look in his eye, and Matthew was almost afraid to tell him about Joy. The last thing he wanted was for Abraham to show her attention — the wrong type of attention.

Matthew took a handkerchief from his pocket, pulled off his hat, and wiped his brow. "It's a *gut* day, that's all. And I'm ready for lunch."

Abraham shook his head, not believing him. "So . . . is *she* that young lady you were talking to after church on Sunday?"

Matthew paused. He cocked one eyebrow. "She?"

"She'll be there, won't she? That pretty young woman? That's why you're in such a hurry." Abraham grinned. "*Ne* man smiles that big because of a sandwich."

"I saw my *mem* making a Florida orange broccoli salad," Matthew offered. "Maybe I'm in a hurry for that."

"*Ja,* but even that doesn't account for the glimmer in your eyes. She's one of the Miller girls, *ja*? Are you courting?"

The twinkle in Abraham's eye was one of excitement for his friend, not interest. Matthew's defenses dropped. A chuckle escaped his lips, and he was amazed how Abraham had been paying so much attention without saying a word. Had everyone in Pinecraft figured it out? It was a small place. With only three hundred year-round residents, everyone knew everyone's business. But they all took care of each other too, when someone needed help or encouragement. Those were two sides of the same coin, he supposed.

Matthew clucked his tongue and shook his head. "I'm not so sure what question you want answered first, but *ja,* I've been fancy on Joy Miller for a while, but things have gotten more serious of late. She's going to be at my parents' house hanging curtains, or at least that's the plan."

Abraham's whistling stopped. "Sounds like your parents like her then." His shoulders squared. More than once Matthew's father had sat down with Abraham to discuss his interactions with *Englisch* girls. His father took his role as bishop seriously.

"*Ja,* both *Mem* and *Dat* approve of Joy — what's not to approve of? But I'm curious," he teased. "Why do you ask? Are you interested in one of the other single sisters? Both Faith and Grace have yet to have a beau."

"Nice try attempting to turn the attention to me." Abraham removed his hat and wiped his brow with the back of his hand, causing his dark hair to cling to his hairline with sweat. "It's just that a lot of folks around here have thought you'd be a bach-

21

elor for life."

Matthew ran a hand down his face. "Am I that homely? Thanks a lot."

"Not because of you, but of your parents. You have to admit your father has high standards."

"He's the bishop. That's his job."

"*Ja.* Just tellin' you what's been said. And" — he shrugged — "they're also saying your standards are right up there with his." Andrew turned back to his work. "But since you seem to have found the perfect Amish girl, there shouldn't be a problem now, should there?"

Florida Orange Broccoli Salad

Salad

1 head broccoli, chopped into bite-size
   pieces
1/2 cup sliced red onion
1 11-ounce can mandarin oranges, drained

Dressing

1/2 Cup Salad-Dressing Mayonnaise
1 Tablespoon Vinegar
3 Tablespoons Sugar
1/2 Tablespoon Vegetable Oil
1/2 Teaspoon Salt

Mix dressing ingredients in a bowl. Toss with broccoli, onion, and oranges just before serving. Makes 6 servings.

THREE

Success in marriage is not only
finding the right person; it's being
the right person.

AMISH PROVERB

Something from outside caught Joy's eye as she smoothed the white fabric of the curtains. It was an Amish bachelor striding down the road. Not just any Amish bachelor, but Matthew Slagel, the bishop's son and the man she was falling in love with. She watched from the window as Matthew walked toward his parents' house. He was tall, lean, toned, and handsome. The sleeves of his homemade blue shirt were rolled up, showing the muscles of his forearms, and the two top buttons of his shirt were undone, allowing her to peek at the tanned skin of his neck. She dropped her chin, embarrassed by the thoughts running through her mind. Thoughts of being kissed by him. Being held.

"Oh, those look lovely!" His mother's voice broke through her thoughts.

Joy turned, caught by surprise. She'd been unaware that the bishop's wife had walked into the living room. Had she seen Joy staring at her son? Heat filled Joy's face, and she quickly turned back to the curtains. If the woman could read her sensuous thoughts she no doubt would quickly usher Joy out of her home. But she seemed to be focused on her birthday gift instead.

Joy dared to turn and peer into the older woman's face. "The curtains do hang nicely, don't they? I'm so glad you like them."

If Jeanette Slagel had noticed Joy's gawking, it hadn't bothered her. The only emotion on the woman's face was happiness.

"*Ja,* just look how much those curtains brighten up this room! So white, and just perfect."

Joy stepped back to take them in. They provided a freshness to the place and were indeed just what the bishop and his wife expected of everything in their lives — flawless, unmarred, and untainted.

"Oh, I see Matthew coming. I have some seafood chowder on the stove and biscuits. I also made his favorite broccoli salad. Would you like to stay for lunch?"

Joy took a deep breath. "Seafood chowder? Is that what smells so wonderful?" She took Jeanette's hand in hers. "If it's not too much trouble." Guilt tinged the corners of her heart. Both she and Matthew had hoped for this invitation, expected it. No Amish woman in Pinecraft would fail to offer lunch when a guest happened to be in their home near noontime.

The front door opened, and Matthew walked in. Joy found him stunning despite the fact he was sweaty and sprinkled with sawdust.

"Let me just get out another bowl." As Jeanette hurried toward the kitchen, she called back to her son. "You better wash up, Matthew, and don't forget to clean under your nails."

Joy chuckled at the chiding.

"Ja, Mem." He offered Joy a humored grin and then watched his *mem* retreat before hanging his straw hat on the hook by the front door. But instead of hurrying to the bathroom to wash up, he moved closer to Joy. The tenderness and care in his blue eyes caused her to squirm. His hair where his hat brim had been was pressed in a circle. His forehead was moist with perspiration, and even his lashes spiked from moisture.

Her heart hammered. Prickles moved up

and down her arms as if she'd just been poked by a thousand tiny needles. "Hot out there?"

"Just a little, but I've already forgotten about the misery of it."

"Really, how?"

He offered a crooked smile and kept his eyes fixed on hers. "Oh, just seeing you makes the whole day better. I'm glad you're here. You must have been at the shop extra early to see that those curtains got done."

"I was at the shop before six and . . ." Should she admit she even skipped breakfast to make sure she got her sewing finished in time to see him? Her stomach offered the smallest growl. "I'm just happy it worked out. It made all the hard work worth it."

Joy dropped her chin. Matthew tipped it up with one finger and studied her face before a grin turned up the corner of his mouth. "You know how to make a man feel loved, you know that?"

Her lips parted slightly, and then closed again. In the three weeks they'd been spending so much time together, neither had used the word *love.* Joy had considered it. She'd believed the growing feelings she had for Matthew were love, and hoped he felt the same. But to hear the words . . . she released a heavy sigh.

"I'm glad you feel that way. Because I —"

"Matthew, *kume* eat your lunch before you run out of time. You know how your *dat* feels about long lunches."

Joy looked around, for the first time realizing who wasn't around — Matthew's father, the bishop.

"Your *dat* isn't here?"

"*Ne.* There's a meeting. It seems a television show about the Amish has permits to film in Pinecraft, and some of the men wanted to talk to *Dat* about it."

A giggle burst from Joy's lips. "*Amish* and *television.* Those are two words that don't usually go together." She motioned to the kitchen and followed as Matthew led the way. "Do you know what this television show is all about?"

He turned to wash his hands in the kitchen sink as his *mem* placed a pot of steaming chowder on the table.

"Not really." He shrugged. "That's what my *dat* is going to find out. And if he can, put a stop to it."

They ate sitting side by side, with Matthew's *mem* sitting across from them, rattling off a list of folks who'd just arrived for the season on the Pioneer Trails bus. "Lydia Hershburger traveled down from Lenora, Minnesota, to Akron, and then she caught

28

the bus with her sister's family. Lydia and I went to school together ages ago. Still, when she got off the bus I nearly ran to her. I would have recognized that face anywhere, especially when she smiled and displayed those two matching dimples."

They listened for a few more minutes, and then Matthew rose. "Well, make sure you tell everyone hello for me, *Mem.* It'll be *gut* to see everyone at church on Sunday." Then he looked at Joy and nodded his head toward the side door.

Joy stood and turned to her host. "*Danke.* Lunch was delicious. Can I help with the dishes?"

Jeanette waved a hand. "Tsk-tsk. You have to be joking. It's *ne* trouble at all. Three bowls. How hard is it to wash three bowls? Besides, I believe my son wants to show you something in the garage." She lowered her voice. "But please don't tell me what it is. My birthday is coming up, and even though he already gave me the curtains, Matthew insists he has one more gift for me. I want to be surprised." She squinted up at her son with a wrinkled nose and wide smile.

"*Mem,* I told you I'm making you a wooden spoon."

"Oh, *gut.* Maybe I'll be able to keep this one for cooking. I never could manage it when you were growing up. Either I used them for smacking your bottom or you used them to dig in the dirt."

Joy crossed her arms over her chest. "Oh, was he a willful one?"

Jeanette chuckled again and checked the hair at the back of her neck. *"Ne,* that was a joke. It was just the opposite. Matthew has always been *gut.* Too *gut.*"

"Too *gut*? I've never heard a mother say that before."

"Well, maybe not too *gut,* but he never did give me a lick of trouble. His older brother, Will, spent enough time bent over my knee for the two of them. But Matthew did like to use all my spoons to dig in the dirt!"

Matthew shook his head, and Joy couldn't help but laugh. Within the small community of Pinecraft, the bishop's family was often treated differently. Everyone was on their best behavior around them. It was nice to see they were ordinary people who enjoyed teasing each other.

Inside the garage, it was dim, the only light coming from a small side window. It smelled of sawdust, oil, and glue. How many projects had Matthew finished in this place? Was giving her a peek into his workshop also giving her a peek into his heart?

30

When Matthew flipped a switch, the overhead fluorescent buzzed and white light flooded the space.

That was another way Pinecraft was different from any other Amish community. Because of the need for air-conditioning in the Florida heat, residents and visitors depended on electricity. Joy inhaled a deep breath and then blew it out slowly. This was Matthew's space, and it meant a lot that he wanted to share it with her.

He shut the kitchen door behind them, and it closed with a click.

"So are you working on something for your *mem*? Another gift?"

"*Ja,* a recipe box." He moved to a high shelf and pushed aside a can of varnish. He pulled down the wooden box and handed it to her. It was larger than most recipe boxes she'd seen, and intricately put together, like pieces of a jigsaw puzzle.

"I made the box wide and deep enough for a magazine page to be folded in half. My *mem* has a habit of tearing recipe pages out of magazines and then folding them super small so they can fit into the box she has. Then she has to unfold each one to find the recipe she's looking for. I'm close to being done."

"I think you're on to something. It's

31

wonderful. I'm amazed, Matthew, by your work. It seems that big or small, you include so many details."

"*Ja*, well, I still have to stain it. But the best part isn't just the box, but what will go into it. I wrote my aunts and cousins and asked them to send recipes. I even rented a box at the post office so my *mem* wouldn't become suspicious of all my mail."

"You put a lot of thought into your plan. It sounds like she's going to love the present."

"She will, and I'm glad. Things get so busy around Pinecraft when the buses start showing up, and she seems to get short-changed every year when her birthday comes around."

Joy turned the recipe box over in her hands before handing it back to him. "You must love woodworking very much. Your face just lights up when you talk about it."

"Whenever I'm in my workshop I feel as if I'm working alongside God, turning trees into useful things. I . . ." He looked at her sheepishly. "I hope that doesn't make me sound like a fool."

"*Ne*, just the opposite. I'd love to hear more. Did you grow up learning how to make things out of wood?"

He placed the recipe box back on the

32

shelf. "You could say that. Before my parents moved to Pinecraft and my *dat* became the bishop, we lived up in Indiana. My grandparents lived right down the road, and my grandfather had a lumberyard out in back. My brothers liked it because they used to climb all over the logs, but I loved looking at the wood. My grandpa would show me a board and ask me what type of tree it was from. I was five or six, and I'd get it right every time." As he spoke he reached over and took her hand, wrapping his fingers around hers.

Warmth spread up her arm, and the connection was strong. She loved getting these glimpses into his soul, into his life. "I bet it was beautiful there."

"Oh, it was. There were walnut trees, some two centuries old. Elms, oak. Sometimes new green shoots would grow out of the bark of felled trees. My grandfather taught me how to strip bark and square logs to prepare them for sawing." He chuckled. "And when I got in trouble, I'd have to fill buckets with dried chips for his stove. I never told him, but I didn't really mind that consequence." He ran his thumb over the back of her hand and looked tenderly into her face. She wondered if he was considering kissing her. Or would he wait? After all, his mother was just on the other side of that door and could open it any minute.

"Sounds like the perfect playground."

"I thought so."

Reaching up, Matthew placed his free hand on her shoulder. Then, tenderly, he let it slide down her arm. Butterflies danced in her chest. Realization dawned that he was waiting for her to respond, waiting for any sign that she was willing to be kissed.

Yet the sound of the water running in the kitchen sink and dishes clanking caused her shoulders to stiffen. Instead of leaning forward or lifting her chin, she placed her free hand on top of his, sandwiching his hand between her palms.

She noted the smallest bit of disappointment in his gaze.

"And how about you?" he asked. "You've told me a bit about your place in Ohio before. Was it hard moving to Florida?"

"I know my sisters have had a harder time. Hope left her garden, and Lovina really struggled for a while before she decided to open that pie shop. Faith is still trying to find her way, I think. And Grace . . ." She grinned. "Grace makes friends wherever she goes."

"And you?"

"Truthfully, I feel like I've been the most

blessed. God gave me a gift when I got the job at the fabric store. Is it strange that a woman in her seventies is my best friend? There are sewing frolics here too. And then I met you." She brushed her thumb against his in a playful caress. It was a simple gesture, but excitement glimmered in his eyes all the same. "But what about you? Do you miss being up in Indiana?"

"To tell you the truth, I'd like to return someday." His voice was husky, low. "My brother bought my grandfather's place a while back, right before he passed, but Will has made it clear that the lumber mill is mine. And he'll give me some land too, to build a house of my own."

Her eyes must have widened in surprise, for he hurriedly added, "All in God's perfect time, of course. How about you, Joy? Do you want to spend the rest of your life in Pinecraft, working at the quilt shop?"

She hadn't really given it much thought, but seeing the hope in Matthew's gaze, she knew her answer. "I like the idea of living someplace like Ohio or Indiana. I'm more like Hope, I suppose. Hope never planned on making Pinecraft her home permanently. I suppose I have *gut* things to look forward to, whether it's here for a season or there for a lifetime."

He squeezed her hand tighter, as if he never wanted to let go. "So you don't mind the cold winters up north?"

Joy chuckled. "I'm a seamstress, remember? Winter is my favorite time of the year. I love sitting in front of a cozy fire, sewing." She squared her shoulders, knowing she spoke the truth. Knowing what he was asking and knowing what she was promising.

"That's *gut* to know." He released her hands and let out a contented sigh. "And what about Lovina?"

"Oh, she's perfectly happy here in Pinecraft. I've never seen her so happy."

"Because of the pie shop?"

"Well, that, but my guess is Noah Yoder has something to do with it too. We're all looking forward to their double wedding with Hope and Jonas."

"And she'll stay in Pinecraft to help care for your father. That's why your family moved down, *ja*? Because of his health?"

Joy glanced up at him curiously. Had he been worried she'd have to stay in Pinecraft to care for her father? She hoped her next words wouldn't disrupt the mood, but she had to be honest about her obligations.

"My father's doing well, but if anything happens, I'll do my part. All of us sisters will."

"That makes sense." He smiled, but the smile didn't reach his eyes. "Speaking of doing my part, I have to get back to work, but would you meet me later for pie?"

"Of course, Matthew." She studied his eyes and offered him a soft smile that she hoped reaffirmed their closeness. "I can't think of anything more I'd like to do. I'll be counting the minutes."

Seafood Chowder

2 1/2 cups diced potatoes
2 cups carrots, chopped
1 cup celery, chopped
1 cup onion, diced
4 cups water
1 pound imitation crabmeat
1 pound shrimp (can be less)
4 teaspoons chicken base
1/2 cup butter (no imitations)
3/4 cup all-purpose flour
2 cups half-and-half
2 cups milk
salt and pepper
Old Bay Seasoning

Using a large stockpot, cook first four ingredients (through onion) in 4 cups water until soft. Add crab, shrimp, and chicken base. In separate pan, melt butter. Stir in flour, half-and-half, and milk. Cook on medium-low heat until thickened. Add to first mixture. Sprinkle with seasonings to taste.*

* Mrs. Bill (Ruth) Gingerich, Sarasota, Florida, in Sherry Gore's *Simply Delicious Amish Cooking* (Grand Rapids: Zondervan, 2013), 146.

Four

For faith to prosper, it must experience impossible situations.

AMISH PROVERB

Joy had a hard time sleeping. She could blame it on *Mem*'s wonderful ham loaf she had for dinner or the pie that topped her off, but that wasn't the truth. She couldn't sleep because of her time with Matthew. Tonight, as they ate pie, he talked more about his grandfather's farm near Shipshewana and the house he wanted to build. Surely he wouldn't talk to her about all these plans without wanting to include her in them, would he?

She'd had a happy life, but the emotions she felt today overwhelmed any she'd ever experienced.

After returning home, Joy struggled with chatting with her parents and sisters. Matthew consumed her thoughts, and a pang of guilt struck as she remembered what Elizabeth had said. She had always loved God it seemed, but not with such an all-consuming love that she lost care for all else. Surely these feelings for Matthew would die down. How would she ever piece another quilt? How would she sit with the other women to work on the quilt top for Hope's wedding quilt tomorrow? How would she ever sleep while seeing Matthew's face and remembering his touch?

She rolled to her side. She'd have plenty of time to think about all these things tomorrow. *Sleep, Joy, sleep.* But even as she chided herself, a loud rumbling interrupted her thoughts. The vibration of it caused the bedroom window to rattle. It sounded like a large semitruck, but what would a large truck be doing in the middle of the night on a small residential street in an Amish community?

"What is that?" she muttered to herself.

She squinted in the dimness, attempting to see whether Faith stirred in the twin bed next to her. "Do you hear that?" she whispered to her sister.

But she received no reply. Faith slept peacefully. That's how it had always been. They could be in the middle of a family gathering, with adults talking and children running around, and Faith could climb onto the sofa, tilt her head back, and fall asleep as if she were in her own bed.

"Faith," she whispered louder.

Joy reached over and lit the small lantern on the side table. Even though they had electricity in their house, both she and Faith used their lantern at night. It was more peaceful. It made Pinecraft feel more like their home in Ohio.

"Faith, do you hear that?" She sighed. "Never mind. Go ahead and sleep. You should just be glad night courting isn't popular anymore, because you'd never get a date." She giggled at her own joke, imagining Matthew tossing stones at her window, urging her to sneak to the living room to talk. *Dat* had admitted bed courtship was popular when he'd dated *Mem.* He'd come to her house after everyone else had retired for the night, and they'd sit on her bed and talk while everyone else was asleep.

Joy shook her head, glad that practice had grown less popular over time. No, she couldn't trust herself if she was sitting next to Matthew on her bed at night. She'd let her mind wander for certain then, further than she should ever allow it to go before marriage.

Outside the rumbling grew louder. Joy

41

climbed from her bed. She put her face to the window, cupping a hand around her eyes. Still not able to see where the rumble was coming from, she turned off the lantern and tried again. Bright headlights filled the narrow roadway, and a rented moving truck rolled past. It was the largest size she'd ever seen. Someone was moving to Pinecraft, but what were they doing at this hour? And on this street?

Now illuminating the yards and small cottages that lined its path as well, the truck stopped just in front of her house, and a light in the cab flipped on. They were *Englischers,* of course. Two men, and they appeared to be lost. The passenger wore a red ball cap and was talking on a cell phone while looking at a map spread in front of him. His free arm flailed in anger as he spoke, but the driver seemed unfazed. He yawned and stared straight ahead, tapping his fingers on the steering wheel to some beat she couldn't make out.

Joy rose and slipped on her bathrobe. She touched her sleeping kerchief, making sure it was in place. The men had no idea where they were going. That was for certain. She didn't want to go out there, but if someone didn't help them, they'd wake the whole neighborhood.

Joy considered putting her dress back on, but that would take too long. Instead, she adjusted her sleeping kerchief one more time and hurried toward the hallway closet, pulling out her *dat*'s winter jacket. She slid it over her nightgown and robe. The heavy wool coat wasn't used much in Pinecraft, but it was useful now. It hung to her knees, and she zipped it up. It wasn't pretty, but it was modest. It would do.

The passenger was still talking on the cell phone when she hurried forward. The truck's cab was high, and Joy stretched to knock on the window. The man jumped, but as he peered down at her, the anger and surprise on his face morphed into confusion. He rolled down the window and leaned out.

"Yes?"

"Are you lost?"

He eyed her, taking in her coat, her face — and then her kerchief.

Joy touched it self-consciously. "Do you need directions?"

He still didn't answer her, and she pointed up to the map he held. "If you give me the address I might be able to point you in the right direction."

He motioned down the street. "Is this Pinecraft?"

The question surprised her. Most *Englischers* had no idea about Pinecraft. No idea of the small Amish community within Sarasota.

"Yes, it is."

"Are you Amish?" Before she could answer, another question rushed out. His brow furrowed. "And do you always wear that scarf when you sleep?"

His second question didn't surprise her. Multiple times a day she was asked if she was Amish, but the third disturbed her. Why did he want to know about her head covering? Why did he care?

She touched her sleeping kerchief. That was one thing different about living in Pinecraft, especially working in the fabric store. Back in Ohio, people were used to the Amish and their ways, but here in Florida they weren't as used to the Amish, and the ways of the Plain people were a mystery. The *Englischers* asked a lot of questions. She decided to answer him as simply as she could.

"I am Amish, and this is my sleeping kerchief. I wear a prayer *kapp* during the day and this at night, in case I want to pray."

"In case you want to pray?"

Joy covered an ear by pressing a hand against the side of her head and then

44

pointed to the truck. "Listen, I don't mind answering your questions, honestly I don't, but if you haven't noticed, this street is lined with houses, and everyone is sleeping — or at least trying to. And that truck is as loud as a freight train. So if I could just help you with directions . . ."

"Yes, of course." He looked down at a piece of paper and read the address to her.

She tilted her head in surprise. "Really? That's where you're going?"

"That's what my assistant told me. She said it's a small house . . ."

"It is, but there isn't really anyplace to park your truck there. I suppose you can park it in the Tourist Church lot. It's close enough." *Then you can figure it all out yourself tomorrow,* she wanted to add.

"Can you show me? If you have a car we can follow . . . I mean, if you can point the way or something."

"Point the way." She tried to think how best to explain the way so they would wake up the least amount of people as the truck rumbled past.

"If it's not too much trouble." He grinned at her, as if attempting to charm her. The man was handsome, but he didn't hold a candle to Matthew. His eyes had dark circles under them. He yawned. The sooner she

45

helped him, the sooner he could get to sleep. Then maybe his charm would work on someone other than her. And maybe this loud truck wouldn't be here long enough to wake the rest of the community.

"It's not too far. I'll ride my bike. Just follow me."

Joy hurried to the carport and pulled out her bike. As she sat on it, she realized her nightgown skirt wasn't as full and flowing as her dresses. It was nearly impossible to straddle the bike seat and pedal, so she hiked up the nightgown just a little. Her bare legs from the calf down showed, but it was the only way. Heat flooded her cheeks, and she was glad the men didn't have a clear view of her face as she rode in front of the truck. She showed more of her legs than she wanted to. Her parents had no idea she was riding off and leading two strangers across Pinecraft. But what else could she do?

After taking a few turns, she finally pulled in to the Tourist Church lot and waited. When the truck was parked, the men got out and walked toward her.

"The house is right down there. The one on the corner. You just passed it," she called, not getting off her bike. They continued forward, and she wondered if she should just ride away, but they paused far enough away not to worry her.

The passenger was just a few inches taller than she was, and he walked slightly bent over as if weary to the core. He held out a large bill.

She eyed it and wrinkled her nose. "What's that for?"

"For your help."

He wants to pay for my help? She placed her foot on the bike pedal. "Oh no, that's not necessary, really. I am glad to help." *And I'll even be more glad to be back in my room, in my bed.*

He slipped it inside the pocket of the Western-style shirt he wore. His sleeves were rolled up at the elbows, but his arms weren't thick and muscular like Matthew's. He wore a watch on his right wrist, and it looked expensive. On both hands he wore a few rings, something she'd never seen on a man.

"I'm just glad I can help. I best get home." She pulled out and offered a quick wave.

"I'd like to see you again. If it's possible. I just have questions, about that sleeping hat . . . and maybe a few other things."

Joy paused again. "Sure. I'll be at the fabric store tomorrow. I work there."

"Can you give me an address?" He pulled

47

out his cell phone as if he was going to type it in.

"You don't need an address. Our community is only eight blocks square. Anyone will know." She rode off then, before he could ask any more questions. From behind her he was calling out something else, maybe a thank-you, but with the soft wind whipping around her face, it was hard to be sure. The sooner she could get home the better. She just hoped the truck hadn't woken up anyone else, hadn't made them look out their windows to see her riding her bike to this house — in her nightgown, of all things. And that news of it wouldn't get back to the bishop.

The wind blew on her face, and a cold shiver raced down her spine. No, that wouldn't do at all.

Ham Loaf

2 1/2 pounds ground ham
1 cup crushed saltines
2 1/2 pounds ground beef
1 cup graham cracker crumbs
3 eggs, beaten
2 teaspoons Lawry's seasoned salt
1/2 cup milk
1 1/2 teaspoons salt

Glaze

3/4 cup brown sugar
1/4 cup water
1/2 tablespoon mustard
1/4 cup vinegar

Pineapple Sauce

1 1/2 cups pineapple juice
1/2 cup brown sugar
2 tablespoons unflavored gelatin
1 teaspoon dry mustard
1/3 cup dark corn syrup
2 tablespoons vinegar

Preheat oven to 350. In a small bowl, mix glaze ingredients. In a larger bowl, combine ham and next seven ingredients (through salt) and half of glaze. Mix well and put in loaf pan. Shape into loaf like meat loaf. (It can also be baked in a roaster pan.) Bake 1 hour, basting with glaze every 15 minutes. Serve with pineapple sauce over the top. For variety, shape into balls and bake on cookie sheet about 15 minutes. Serves 15 to 20.*

* Ann Mast, Sarasota, Florida, in Sherry Gore's *Simply Delicious Amish Cooking* (Grand Rapids: Zondervan, 2013), 108.

FIVE

Life is like a calendar — when a page is turned, it's gone. No matter what you do next week, no yesterdays will dawn.

AMISH PROVERB

Alicia Lampard opened her eyes, attempting to adjust to the brightness of the room. "Where am I?" she mumbled, knowing she wasn't going to get an answer. Or at least hoping she wasn't. Her mouth felt full of cotton. Her tongue was thick and sticky. She'd had too much to drink again, which didn't surprise her. The question was where and with whom? She didn't need to ask *why* she drank. The ache deep inside, the painful memories, and the regrets were always a heartbeat away. Alcohol released her from their suffocating grasp for a time. If only she could keep the pain at bay without it.

The roar of ocean waves interrupted her thoughts, and then she remembered. Sarasota, Florida. A new state. A new show. A new start.

She closed her eyes again and then opened just one, taking in the view of the bay through a window framed by beige curtains. She stretched, her bare legs rubbing against the cool of the sheets. Filming would start in a few days. Her manager, Reagan, suggested she come to Florida a few days early. He claimed it would give her a chance to relax and get her mind into the new role. But she had agreed because she needed to get her mind wrapped around the idea of seeing Rowan again.

She hadn't seen her estranged husband at all in the past year. Well, unless you could count his face splashed on the pages of the tabloids. She ached, knowing what she'd thrown away. One night with an old flame, and she'd set fire to their marriage. She and Rowan had been good once. They'd had great times. But like everything in her life, she'd managed to destroy it all — destroy them. She was good at lighting the matches and throwing on fuel. She was not so good with rebuilding her life from the ashes.

She just didn't understand why Rowan still hadn't filed for divorce.

A glimmer of hope tinged her heart, and Alicia sat up. Rowan had cast her for this role. He'd asked for her by name. If they couldn't live together as husband and wife, perhaps they could still be friends. She'd take that if it was all she could get.

Rubbing her eyes, she leaned over the bed, reaching for her notebook bag on the floor. With frenzied movements she riffled through her papers and magazines. She pulled out a copy of *People* and tossed it into the small wastebasket. "100 Most Beautiful People," the title read. She'd flipped through it on the plane. She'd made the list once, but it was during the most horrific year of her life, which proved one thing: It was possible to be beautiful on the outside but filled with darkness and despair within. If her fans could see inside her — then and now — no one would ever call her beautiful.

Then, finding her small journal, Alicia set it on the bedside table. The words built inside her. She needed to write down her thoughts in the only place she could truly be honest with herself. But first she had to brush this taste out of her mouth, take some Advil, and breathe in some fresh air.

She rose, stretched again, and then slipped on the white hotel bathrobe over her T-shirt pajamas. The room was simple and classic with clean lines and a soft palette, but

instead of calming her, it seemed too imper-
sonal and quiet. What she wouldn't give to
hear the shower running or the television
click on, knowing she was sharing the space
with someone who wanted to be there.
Someone who truly cared about her.

She walked stiffly toward the sliding glass
door and opened it to the balcony. A warm
ocean breeze blew in. She gazed out at the
pool, with its colorful umbrellas, and the
ocean beyond. Was Rowan staying at this
hotel too? She'd forgotten to ask.

With a renewed energy she unpacked her
things, leaving out her swimsuit and cover-
up. Suddenly, a late lunch at the pool
seemed like the perfect idea. She could
almost picture Rowan showing up there,
seeing her. Sitting down on the chaise
lounge chair next to her and catching up.
But as Alicia brushed her teeth, reality set
in.

She'd shamed him. She'd hurt him, and
trying to defend her actions, she'd said
things he didn't deserve. She also knew,
deep down, that he asked her to star in this
new show for only one reason — he needed
to please the network. Rowan cared about
many things, but nothing as much as his
reputation. If she wanted to gain his attention, she'd need to prove the network had

chosen well, even if that meant putting on a bonnet and playing the part of an innocent Amish woman. Alicia just hoped viewers wouldn't look too closely into her eyes, because then they'd discover the truth that she was anything but pure.

Taking a long drink of water, she returned to the bed and the journal. She picked up the hotel pen and began to write.

I'm in Florida, and I wish I could share it with you. The ocean breeze coming through the balcony door reminds me of childhood summers going to Disney World and stopping over one night at the beach. My hair tends to curl in humidity, and trying to keep it tucked under a bonnet will be interesting. I read the script, and it's good. It's about a young Amish woman trying to make a new start in Florida after losing the man she loves to death. Did they model the script from my life? My husband didn't die, but my soul feels the loss as harshly. I've been attempting that new start thing but have been failing more than succeeding. Maybe I'll learn something through this character, through this place.

Alicia stared at the page, wondering what

to write next. Or if she should continue. Taking a deep breath, she decided there was just one more thing she wanted to say.

Today I will try to think about living, not dying. Today I will trust that somehow I've ended up in this place, on this set, for a reason. Even though I have no idea what the reason could be.

Six

One reason a dog is such a lovable creature is that his tail wags instead of his tongue.

AMISH PROVERB

Joy stifled a yawn and took her place by the quilting frame at the Slagel home, remembering her grandmother's words: "Many hands make quick work."

She took a needle in her hand and began rocking the sharp point through the quilt layers. She tilted her head down, and soon the tiny stitches lined up in a neat row. Glancing up, she scanned the circle of women doing the same. Most she knew, but Jeanette had invited two longtime friends from Indiana to the sewing frolic as well. The more the merrier was Joy's opinion. There was always a sense of accomplishment when the group was able to finish a quilt top by the end of their gathering.

While the women stitched in the living room, a half-dozen young teens prepared lunch in the kitchen. Up north most Amish girls finished school at fourteen. After that, they worked alongside their *mems* in caring for the home and family. But they also joined their *mems* in outings like this, though most girls were not allowed to quilt with the women because of their many mistakes. Even if they could sew well, though, most didn't want to be welcomed into the sewing circle anyway. Not yet. Why sit around and listen to the older women share news about the community when you could hang out with your friends and talk about boys? They talked about other things too, like jobs and trips, but mostly about boys.

Had it already been nine years since she was their age? How many sewing circles had she been part of since that time? Too many to count.

Joy had always loved gathering like this with her sisters and cousins, her mother, and her aunts and neighbors. Sometimes Lovina would sneak out to help in the kitchen with the other teenage girls who prepared the meal, and most of the time Hope was allowed to stay home and work in the garden, but Joy couldn't get enough of the stories the older women shared. She practiced at home with any scrap of fabric she could find, working to get her stitches just right so she'd become a seamstress worthy of inclusion even at a young age.

A soft smile touched her lips, sure she'd someday have a daughter to teach. And for the first time in her twenty-three years she had a fuzzy picture of what that could look like in her mind. Spending time with Matthew had made all those "someday" dreams of a young girl seem more possible.

Joy wished she could go back and tell the young girl she'd been not to fret so much about when the right man would arrive. *Because in God's good time, he's come.* Matthew was even more wonderful than she could have imagined. Her smile broadened at the voices around her rising and falling with stories filled with good humor and delight. Even those who lived in Pinecraft had a holiday spirit when the vacationers from up north started arriving.

Lately, with her work at Pinecraft Fabric and Quilts, she hadn't been to as many quilting frolics as she would have liked. But today Elizabeth had surprised Joy by bringing in one of their part-time workers to take Joy's place, insisting she needed a break from the store. More than that, Elizabeth had also joined the circle.

"Anna, before you leave, please write down your recipe for Hello Dolly Apple Bars." Vera Chupp leaned out to look around Joy, talking to her *mem* on the other side. Joy shifted back slightly to make it easier for the women to talk.

Mem chuckled. "Oh, *ja,* of course. It's the easiest recipe yet."

"It may be easy," Vera said, "but Howard didn't stop talking about them. He was raised on an apple orchard in Ohio, you know, and he loves anything with apples."

"Granny Smith." Joy's *mem* paused and pointed her finger into the air for emphasis. "The recipe works best with Granny Smith apples."

Laughter spilled out from the kitchen, and the way the young women spoke in hushed tones afterward, Joy was certain one of them was daring to share the dreams of her heart. Was the young man here in Pinecraft for the season or up north? Time would tell.

The bishop's wife cleared her throat, gaining everyone's attention. "Did you hear a television show is coming to Pinecraft?" Jeanette paused her stitching and let her gaze slowly scan the room, meeting each woman's eyes. The sewing paused.

One of the ladies Joy didn't know from

Indiana gasped. "A television show?"

"*Ja,* it's about an Amish family. They're filming it here, if you can believe that."

"They're coming to Pinecraft?" one woman asked. "With television cameras?" She huffed. "It's bad enough with the cameras coming to the Haiti auction and any other event we have. It seems any gathering of Amish is news in these parts."

"And I came on vacation," one of the women from Ohio commented. She had red hair and a smattering of freckles across her nose. "It's *ne* vacation if I'm always having to skirt cameras."

"From what I heard it's a sweet family show." Ruth Eash jutted out her chin. "Clyde went to the meeting about it yesterday. He talked to the producer afterward. He said the producer was wanting to make sure they got it right — about our community and all. At least they're talking to us and aren't trying to sneak cameras in."

Mem clucked her tongue. "As if any *Englischer* could understand our Amish ways. It would be silly for them to even try."

"No one we know is going to be in it, are they? Be filmed? I can't even imagine," the red-haired woman said. "I'm sure being a movie star doesn't align with humble living."

Ruth straightened her shoulders and leaned forward in her chair. "Oh *ne,* the actors are not Amish people. They are just playing Amish, probably from Hollywood, is my guess."

Joy turned her attention to Jeanette for a response, knowing there would be one.

Jeanette's eyes grew round. Her eyebrows lifted into two pointed arches. "That doesn't seem right — *Englischers* dressing up and acting like us. We do not dress plain for show."

"They'll never get it right," Vera echoed.

"*Ja,* we'll know the difference," Ruth's daughter Hannah admitted as she stitched, head bent down, "but I suppose no one watching television would. And of course, since we don't watch television, how would we ever know?" Hannah was just a few years older than Joy and the mother of twins. Yet even though she was younger than the rest, she had no problem speaking up. The room grew silent, as if each one was considering her words. Hannah was right. Since the Amish didn't watch television, they'd have no idea how they were being portrayed.

"It still doesn't seem right," Vera Chupp finally said.

Elizabeth cleared her throat, and the others paused and turned. She continued sewing with slow, even stitches, and from the concentrated look on her face, Joy knew she was trying to find the right words.

"The *gut* Lord uses many ways to share His story." Elizabeth's words were even and measured, just like her stitches. "Don't you think that's what people are curious about — why we've chosen to live this way? We are different, and they wonder why. They are curious, maybe because their lives have become filled with so many other things. And we do it because of God's directives. His Word tells us to live plain lives."

Elizabeth pulled her needle through the fabric, holding it gingerly between her fingers, and then she looked around the room, gazing at each one. "Say they do make this program. And say we are inconvenienced — as we most surely will be. But if this television program shares why we do these things, why and how we serve God, then maybe people out there will learn about Him. Maybe someone we'd never get to meet in person will hear about our faith and desire to know God better."

"But it's *television.*" The last word came out of Vera's mouth with a hiss. "If you add a little bit of *gut* into a pot of poison, does it change the fact that it's still poison?"

Joy didn't add her thoughts, but she

tended to agree with the others. In fact, it was one of the only times she didn't completely agree with Elizabeth. It didn't seem right that someone's job was to put on a dress and *kapp* and mimic her life. Mimic her faith.

And then, a new realization hit her, and her heartbeat quickened within her chest. She thought of the truck and the loud rumbling on the street, of *Englischers* bringing a moving truck into their small Amish community.

I bet that's what those men were doing last night! They had to be part of this television show. Were they going to be filming in that cottage? Was that truck filled with cameras and equipment? A shudder traveled down her spine, remembering the passenger's questions. *"Are you Amish? Do you always wear that scarf to bed at night?"* No wonder he was so interested in her sleeping *kapp.* He was creating Amish characters for a fictional show!

Joy lowered her head and continued her detailed stitching. She was just glad no one saw her last night. How could she explain?

If that man did come and find her, asking questions, she'd turn him away. The last thing she needed was to get on Jeanette's bad side. She wouldn't risk her relationship with Matthew for anything, especially not a television show about the Amish being directed by *Englischers* who wouldn't be able to tell the difference between a scarf and a *kapp*. Surely the bishop would not be happy about this.

Hello Dolly Apple Bars

4 cups diced apples (Granny Smith apples
   are best for this recipe)
1 1/2 cups sugar
1/2 cup oil
3 eggs
2 cups flour
2 teaspoons baking soda
1 1/2 teaspoons cinnamon
1 teaspoon salt
1/2 cup chopped nuts
1/2 cup raisins
1 cup chocolate chips

Preheat oven to 350 degrees. Mix all ingredients together and spread into 13 by 9-inch pan. Bake 35 to 40 minutes. Makes 18 bars.*

* Mrs. Homer (Martha) Gingerich, Pinecraft, Florida, in Sherry Gore's *Simply Delicious Amish Cooking* (Grand Rapids: Zondervan, 2013), 170.

Seven

Only after the rain falls do things begin
to grow. The same is true in life —
there must be some rain in order for
us to grow.

AMISH PROVERB

The sewing frolic had been a success, and while they hadn't quite finished Hope's wedding quilt, it was getting close. After enjoying lunch with the other women, Joy bundled up the quilt top and carried it home. Matthew had mentioned taking a walk in Pinecraft Park together after supper, and she couldn't wait to see him. Couldn't wait to be with him. Couldn't wait to hear more about the plans he had for building a house in Indiana. Each conversation stitched them together. Each dream shared united them in an undeniable way.

Joy couldn't help but whistle a tune as she entered their living room. It was dimmer

67

than usual. The shades had been drawn. Joy moved to the window to open them, but then she stopped short. Her *dat* was lying back in his recliner, and his eyes were closed. He was napping, just as he had been yesterday. Yet something was different. He was still, unmoving, and even in the dim light he looked pale and thin. When had he gotten so thin?

A sinking feeling hit the pit of her stomach, and memories of how ill he'd been in Ohio flashed through her mind. Was her *dat* getting worse?

She stepped toward him. *"Dat?"*

He stirred from his sleep, and his eyes drifted open.

"Are you all right?"

"Ja, just tired, that's all." His voice was scratchy. His breathing labored. "Some days a body just calls for a nap."

Joy placed her hand on his. His once powerful hands lay limp, crossed on his chest. She grasped one. His skin was soft and the fingers bony — opposite of the hands that had once commanded a team of horses or stacked tall rows of wood for the fire. They'd moved to Florida because of his health, and an ache pulsated in her chest, making it hard to breathe. For a time it had seemed he was getting better. Had that been only her imagination?

She offered what she hoped was a re-assuring smile. "Just a nap. *Ja,* of course. I'm sorry I woke you."

He squeezed her hand, smiled, and then released it. She stepped back as his eyes fluttered closed again, as if he was unable to resist the pull of sleep.

She hurried to her bedroom and was surprised to see Faith there. She usually worked as a waitress at Yoder's Restaurant during the day, and when she wasn't working that job she often set up her easel at the park or near the creek — anywhere she could find nature to inspire her paintings.

Joy set her quilt top and supplies on her bed. Faith's brow was furrowed as she studied five of her paintings spread out on her bed in front of her.

"You've been doing a lot of paintings lately." Joy stepped closer to get a better look. "I've hardly seen you around. Something must be inspiring you."

Faith smiled guardedly. "There are so many beautiful things to paint." She still wore her painter's smock over her dress and apron and smelled of oil paint. Yet the peaceful look usually on her face when she was immersed in her art was missing.

Joy studied her sister's furrowed brow and

tightly pressed lips. "Is something wrong?"

Faith looked at her briefly, shrugged, and looked back to her artwork. They stood quietly for a moment, and then Faith shifted her weight to the opposite foot. "These are *gut*, but none really stands out. There isn't one I can expect a big price for," she said, sounding self-conscious.

"So you're going to sell them . . . all?"

The question caused Faith's eyebrows to turn down. "*Ja*, I am." She squared her shoulders. "I'm getting ready for the season — the tourists mostly. Lovina said I can hang them on the front wall of the pie shop to sell."

An unsettled feeling caused the hair on the back of Joy's neck to stand up. She leaned forward earnestly and lifted up a painting of a white farmhouse. It was the house she and Joy could see from their bedroom window back in Ohio. How many days had they awakened to that view? The farmhouse surrounded by a sea of green in spring or golden wheat in summer. Standing out among the red and golden hues of autumn or hiding amid the gray skies and snow-covered ground of winter. Emotion caught in Joy's throat. No one else who viewed this painting would know its meaning. She attempted to swallow the emotion away. "I thought you weren't going to sell this one. It's your favorite."

Faith released a sigh. "I do like it, but if it brings a little bit of money . . . well, everything would help."

"Help for what?" Joy returned the painting to the bed. "Are you saving up your money to return to Ohio? Or . . ." She searched her mind, thinking of why Faith would need money. "Or do you have a secret love and you're planning on running away together?" Joy chuckled, but the expression on Faith's face didn't change. Out of all the sisters, Faith was most vocal about what handsome bachelor had caught her eye. She enjoyed playful bantering over the many ways to capture a guy's heart too, but not today.

"I told Lovina we needed to sit down with you and Grace and, uh, talk." She bit her lower lip.

A stab of worry knifed through Joy's stomach. She stepped closer to her sister. "What's going on? You have to tell me."

Faith released a heavy sigh. She finally turned and caught Joy's gaze. "I heard you asking *Dat* if he's okay. The truth is, he's not."

"What do you mean?"

"I overheard him and *Mem* talking the

71

other day. The medication he was using isn't effective anymore. The doctor has given him a new prescription."

"Will it help?"

Faith shrugged. "I'm not sure if we'll find out. He's refusing to fill it because it costs so much. He doesn't want to turn to the church for help either — he thinks others have more important needs."

Joy pushed aside her things and sank down on her bed. She'd been so focused on the quilt shop and on Matthew that she hadn't spent much time with her parents lately. Sometimes when she got up in the morning, *Dat* was still in bed. Other times, when she returned home from an outing or walk with Matthew, *Dat* had already retired for the night. Both of those things should have been clues to her that something wasn't right.

"Do you know how much the medication will cost?"

"*Ne.* But I plan on talking to *Mem* tonight." Faith scooted over one of the paintings, sat down on her bed, and jutted out her chin. "I hope she's not going to be stubborn and refuse to let me help pay."

"Do you mean let *us* help pay?"

Tears welled up in Faith's eyes. She reached over and grasped Joy's hand.

Joy squeezed. "You didn't think I'd let you carry this burden alone, did you? In fact, we can talk to Grace, Lovina, and Hope, and —"

"*Ne.*" The word shot from Faith's mouth. "I don't want you to talk to them about it. Not yet anyway. Let's at least figure out how much the cost is going to be. Grace doesn't have a regular job, and both Hope and Lovina are getting married soon — right before Christmas. It's a special time in their lives. I don't want to take away their joy. We'll have plenty of time to talk to them after their weddings. Besides, we don't even know how much money is needed."

Joy nodded, but she wasn't convinced. If her *dat*'s health was failing this much now, what would he be like in a few months? What if things got worse quickly? Would they regret not telling her sisters, getting more help?

Then again, she could easily picture both sisters postponing their weddings to make sure *Dat* had what he needed. And he would hate that. It would hurt him to know he was a burden. Faith was right. They needed to know the cost first and then make a plan. She had saved up money from her job. She also had some quilts she could sell if it came to that. They'd somehow scrape it together

— they just had to.

"*Ja,* we'll wait to tell them, but find out how much is needed as soon as you can. I can give you most of my next paycheck, and Lovina has asked me to make more aprons to sell at her shop. I've been meaning to do that."

Joy stepped forward and pulled her sister into an embrace. Faith's shoulders felt tight and tense. How long had she been carrying this burden alone? Too long.

"Please, don't get worried," Joy whispered in her sister's ear. "I know how you tend to do that." She offered a soft smile. "Have faith, Faith."

"*Ja,* I'll try. It's just . . ." Faith lowered her head and focused on her paint-splattered tennis shoes. "I just don't know what we're going to do around here without *Dat.*"

Joy flashed a bright smile and hoped it made her look more confident than she felt. "Let's not think of that. We'll figure it out. God will provide. I know He will."

EIGHT

When life gets too hard to stand, kneel.
AMISH PROVERB

Joy knew *Mem* was going to stop by Yoder's Produce after the sewing frolic. Her plan was to find her, help with the groceries, and then ask about the medication cost. She not only needed to help *Dat,* she needed to help her sister Faith too. Faith tended to take on everyone else's burdens as her own. The sooner Joy could find a way to help, the better for everyone.

As she turned down Kaufman Avenue, she stopped short. The garage door was open at the Slagel house. Was Matthew home? Warmth filled her. She placed her right hand over her chest and noticed the quickening beat.

The sound of a saw filled the air. She followed it into the open garage, and the scent of fresh-cut wood greeted her.

Over the last few weeks, Matthew had been busy working on home construction around Pinecraft. A lot of building had been going on lately. Old houses were demolished and beautiful new ones were built in their place, but it appeared Matthew was working at home today. He concentrated on the wood and saw in his hands. She paused and waited until the saw blade stopped so she wouldn't distract him.

He glanced up as she neared and a smile filled his face. "Well, hello there." A quiet stillness invaded the place where the saw's buzzing had been a moment before.

"I was just here not thirty minutes ago at the sewing frolic. You must have arrived just after I left. A change of pace today?"

He ran a hand down his face, brushing off sawdust — or at least attempting to. "I do have some landscaping work to do later, but I gave one of my construction projects to Noah Yoder's nephew Mose. He and his friends are saving up money to buy their own place, and I thought I'd help them out."

She wrinkled her nose as she smiled. "*Ja,* you say that, but I know you were just wanting to get back to your shop. Have you finished staining the recipe box for your *mem*'s birthday yet?"

"Shh." Matthew held a finger to his lips.

He glanced to the door that led into the kitchen. "She might hear you."

Joy covered her mouth with her hand, and then laughter spilled out. She stepped forward. "I'm so sorry. I'm the worst about keeping secrets. I should let you know that now. I usually make homemade gifts for my family every Christmas, but none of them stay hidden long enough to get wrapped for Christmas Day. Mostly because I either can't wait to share or I spill the beans before it's time."

Matthew stepped around the saw, moving closer to her. "That'll be *gut* to know for the future. I'll have to resist telling you any secrets from now on."

She glanced to the shelf where the recipe box was hidden. "You know, I've been thinking," she said only loud enough for him to hear. "I've been making aprons and dish towels for Me, Myself, and Pie, and they've been selling well. What do you think about making recipe boxes, and maybe even cookbook stands? I imagine they'd be popular with the tourists — taking a little bit of the Amish community home with them and all that. You do such a beautiful job."

Matthew's eyes brightened. "Do you think people would really be interested?"

"I do. But you might have to quit your construction work, because if they sell as well as my aprons and towels, you'll have trouble keeping the recipe boxes in stock."

He got a queer look on his face, and it was hard to read his thoughts. He brushed his hands on his overalls, trying to brush away more sawdust, but it didn't help. His pants were just as dirty as his hands. Then he reached for her hand, and she placed it in his, not caring they weren't clean. His gaze kept steady on hers. Finally he tugged on her hand. "Come here," he whispered. He pulled up two chairs, and they sat down.

"Did I say something wrong? I'm sorry if you thought I wasn't appreciating your construction work, because I do. I just know you like —"

"Shh." Matthew placed a finger near her lips. "You don't need to worry. That's not it at all, Joy, just the opposite. I'm not mad, but pleased. And you surprised me, that's all."

She studied his eyes for a long moment, and he didn't move so much as an eyelash. There was intimacy in his gaze. He wanted to tell her something and was building up the nerve to do so.

He looked away, as if studying the pile of lumber stacked against the wall, and then looked back at her. "I've never told you this before, but I can't picture myself doing construction my whole life."

She threaded a stray hair behind her ear and leaned forward, letting him know she was listening.

"I want to have a farm, but my shop is my favorite place. I would love to do more woodworking and make small things others might enjoy, but I just thought it was a silly dream."

"It's not silly at all."

"Yeah, well, my *dat* thinks it is." Matthew paused before explaining. "He doesn't understand why I'd give up a *gut*-paying job like construction to spend my days in a workshop with *ne* guaranteed income — especially if I'm thinking of supporting a wife soon."

Joy placed a hand over her heart. Matthew wasn't the type to give her a flowery proposal, telling her why he wanted to spend his life with her, and she didn't need that. It was romantic enough that he was pondering all these things and figuring out what made sense for a future with her.

"I don't have everything figured out yet." Matthew shrugged. "And despite my *dat*'s opinion, I don't think I have to know yet. Mostly, Joy, I'm not as concerned with *what* to do with my future as I am with *who* I want to spend it with."

"And?" Her breath balled up in her chest, and in her excitement it was as if she'd forgotten how to exhale.

Matthew leaned forward, and Joy's eyes fluttered closed. He placed the softest kiss on her lips. His lips were warm, and he smelled like the sawdust that dotted his clothes. Tingles moved through her lips and down her arms. She lifted her face and encountered his blue, blue eyes, a deep blue like the color of the Florida sky just after a storm. She immediately remembered the first time she saw him. It was their first Sunday in Pinecraft. She thought he was handsome then, but she'd never imagined her first kiss would be from him. And she never imagined the emotions running through her would be so intense.

"And I know who that is," he whispered, still only inches away from her lips. "I have *ne* doubt. You're exactly the type of woman I've been searching for."

Joy saw the love she had hoped to see in a man's eyes someday.

The sound of voices interrupted the moment. Matthew glanced over and pulled back when he saw a small group of men riding by on bicycles. Joy did the same. As much as she wanted to revel in this moment, such exhibits of affection weren't approved of in public.

"How about we pick up a snack at Yoder's and take it to the park?" Matthew's voice was husky, and she knew all the heated emotions racing through her were affecting him too.

"That sounds like a perfect idea."

And it wasn't until they were walking down the street to Yoder's that Joy remembered she had first set out to find *Mem*.

I'll wait until tonight to talk to her. Just like Faith had planned. We'll get it all worked out. Somehow we will.

And as she glanced up at Matthew walking in step with her, she knew God hadn't brought them this far to fail them — fail her — now.

NINE

Listening is 50 percent of our education.
                    AMISH PROVERB

Joy followed Matthew through the front door of Yoder's Restaurant — one of the favorite places to eat in Pinecraft, Amish or not. The aroma of fried chicken and fresh cinnamon rolls greeted her, and her stomach rumbled a little despite the lunch she'd had earlier. A cell phone chimed, and Matthew reached inside his pants pocket. Up north, cell phones were only used because of work-related needs, but in Pinecraft it seemed almost everyone had one. The Amish snow-birds often proclaimed, "What happens in Pinecraft stays in Pinecraft."

Matthew checked the number, and his brow furrowed. "Sorry . . . do you mind if I get this? It's Mose."

"*Ne,* of course not. There's a line anyway. It'll be a while before we can get a table."

Matthew stepped out of line and hurried outside. From her place in line she saw him talking, and then a worried expression came over his face.

"Joy?" The Amish hostess waved her forward, and Joy recognized one of Faith's friends. "Will there be two of you today?"

"*Ja,* but give us a minute . . ." She glanced outside again. Matthew blew out a heavy sigh as he tucked his cell phone back into his pocket. She could see worry on his face and noticed a stiffness in his shoulders.

She offered a quick smile to the hostess. "I'll be right back."

Joy hurried outside, the warm breeze dancing across her face. "Is everything all right?"

Matthew released a sigh. "I'm afraid not. It sounds like Mose was using a temperamental chain saw when he was tearing down the old structure. It jumped and got his leg real good. Abraham took him to the ER. They've been trying to get hold of me for an hour, but over the noise in my own shop I didn't hear my phone."

"Do you need to go?"

"*Ja.*" He removed his hat and ran a hand through his hair. "Not only did we lose Mose's help, but Abraham's too. I need to get back to that project. I'm afraid I'm going to be working late. And I was hoping to see you this evening."

"I understand. But I actually need to spend time with my *dat* and *mem*. Lunch tomorrow?" She offered a bright smile, even though thoughts of her *dat* caused her chest to resume its ache.

"That sounds perfect. Maybe a picnic at Phillippi Park?"

"I'll prepare a basket."

Joy watched him go, moving with long, purposeful steps. She considered picking up a snack to go, but there were plenty of leftovers at home. Besides, she needed to spend her money more wisely now.

As she walked toward home, Joy said a quick prayer for Mose. Then she considered how best to approach the subject tonight with her *dat*. She knew he could be stubborn, but he'd raised five girls who could be equally so. She just hoped *Dat* would allow her and Faith to pitch in. Their family needed him — needed him around, needed him to be well. *Ja,* there were many needs within the Amish community, but that's what God designed family for, wasn't it?

Dat and *Mem* sat side by side on the couch. The evening sun slanted through the windows, highlighting the white of *Dat*'s beard.

They'd just finished dinner, and *Mem* had made an orange cream pie — *Dat*'s favorite — but no one had touched it. *Dat* narrowed his gaze at them as Faith asked about his illness.

"So tell us the truth, *Dat.* How bad is it? I know you need more money to get the type of help you need."

"It's not something you need to worry about." His reply was sharp.

Mem almost seemed relieved by the questions. "John, please. They are concerned. As I told you before, it's not right that you keep so much from them. They are women now, not children."

"Just tell us what we can do to help," Joy said, jumping in. "*Mem*'s right. We're not little girls. None of us can do much alone, but together —"

Dat waved his hand in the air, acting as if they didn't need to have the conversation. "I'm fine, I'm fine," he mumbled under his breath. He shook his head as if they were making a big deal out of nothing, but his thin frame and the concern in *Mem*'s gaze told a different story.

Joy clutched her hands on her lap. "Tell us the truth, *Mem.* We want to know what to expect. How to help."

Faith's chin trembled slightly. Joy reached

over and took her sister's hand.

"I thought *Dat* would be better after the move." Faith sighed. "It did seem as if he was better for a time."

"Listen to yourselves." *Dat* stroked his chin. "*Dat* this, *Dat* that . . . I'm not dead. I'm sitting right here."

"John, please," *Mem* said again. "They are just concerned. I'd be more worried if they didn't want to fret after you." *Mem* leaned forward, as if letting them into a secret.

"We didn't want to worry you girls. The weather in Pinecraft has helped some, but the lack of manual labor and the rest are what help the most."

"But Faith says there is a medication that could help."

"Not medication, but therapy. It's experimental and expensive. Your *dat* has a lung disease that has *ne* cure."

Joy straightened in her seat. "*Mem*, how come you haven't told us before? You let us assume it was simply a chronic respiratory condition. Are you saying it's something more?"

Mem's eyes grew round. A film of tears caused Joy to sigh and sink back on her heels, waiting for the blow *Mem*'s words were sure to bring.

"It's called chronic obstructive pulmonary

disease," *Mem* said. "Or COPD. A lot of things cause it, but what your *dat* has is an inherited disease. It's not common, but not uncommon either. Both of your paternal grandparents had a faulty gene, it seems. These genes tell cells how to make AAT proteins. To state it simply, AAT proteins are made in the liver. These proteins protect organs, such as the lungs."

Faith held up a hand, halting her words. "That sounds complicated, but what does it mean?"

"Your *dat*'s protein gets stuck in the liver, and it never gets to the organs it needs to protect. The therapy takes donor proteins and injects them into the patient."

Joy's mind reached for any bit of hope. "But the infusions will help, right?"

"They could." *Mem*'s face relaxed as she spoke, as if sharing the information was also sharing the burden. "The therapy involves getting infusions of the AAT protein. It raises the level of protein in a person's blood and lungs. The doctor mentioned it, but there is not enough research to know how well the therapy works. That's why we can't possibly think of approaching the bishop. If we knew it could work . . ."

"Is it expensive?"

Dat nodded. "Too expensive to consider."

Faith's eyes were wide. "But if you got this, then you'd be better?"

"As I said, there is *ne* cure for this type of lung disease." *Mem* glanced at her husband with tender love. "The therapy is considered preventative. The parts of his lungs that are destroyed will never be healed. The therapy would only stop his lungs from getting worse."

Joy looked at her sister and noticed determination in Faith's gaze. *Mem* must have seen it too.

"I know what you're thinking, but it would take us years to save that much money." *Mem*'s words carried emotion, and Joy thought she saw her try to swallow it away. "As your *dat* says, God knows the number of each of our days. We both have peace with that. This is not something to take into our own hands. Even without the treatment, the doctor believes we still have years left together."

Years of sleeping all day? Years of just getting worse and worse? Joy didn't say the words, but she thought them. *O Lord, please show us a way.*

Orange Cream Pie

1 9-inch baked pastry piecrust

Orange Filling

2 cups water
1 cup sugar
2 tablespoons cornstarch
1 teaspoon orange-flavored drink mix (like Tang)
3 oranges, peeled and chopped

Cream Cheese Filling

4 ounces cream cheese, softened
2 cups confectioners' sugar
8 ounces whipped cream (optional)

To make the orange filling, bring 1 1/2 cups of water to a boil in a saucepan. In a bowl, mix together sugar, cornstarch, and drink mix. Add 1/2 cup of water into the sugar mixture and stir. Pour into boiling water, reduce to medium heat, stirring as it cooks. Remove from heat when it begins to thicken a bit. Cool. Stir in orange pieces.

Next, for the cream cheese filling: In a bowl, stir together cream cheese and confectioners' sugar until creamy. Add half of the whipped cream to the mixture. Spoon into baked piecrust. Top with orange filling. Refrigerate overnight. Decorate the top of the pie with the reserved whipped cream, if desired. Makes one 9-inch pie.

TEN

A friend is one who knows all about you
and still loves you.

AMISH PROVERB

Alicia had just gotten to the beach with
script in hand when her cell phone rang. It
was a custom ring that sounded like an Irish
jig. How many months had it been since
she'd heard that ring? Too many. She answered it with a quick release of breath.

"Hello."

"Hey, I like yellow on you. It always looks
good with your creamy white skin. But did
you really think you could hide behind those
sunglasses, especially when ET spilled the
news about the upcoming series last night?"

Alicia glanced down at her yellow sundress
and flip-flops and then looked around. A
family with three small children played near
the water. Behind her, two older women
strolled by wearing windbreakers and sun

visors. Then she noticed a man standing close to one of the red umbrellas near the hotel. Even though it was too far to see his face, Alicia would know Rowan's stance anywhere. She also noticed a hint of smile in his voice. That surprised but pleased her. The last few times they talked, all they managed to do was scream at each other. Then again, maybe he was more pleasant because their relationship was different for this job. He was the director and she the actress. They'd always been professional in those roles, and maybe he, too, was hoping to be friends.

She moved his direction, telling herself to act natural. But as she neared and noticed his smile, a hundred happy memories flashed through her mind. They'd been married almost five years before separating, so she had many good memories to choose from. Maybe for a time she could forget how they'd grown apart, and how she'd let temptation get the best of her.

Alicia walked up the concrete steps and then sauntered toward the table near where he stood.

"I hope you don't mind, but when I saw you on the beach I ordered lunch for both of us."

She pushed her sunglasses to the top of

her head. "You did?" She placed a hand over her stomach. "That's good because I'm starving."

He laughed. "You're always starving."

Rowan motioned to the table, and she sat down. He was thinner than the last time she'd seen him. Maybe there were a few more wrinkles around his eyes too, but he was just as handsome as ever. His easy manner relaxed her, making it hard to believe they hadn't spoken in a year.

She took a sip of her ice water with lemon. "So, what did you order for me?"

"What do you think? Caesar salad with anchovies, dressing on the side, and broccoli cheddar soup."

She chuckled. "Am I that predictable?"

"Of course you are, and you're not going to spend the day with the script as you planned."

"I'm not?"

"No. Instead, we're going to Pinecraft. I want us to go spy on some Amish."

"As if they're not going to notice us watching them?"

"They get a lot of tourists there. We're just going to pretend we're in Florida for the weekend or something."

"Why, Gaston, you are positively primeval," she stated, using her nickname for him.

He pointed a finger into the air. "I won't argue with that, and in addition to research I have another motive too. I heard there's a shop that makes the best pie."

Joy leaned forward and rested her elbows on the top of the picnic table. Phillippi Park was busy today, and the noises of a community at play were all around her and Matthew. Everyone but the Swartzentruber Amish wore flip-flops. A couple of young people sat at a far table with cigarettes in their hands. Joy shook her head. Even though they were in *rumspringa,* they had no right to be smoking in public. It was a bad example to the *Englisch* who didn't understand. A group of girls walked by, and right away Joy noticed their pierced ears and sleeves rolled up.

Instead of getting upset, she decided to focus on the happy sights. Toddlers ran in circles. Older men gathered at the shuffleboard court. Teens too old for school sat on a nearby quilt on the grass and chatted. Youth from different Amish communities around the United States were catching up after not seeing each other since last year.

Even though there was so much going on around them, Joy was attuned to Matthew's every motion as they ate chicken salad sandwiches from Yoder's. He drank half his lemonade in one tilt of his head. The chocolate chip cookies seemed small in his large hand, and he ate each one in two bites. Yet despite his size, he ate with care, like she imagined a king eating at a banquet. Growing up, Joy loved reading stories from history, and that's how Matthew appeared to her. He wasn't like a lot of the other young men, who liked playing practical jokes or who, up north, would get into trouble racing their buggies. He had a boyish face, yet he was responsible, mature. And he was exactly the type of husband she was looking for.

Joy also knew her parents approved. Unlike Lovina's beau, Noah, who had trouble in his past, or Jonas, Hope's intended, who was a widower, Matthew's life had no complications. He was the bishop's son. A son the bishop could be proud of. Joy had no doubt most of the mothers in Pinecraft had hoped Matthew would choose their eligible daughters to court. Joy didn't know how she'd been so blessed.

"So Mose is all right?" she asked, thinking about yesterday's phone call.

"He has a mess of stitches, but the doctor says he's lucky. It was close to hitting a major artery. God's hand was protecting him for certain."

The sun moved over the trees, cascading bright light onto them. Matthew rolled up his shirtsleeves and leaned both elbows beside his empty paper plate. The wind picked up, ruffling their napkins on the table. Both of them reached for the scattering napkins, and his hand bumped hers. "Sorry." He captured her hand, clinging to it. "I didn't mean to bump your hand."

Joy laughed. "It's okay. You've made it all better, see?" She squeezed. She considered telling Matthew about *Dat,* but she didn't want to make him feel as if she were asking him to help financially. She and her sisters would figure it out somehow.

Matthew's hand completely covered hers. It was rough, like *Dat*'s used to be. A twinge of pain touched her heart as she thought about last night's conversation with her parents. She and Faith still wanted to know the costs involved, and *Mem* said she'd get more details. They determined to do what they could to find a way to get the money. Yet this moment she simply wanted to enjoy the smiling face across from hers.

"So was there any interesting news at the sewing frolic yesterday?" Matthew asked. "Any news of who's getting married or having a baby? I think that's what my *mem* likes best about sewing."

"There's always news like that, but mostly about people I don't know. But" — she leaned forward — "there was quite the excited discussion about the television show that's coming to town."

Matthew's brow furrowed. "So I heard. It sounds like complete nonsense to me. I have *ne* doubt they'll be adding all types of Hollywood drama to a show like that. Otherwise who would watch a program about sewing frolics, baking, and woodworking?"

Joy wanted to point out that it was sure to have a romantic plot, but she knew that wouldn't please Matthew either. Instead, she looked around. "Do you think they'll be walking around with their cameras? They can't do that without permission, can they?"

"*Ne.* I'm sure they can't. From what I hear, the main production studio is a few blocks over, but they are going to be doing some filming in a house close to Pinecraft Park — a rented house where these fictional people supposedly live."

"It's on the corner of Good Avenue and Fry Street. That little white house that's been empty for at least a year." The words came out before Joy realized what she was saying.

"Really? How do you know that?"

Joy nibbled on her lower lip. The last thing she wanted to tell Matthew was how she'd led the *Englischers* to the place in her nightgown when she should have been in bed sleeping. "Uh, there was a big truck on our street. It was a supply truck I suppose, and they were lost. I gave them directions."

Matthew nodded, and Joy was thankful he hadn't asked more questions. Heat warmed her cheeks even now thinking about how she'd thrown a coat over her nightgown.

"Lucky it was you they asked." He chuckled. "I know many Amish women who would have just walked away."

"Oh!" Joy sat straighter. "Speaking of Amish women, I have cousins coming on the Pioneer Trails bus today. It's an unexpected trip. *Mem* just found out this morning. Could you walk me?"

"Is it three o'clock already?"

"Almost."

"I'd be glad to, but then I need to head back to work. Although . . ." He smiled at her. "It's hard to do when I have such lovely company."

They walked side by side and joined numerous others traveling the same direction. Within a few minutes they were part of a crowd waiting for the Pioneer Trails bus to come in.

Matthew stood shoulder to shoulder with her. They were not touching, not holding hands, but anyone who saw them would know they were a couple.

Up ahead, *Mem* scooted closer. She paused, lingered a few steps away, and eyed them before turning north to watch for the bus.

Matthew glanced around. "It seems everyone is trying to pretend they're not watching us, not whispering about us."

"Well, it's not every day that one eats lunch with the most eligible bachelor in town."

"I'm not sure about that."

"I am, and I'm not even going to look. If they see my eyes, I'm sure to give everything away."

"Everything? What's everything?"

She wanted to say, *That we are falling in love. That we are both hoping for a future together.* But instead Joy simply shrugged and glanced down at the paper bag in her hand. "That I've been so busy at work that I didn't make you a lunch, but instead we purchased it from Yoder's."

He chuckled. "That sounds like a scandal to me, but I think we'll get through it." He flashed a smile totally bereft of worry. "But even more important than that . . . I can only stay a few minutes."

"*Ja,* I understand. A man's got to do what a man's got to do."

Beside Matthew two older men with white beards sat on three-wheeled bicycles. They wore straw hats with a black band. They each chatted with one foot on a pedal and the other on the ground. Another man sat in a motorized wheelchair, with his basketball-size belly pushing out. It was hard to picture him as a young farmer or factory worker from up north. She guessed that twenty years ago he'd never imagined himself here, hardly able to walk or get around well. Just like her *dat* never pictured himself in such a weakened state. *Lord, help me to focus on what matters. Even though it may not seem like it, the years are short.*

On the other side of Joy were women on bicycles. While one woman sat, the other two stood, arms crossed and eyes intent on the roadway, as if just watching it would make the bus come more quickly.

Mem scooted closer and joined them just as the bus pulled up. One by one, weary travelers exited. They were met by friends and family eager to help with their luggage and welcome them to this haven of rest. Most of the visitors were factory workers, here to enjoy their two-week vacations. Older men and women, younger women with children, and piles of suitcases filled the street.

Joy introduced her cousins to Matthew, and both Rosella and Sylvia eyed her curiously. Joy knew she'd get lots of questions later. A handsome bachelor at their cousin's side was news for certain.

Hugs were given, and Joy looked around. "Where's Esther and her family? Aren't they coming?"

"Actually" — Rosella lifted an eyebrow — "they took the train out West and got on a cruise ship. They're sailing through the Panama Canal and will be landing in Fort Lauderdale tomorrow."

Mem clicked her tongue. "Well, that's a fancy enough way to travel. I —"

"Excuse me." A man stepped toward them, an *Englisch* man. He wore jeans and a light blue T-shirt. He stepped past *Mem* and turned to Joy. "I'm so glad I found you. I was hoping to introduce you to my . . . uh, my friend."

All eyes turned Joy's direction. She pulled back in surprise. "Oh, are you talking to me?"

"Yes, don't you remember . . . from the other night?"

Joy's eyes widened, and then she realized he was the man from the moving truck. He was hard to recognize without his baseball cap. He looking happier, refreshed. A woman stood behind him. She had dark hair pulled up in a ponytail and wore a yellow sundress with thin straps. She rubbed her arms, seemingly uncomfortable by the way she was dressed around these plain women. Seeing that, Joy took a step their direction. The sooner they said their piece and were on their way, the better for everyone.

"I do remember. I hope you found the place all right." She extended a hand to the young woman. "I'm Joy." She glanced behind her. "The bus has just arrived with friends and family from up north. It's like a family reunion." The woman looked familiar, but Joy wasn't sure why.

"It looks like we arrived just in time," she said, offering a smile. "I'm Alicia."

The man's smile was brilliant as he scanned the group. He placed a hand on the woman's bare shoulder. "Alicia is one of the actresses here. She's part of the television show we're filming." His voice boomed. "I would ask you if you've seen some of her other projects, but we all know that's not allowed, don't we?"

The voices around them stilled, and the

expressions on the crowd's faces darkened. The joy of the moment slipped behind cautious masks. They didn't trust this man and didn't like that he'd interrupted their reunion. Joy glanced at the faces of the older gentlemen and saw more than one furrowed brow. It was clear that most people felt the same as the women at her sewing frolic. The atmosphere of the gathering turned icy despite the bright sunshine outside.

The woman, Alicia, saw it too. Her smile slipped away and she pushed the man's hand from her shoulder. "Maybe we should leave these wonderful people to their reunion. Didn't you promise me pie? I see the sign for Me, Myself, and Pie just across the street."

Joy didn't hear the man's response. Instead, she felt the softest touch on her arm, and a cold chill traveled up. She looked to Matthew, and anger tightened his face into a scowl. Joy took a step back. She'd never seen him like that. Fear struck within her. A cold fear that cascaded over her, causing goose bumps to rise on her arms and her heart to lurch. He was angry with her. For what? For the interruption? For not telling him more about her interaction with the *Englischer*? Maybe both.

"The other night?" Matthew mouthed

only loud enough for her to hear.

Joy didn't want to explain. Not here, not now.

She turned back to the *Englischer.* "I, uh, hope you enjoy your, uh, work in Pinecraft," Joy commented, and then she glanced back over her shoulder in the direction of her cousins. "I'm going to help my cousins get settled in."

The smile on the man's face faded. "Yes, of course."

Joy turned, wondering what to do, what to say. She hoped they weren't going to say anything. Weren't going to follow her. She also hoped Matthew wasn't going to ask too many questions, especially about her giving the man directions.

She moved to help Rosella with her suitcase, and when she turned around Matthew wasn't following. He still wore an angry expression as he watched the man and woman strolling away. Joy released the handle to the suitcase and hurried back to Matthew. "I'm so sorry. I forgot you have to leave. I hope you enjoy your time at work."

"Ja, danke." His words were simple, and she missed the warm smile from earlier that day.

"Do you think we can catch up after work?"

"Maybe." Matthew licked his dry lips. "I've taken an extra-long lunch. I might need to work late."

"I understand." She resisted the urge to reach out and touch his arm, to reassure him. She resisted the urge to explain. He wouldn't like it if she did.

Rosella moved with slow, unobtrusive steps, clasping her hands together. "I think we're ready."

"I'll see you later then, Joy." Matthew turned and walked back in the direction of his house, most likely to get his tools. He looked both sad and angry, even from behind.

The bright summer sun overhead now seemed too overbearing. The ache of disappointing Matthew spread from her shoulders up her neck. Compounding it was the fact that her cousins and *Mem* had witnessed the whole thing. They not only saw her interaction with the *Englischers,* but also Matthew's reaction. *I feel like such a fool. Why did I have to help them?*

Joy looked to her mother, and she noted curiosity there too. *Mem* walked by her side as they followed the two others with their suitcases.

"Why didn't you tell me about the other night? About giving them directions?"

"Oh, I . . . well, there were so many other things to talk about," Joy said. It was the truth, but the deeper truth was she was afraid of these very responses.

Stupid, stupid. Joy's fingers tightened around the handle of the suitcase that she pulled. Yes, it was good to help people, but she didn't need to help everyone, especially not *Englischers.* The men in the truck would have eventually figured it out, she was certain. Or maybe someone else would have stepped forward to help. It was a small community, and everything people did came to light. She had to make sure to be more careful next time. She cared for Matthew, and nothing was worth the risk of losing him.

"Kume." Mem motioned her cousins forward. "We'll drop off these things at your rental, and then you must come to our house for ice tea and Tasty Treat cakes. I baked them this morning, and I have to hear how everyone in Ohio is doing."

Her cousins nodded, but their eyes were still on Joy. Dozens of questions filled their gazes, and she prepared herself to be peppered with them later. Joy didn't mind answering. What she did mind was that she had no doubt her answers would make it back up to Ohio by tomorrow night. And

then spread to sewing frolic after sewing
frolic after that.

Tasty Treat Cakes

2 cups sugar

2/3 cup butter, melted

1 teaspoon vanilla extract

1/4 teaspoon salt

2 teaspoons baking soda

3/4 cup cocoa powder

2 cups water

2 teaspoons vinegar

3 cups all-purpose flour

Preheat oven to 350 degrees. In a large bowl, mix the wet ingredients into the dry. Pour batter into two 10 by 15-inch jelly roll pans. Bake for 15 minutes. Cool and frost.

Snowy White Frosting

2 pounds confectioners' sugar

1 cup solid vegetable shortening

2 tablespoons butter, softened

1/4 teaspoon salt

2 teaspoons vanilla extract

1/2 cup milk

Fill large mixing bowl with confectioners' sugar. Add shortening, butter, salt, vanilla, and milk. Mix for 5 minutes, until smooth and creamy.

Tip: This frosting works great for doughnuts and as a cream filling for whoopie pies.

ELEVEN

It's better to hold out a helping hand
than point a finger.
AMISH PROVERB

Joy brushed the feather duster along the rows of fabric, but today the duster felt as if it weighed twenty pounds. The heaviness on her heart was even more. Every breath hurt, and an ache had started in her temples. She'd attempted to enjoy her visit with her cousins yesterday afternoon and evening, but her mind kept flitting back to Matthew. She hadn't seen him last night, and when she'd walked by his house this morning he hadn't been there either. She knew she had to explain — she just hoped it would be enough to calm the troubled waters. This was no way to start a relationship. That she knew.

The bell on the front door jingled, and a tall woman entered the fabric shop. She paused inside the doorway and pushed her sunglasses up on her bright red hair, letting out a low whistle. Without hesitation she hurried over to a stack of quilts displayed on a deep shelf.

"Wow, these are beautiful. Just what I was looking for!"

The woman's excitement pushed aside Joy's worries for a time. She hurried over to the woman, adjusting her *kapp* as she did. "Can I help you?"

The woman turned, and her eyes widened. "You . . . you're Amish." She reached out and gently grabbed Joy's wrist as if she were afraid Joy was going to slip away.

Joy broadened her smile. "Uh, yes. Would you like me to help you with one of these quilts? They're all hand-quilted by women in our community."

"Hand-quilted?" The woman released Joy's wrist and reached for the closest quilt. It was white and purple with a dahlia design in the center. The woman trailed her fingers over the gorgeous, colorful border. "You're not telling me that each one of these stitches was done by a human hand and not a machine, are you?"

"Yes, that's what it means. These Amish quilts are entirely hand-quilted. The top is pieced together, and then the top, batting, and backing fabric are layered and held taut in a quilting frame."

The woman's eyes were lined with dark makeup, and they widened with the explanation. "And they use a needle and thread to sew it?"

"In a quilting frame, yes. This is a queen-sized quilt, so it will have forty to fifty thousand stitches. Once that's finished they bind the edges."

The woman reached into her purse and pulled out a pair of reading glasses. "Don't tell anyone I wear these." She chuckled. "But I have to take a closer look." She gaped as she studied the tiny stitches. "It's just unbelievable." She returned the glasses to her purse, sliding them into a small black-and-gold trimmed case. "I bet they cost a fortune. All that time. With all those children running around, it must take years to finish that."

The woman seemed to be talking more to herself than Joy, and Joy couldn't help but smile. "Well, this one cost —"

"Or are these made in those sewing bees, or whatever you call them? That would go much faster, I suppose, if there was someone around to watch all those kids."

Joy just smiled, unsure of how she was supposed to answer the part about kids.

Amish kids did go to school, and there were always older ones around to care for younger ones. But she did know how to answer about the sewing bee.

"Sometimes quilts are made at quilting frolics, but these are hand-quilted by one artist. They are made from high-quality cotton and will last a lifetime. They do cost a lot, but they are worth the investment."

"But some quilts are made by more than one artist."

"Oh yes. I was just working on a quilt for my sister at a sewing frolic. A nice number of us were gathered around the quilt frame." Joy ran her hand over the stitching. "Some people like quilts that are more uniform. Quilting businesses tend to use the putting-out system or factory production because those are more efficient."

"Putting-out?"

"Oh, that's what the textile industry called it when subcontractors completed the work off-site. Women took the work home with them."

The woman leaned closer to eye the stitching. "I suppose I've never really thought of this before. Fascinating."

Joy turned the quilt over so the woman could see the underside. "Personally, I like it when all the stitches don't match. I like to imagine the conversations that took place when women were working together. Quilt stitches are like handwriting, you know. Each woman has her own distinct, recognizable style. That's one thing collectors love about old quilts."

The woman wrinkled her nose. "And how much would this one be?"

"This one is $1,200, and I wish I could give you a discount, but the season has just started and we get a lot of tourists. Maybe if you come back in May we might —"

The woman waved a hand. "Twelve hundred — you've got to be kidding. I could buy them and sell them in California for so much more. Vintage, retro quilts would be all the rage."

Joy nodded, not sure what the woman meant or whether she was still interested in the quilt. "We have others." Joy pulled two more quilts off the shelf and set them to the side, and then she pulled out a third one for the woman. The quilt top was made of tiny shapes in various colors, and when put together they made a scalloped pattern. It reminded her of rolling ocean waves reflecting a rainbow.

"Oh, look at this one," the woman cooed. "So detailed."

"This is the bargello pattern, and putting

it together is as tricky as putting together a puzzle. See how the colors and pattern vary to give it this swooping effect? The quilter has to be precise with the various shapes, or it turns out a mess." Joy didn't want to admit she took on one of these quilts when she was young and it led to disastrous results.

"Oh, yes, the bargello design. I learned about that in art school. Some call it a flame stitch. There was a story about a princess who designed it. They don't just use that pattern for quilts. I've seen it in both textiles and paintings." The woman pulled out her glasses again, slipping them on her nose, and studied the design. "Amazing, just amazing." She straightened up and peered over her glasses, looking at Joy. "And I assume this one cost more, because of the extra work."

"Yes, one hundred dollars more, but it's my favorite quilt. If you'd like to look at some less expensive ones . . ." Joy reached down farther into the pile.

A beeping sound erupted from the woman's purse, and she pulled out her cell phone, hitting a button. The beeping stopped, but her eyes widened, noting the time. "Listen, I need to run, but . . ." She typed something into her phone with her thumbs, and Joy waited for her to finish.

"Oh, I understand. It's a big investment. If you'd like to return later, we're open between ten and four o'clock every day."

The woman glanced up. "Actually, I'm supposed to be meeting one of my assistants who just flew in, but if you can ring up these two quilts and four more that you like, that would be great."

"Six?" Joy gaped. "You want to buy six quilts?"

"Are they all around $1,300?" The woman looked down at her phone again. "I really need to get going."

"Yes. I can ring them up, but it'll take me time to fold and bag them too."

"Do you think you could have someone deliver them? Our place is just down the road. I won't be there. I'm flying out to work on another project in the morning, but I'll let everyone know you're coming."

Joy nodded and then took the credit card from the woman's hand. She rang up the sale for more than they usually made in two months' time, still not believing this was really happening.

The woman signed the receipt and then handed it back.

"If you'd like to come back later and check my choices, I can stay open a little later —"

"No, no. I trust your judgment." The woman flashed perfect, white teeth. "And I really need to go. We have to be in a meeting in ten minutes. Thanks for delivering them!"

The woman grabbed one of Elizabeth's business cards, turned it over, and scribbled down the address. "Here is where they need to be delivered. If you could get them there before eight tomorrow morning, that would be marvelous. I really appreciate your help."

Then, sliding the glasses back into her purse, the woman strode out of the store. As soon as the door shut, laughter spilled from Joy's lips. "Well, that's not something that happens every day." She looked at the credit card receipt in her hand and then at the quilt shelf. Two quilts were pulled out, and others had fallen to the floor. It looked as if a raccoon had dug through them, trying to build a nest. Then a new thought caused a twinge of excitement. Elizabeth paid her an hourly wage, but Joy also got a commission from quilt sales. She usually sold only one or two a month, and it was a nice little bonus in her check though nothing to get overly excited about. But this . . . this would help with her *dat*'s therapy. She clasped her hands to her chest. *Thank You,*

Lord. Thank You for providing!

She couldn't wait to tell Faith. She couldn't wait to tell Matthew.

"Oh." The word slipped out. She remembered how they parted yesterday. She also remembered that she hadn't yet told him about her *dat*'s medical issues. Pain pierced her heart, and she let her eyes close. They couldn't lose *Dat;* they just couldn't. She opened her eyes again, willing the tears to stop. She quickly wiped them away and then moved to the quilts to pick four more to deliver. She chose her favorites and then started to wrap them. She couldn't carry all of them at once, but if she borrowed *Mem*'s garden wagon — the one she used when she went grocery shopping — then she'd be able to deliver them all early the next morning.

Just a few weeks ago, she seemed to be living in a dream as she started her relationship with Matthew, but in a matter of days things had changed. She'd found out about her *dat*'s true condition. He needed her. She couldn't simply think of herself. Then there was Matthew's anger. She felt an ache in her gut, thinking how he'd been cross with her. His reaction surprised her. He'd gotten angry so easily. She wasn't used to that. Her father had always been so even-tempered. Very few things made him really upset, and most of the time he was merely frustrated, just as he'd been the other night when both she and Faith asked questions about his health. But the anger that had flashed in Matthew's eyes had been different. *Is it something I need to be worried about?*

Joy pushed that thought out of her mind. No one was perfect. If this relationship continued, sometimes she would do something to make Matthew angry. And sometimes he would make her angry. Everyone had a bad day now and then, even the most eligible bachelor in Pinecraft. She also had to think through her actions before acting on a whim. It wasn't just her she had to think about now, but Matthew too. If they were going to spend their lives together, everything she chose would impact him.

I need to be more careful. I need to make wiser choices. She didn't want anything to risk the life they were starting . . . together.

TWELVE

A true friend will place a finger on your faults without rubbing them in.

AMISH PROVERB

Laughter spilled from Alicia's mouth as she stepped in front of the mirror and eyed herself in her new wardrobe. She was told to come to the set today without a stitch of makeup on. And then the wardrobe designer, Georgia, helped her carefully put on the Amish clothes. She wore a long, dark-blue dress with three-quarter sleeves. A white apron was over her dress. And over her pulled-back hair she wore a bonnet that she learned the Amish called a *kapp.*

"I got all of these things on eBay. I was hoping they would fit." Georgia stepped back and placed her hands on her hips. "Actually, I think they look pretty good." Georgia was three inches shorter than Alicia and plump around the middle. They'd

119

worked together before, and Alicia was pleased when she arrived to see who Rowan had hired to help with wardrobe. Alicia trusted Georgia — trusted that whatever they talked about wouldn't be in the tabloids. Trust like that was hard to find.

Alicia swayed from side to side, studying her reflection. *I look like my grandmother.* Emotion pinched her heart. Out of everyone in her growing-up years, Granny had been the stable, caring one — but that didn't mean she wanted to dress like her.

"This dress is baggy and so plain. Can we pin a flower up by my collar or something? Or maybe I can find a necklace?" She glanced down at her hand. "At least this wedding ring gives me some bling, although the plain gold band isn't really my style."

She didn't know how she felt about playing the role of a widowed woman, especially in front of Rowan. It's almost as if she had FAILURE tattooed to her forehead. *Don't think of that now. Don't go there.* She was here to work, not to dwell in the past. That would get her nowhere.

A ripple of laughter bubbled up from deep in Georgia's chest. "I'm sorry that we had to ditch the bling for this one. Amish don't wear jewelry, except for wedding rings. They don't pin flowers on their dresses. They

120

don't like all those fancy things. Weren't you paying attention when you and Rowan were walking around the village yesterday?"

Alicia nodded, but she could tell from Georgia's eyes that she didn't believe that. Georgia had spent enough time with her to know when she wasn't telling the truth.

"Mm-hmm." Georgia used a small comb to brush stray strands of hair under the *kapp* and then sprayed them into place. "You can't fool me, Ali. You weren't paying attention to the Amish at all. Do you even remember what state we're in, beyond the state of confusion?" She laughed again at her own joke, and then her motion stopped. She paused, looking deep into Alicia's eyes. "I'm sure it was just nice being with Rowan again." Her voice was soft, tender.

Alicia leaned forward, speaking loud enough for only Georgia to hear. "I don't know what to think about it all. Rowan is acting like . . . like we're friends."

Georgia hadn't been working on the foreign set with Alicia when the event that had shattered her marriage happened, but Georgia no doubt had seen the steamy photos the paparazzi had captured at the bar before Alicia and her costar retired to her hotel room. Georgia had probably read the many stories in the newsstand tabloids, stories that unfortunately had no need for exaggeration to be shocking. It was a scandal Alicia was sure would be the fall of her career, but she'd highly underestimated the wonders of the crisis-management expert her manager hired. A few tearful pictures, a good publicist who guided her actions and responses in the months after, and a Barbara Walters special that dove into her painful childhood and heartwarming rise to stardom . . . these tactics helped her retain her role as America's sweetheart.

"Rowan's had time to get used to the idea of working with you again." Georgia attempted a smile. "And he knows you well. He knows that whatever's on your heart shows up on your face. Maybe that's why he doesn't want to stir the waters. After all, I've never seen a ticked-off Amish woman."

Alicia gasped and placed a hand on her hip. "Are you calling me a bad actress? A good actress can act pleasant even when she's seething inside, right?"

One perfectly arched eyebrow cocked in the air. Georgia clucked her tongue. "I'm just saying how things are."

Alicia's heart sank, and the warm feelings that had bubbled up yesterday popped, leaving just an emptiness in their place. Georgia was right. Rowan knew her — knew how she responded to stress and sadness. Of course he'd want to keep her as happy as possible while she was on set.

She gazed into her face in the mirror. Pale, with brown eyes that were too large and lips too thin without lipstick. An ordinary woman who'd experienced an extraordinary love and thrown it all away.

"So you don't think he's forgiven me?"

Georgia moved to a clothes rack, flipped through some garments, and then turned back to look at Alicia. She still didn't answer right away, but instead she studied Alicia's face as if testing to see if she should answer truthfully. Georgia bit her lip and again raised her eyebrow. "Would you forgive yourself if you were in his shoes?"

And like a rush, the memory came back. The sound of the church bells ringing across cobblestone streets. Her costar and former boyfriend lying in her bed asleep after a long day of filming and too much drinking at the hotel bar. The knock at the door — housekeeping she'd presumed. Opening the door to see Rowan's weary but smiling face. "We wrapped up filming yesterday. I thought I'd surprise you," he'd said. And then the hurt and horror to realize what she'd done as her costar exited the bedroom.

Though she now held in the tears, the trembling of her fingers gave away her emotions. She covered her face with her hands and pressed her chin to her chest.

Georgia placed a hand on her shoulder. "I'm sorry. I shouldn't have been so blunt. It's something I need to work on."

Alicia swallowed down her emotion. "I'd rather have someone tell me how it is."

Georgia leaned forward, resting her forehead on the top of Alicia's head, whispering into her ear. "At least you can be friends, right? At least you're both here."

Alicia nodded, wondering how both thankfulness and regret could fill one so completely.

She was here in Florida with Rowan. She didn't know why, but she was. And the first thing she had to do was prove Georgia wrong. She could play her part without everyone knowing her heart was breaking in two. She was an actress, after all.

Taking a deep breath, Alicia squared her shoulders.

Georgia pulled back. "Good girl. That's the way to tuck all those emotions away. Are you hungry?"

"What do we have?"

"Craft services set up a table. There's some yogurt, granola, and juice. Or" —

Georgia's eyes sparkled — "I picked up some whole wheat oatmeal bread and strawberry jam from a neighbor. Both are homemade."

"From a neighbor? How did that happen? Did you already go visiting up and down the street?" Alicia chuckled, hoping it sounded convincing. "To research Amish dresses, I'm sure."

"No. There's actually a place a few houses down with a sign in the yard that reads Amish Baked Goods for Sale." Georgia placed a hand on her hip and stuck it out. "I didn't get this figure by passing up baked goods."

"I'll have the bread and jam, please."

Like two girls sneaking into a candy jar, Georgia led Alicia to a corner of the wardrobe room where a tote bag sat. She pulled out the bread, still warm, and a jar of jam.

"I don't have a knife, but they gave me a plastic spoon for the jam."

Alicia picked up the bread. "Who needs a knife?"

She unwrapped the bread from the wax paper and pulled off a thick chunk. The aroma rose, filling her nostrils. She breathed it in. Few things were more wonderful than the scent of fresh-baked bread.

She pointed to the jar of jam. "Do you mind?"

Georgia waved a hand. "Go ahead."

Alicia picked up the jar and opened the lid with one twist. She placed it on the table and then spooned jam into the soft center of the bread.

Closing her eyes, she took a big bite. The yeastiness of the bread mixed with the fresh strawberry taste of the jam exploded on her taste buds. "Oh my goodness. You have to taste this." The click of a photo being taken caused her to open her eyes, and when she did she saw it wasn't Georgia who'd snapped the shot. Rowan stood there, dark-haired and handsome, holding his cell phone in his hand. There was a mix of tenderness and humor in his gaze.

He chuckled as he glanced down at the shot he'd taken. "You should see yourself. A true Amish beauty indeed."

"No, Rowan, please." She extended her jam-covered fingers toward him. "I'm not wearing a stitch of makeup."

He pulled his cell phone closer, out of her reach, and typed in something with his thumbs.

Alicia finished chewing and then took a step toward him. One hand held her bread, and she stretched out the other even closer.

She pointed to his phone. "You're not posting that —"

"Oh yes. Yes I am."

"Seriously, Rowan. I look so plain."

He glanced up, and his eyes twinkled. "Which is how you're supposed to look during filming."

"No." She jutted out her chin. "No, during filming I'll only *look* like I don't have makeup on. But my blemishes, my —"

"Tsk-tsk, I don't want to hear it." He put up a palm, blocking her words. "You know your adoring fans want a glimpse of what you're working on next."

"Rowan, please!"

He pretended not to hear her and pushed Send. Then he tucked his phone into his front jeans pocket.

Georgia glanced at her watch. "It's 7:35. My guess is 8:07."

"8:07? What do you mean? What are you talking about?" Alicia took another bite of her bread, pretending her insides weren't fluttering with Rowan's closeness. Pretending she was shocked by his actions, when she was really pleased with the attention.

Georgia shrugged. "Oh, it's my guess for how long it'll take before you make the home page of *People.*"

"You're kidding, right?" Alicia mumbled

127

between bites of bread. Just then her phone pinged on the table next to her.

Rowan reached for her phone. "I recognize the sound of that notification. I'm honored that you still keep track of me."

Alicia shrugged. "I just haven't turned it off." Should she tell him she still had his unique ringtone, and their last vacation photo was still her wallpaper?

"In over a year you haven't turned off the notifications for my Twitter posts?"

She shrugged again. And unlocked her phone. She opened his tweet, and her face popped up. Well, at least part of her face. Half of it was hiding behind the large chunk of bread.

In Pinecraft. Filming starting soon. #Amish-beauty

Heat rose to Alicia's face, and she returned her phone to the table. "I can't believe you're making me wear this bonnet," she mumbled. "And I can't believe that hashtag. People are going to take that the wrong —"

"And I can't believe you haven't offered me any of that," Rowan interrupted. He tore off a chunk of bread.

Alicia didn't know what to say, what to do. Georgia made some excuse about checking on a delivery and left. As they chewed their bread in silence, Alicia pretended things were as they used to be. For a moment she forgot she was wearing an Amish dress and *kapp.* She just wanted to enjoy the quiet moment with Rowan by her side. She wanted to forget the ache and loneliness of the last year, and enjoy what it felt like to listen to his laugh, to see his smile.

Whole Wheat Oatmeal Bread

4 cups quick oats
1 cup brown sugar or honey
1/2 cup butter
4 tablespoons salt
3 packets yeast
18 to 20 cups bread flour

In a large bowl, mix together the oats, sugar, butter, and salt. Add yeast to 8 cups boiling water and mix into batter; add 18 to 20 cups bread flour. Cover bowl with a towel and put in a warm place. Let rise until double in size and punch down. Let rise a second time until double in size and punch down. Preheat oven to 350 degrees. Divide dough into 6 or 7 pieces. Place in greased loaf pans. Bake until tops are nice and brown. Makes 6 or 7 loaves.

THIRTEEN

A house is made of walls and beams; a home is made of love and dreams.

AMISH PROVERB

A knock at the door announced a visitor. Joy stopped her foot on the sewing machine pedal and set the dish towel to the side. She'd come up with a unique design for Lovina to sell at her pie shop not long after Me, Myself, and Pie opened. She started by making aprons, and it was Grace who'd suggested the towels. Joy sewed a strip of fabric with a quilted pattern on the bottom seam and added rickrack edging. Over the last ten months she'd lost track of how many she'd made.

She hurried to the front door, expecting her cousins. Instead Matthew stood there, hat in hand. His wide eyes were hopeful. "Joy, I was hoping you were still up. I saw the light on, and when I neared the door I heard the whir of the sewing machine."

"*Ja,* I'm up. Just trying to fill an order." She stepped to the side and waved him in. "Lovina is a slave driver." She smiled, releasing a breath. Thankful to see his smile. The last look she'd seen on his face was one of anger, anger over her interaction with the *Englischers.* She didn't have to worry about that anymore though, because she'd determined to stay as far away from those *Englischers* and their television show as possible.

Matthew eyed Joy's face, her hair. "You certain it's okay for me to come in?"

"*Ja, Mem, Dat,* and Faith have already retired for the night, but I was waiting up for Lovina. She's working late tonight . . . which really means she's enjoying a piece of pie with Noah after the shop is closed for the evening."

He stepped inside, shut the door behind him, and followed her into the kitchen. Then he paused and gazed at her hair again. "Honey-brown hair," he whispered, barely loud enough for her to hear.

"Excuse me?"

"Last night, when I was thinking about the color of your hair, I couldn't quite remember. At first I thought golden brown, but that didn't seem quite right. Honey brown . . . *ja,* that suits you better."

She motioned to the table and they sat down. "Speaking of honey, how about something sweet?"

She pulled a plate from a cupboard, opened the storage container on the counter, and took out two lemon bars. She set the plate before him and then scooped two forks out of a drawer. She couldn't hide her smile as she sat down. With three bites Matthew's lemon bar was gone. Joy picked up her fork, but her stomach was flipping around, and she couldn't take a bite. Instead, she returned her fork to the table, thankful he'd stopped by.

Under Matthew's gaze, Joy captured one of her *kapp* strings and twisted it around her finger. She felt his eyes on her, deep down in her core.

Heat rose to her cheeks, and she resisted the urge to fan her face. She glanced away, unsure what to do or say.

He chuckled. "I like that I can see what you're feeling just by looking at your face."

"You do?"

"*Ja,* and your name suits you well. It always seems as if you're smiling. Well, except for the other day." He cleared his throat. "I'm sorry, Joy. I didn't mean to get so angry."

"I understand. I —"

"*Ne.*" He held up his hand. "Don't forgive me so easily. It's not right. It's just that there were so many people, and it seemed like everyone was looking at us. And . . . well, when that *Englischer* came up, they all saw that too. I was more confused than anything."

Joy nodded as if she understood, but she really didn't. It's not as if she got the attention of the *Englischer,* desiring to talk to him. It's not as if she knew him or had expected him to approach her.

"*Ja.* I suppose those *Englischers* are just used to the attention. Being in television and all."

Matthew nodded, and then seeing that she wasn't eating her lemon bar, picked up his fork again.

"Go ahead," she said with a chuckle.

He ate that one in three bites too and then accepted the glass of water she offered.

"So do you think you can meet me for breakfast tomorrow?" he asked. "We'll be starting a new job, and I don't have to be there until after ten."

"I'd love —" She stopped the flow of words spilling out. "Oh *ne.*"

"What?"

"I have to make a delivery tomorrow

134

morning. Six Amish quilts before eight o'clock. I don't think it'll take much time for me to drop them off, but I wouldn't want to tell you I'll be there and then not show up."

"Someone ordered six quilts?"

"*Ja,* they . . . or rather *she* did. This lady walked into the fabric store and pointed out the quilts she wanted. The price didn't even seem to be a concern."

"And she's staying around here?"

"*Ja.* She wrote down the address for me. I remember it being around Pinecraft, but I didn't pay much attention to it."

"It's not for that television show, is it? Because if you'd like me to go with you . . ."

A tension built in her chest. Was it for the television show? She didn't think so. Joy bit her lower lip. But what if it was? *I'd better handle this errand on my own.*

"How about this . . . Why don't I make the delivery and then stop by your house? I want to drop off a dish towel for your *mem.* A birthday present of sorts. My delivery shouldn't take too long."

"*Ja,* that's a *gut* idea. I suppose I should be around for *Mem*'s birthday breakfast, and she would love to have you there for it too. She cooks one for herself every year, and *Dat* always surprises her with flowers."

135

"If he always does it, is it really a surprise?"

"He likes to think so."

"Well, if you're sure neither of them would mind me being there, I wouldn't want to miss seeing her act!"

Their laughter merged and danced around the table.

"Speaking of her birthday, I know she'll love the recipe box. I also talked to Lovina about it, and she would love to have some for the store. Do you think you could make twenty?"

"Twenty!" He choked out the word.

"*Ja*. Is that too many?"

"Well, if I didn't have a full-time job . . ." He let his voice trail off, almost with a wistful tone.

"Maybe you should try woodworking as a job. Once Mose is up on his feet again, I bet he'll appreciate extra work. Not to tell you what to do . . ."

"Telling me what to do? I don't see it that way. It's more like believing in me." He smiled. "You always surprise me, Joy. I was afraid to share my dreams with you — dreams of doing more in my workshop."

"Well, one thing is for certain — we like to dream around our home. With Lovina's pie shop and Hope's garden . . . all sorts of

136

dreams are coming to light."

"And what about you?" Matthew leaned closer, reaching his hand across the table. His palm was open to her. Seeing that, she knew his heart was too. "What do you dream about most?"

Joy placed her hand in his, allowing her small hand to be engulfed in his larger one. "I've never been one to have big, fancy dreams. I never wanted to open a shop or create something big. I do enjoy sewing, but mostly" — she squeezed his hand — "all I've wanted is this. Just knowing I have someone to care for and knowing he cares for me back."

"It's grown into much more than care, and you know it." Emotion seemed to tighten Matthew's throat, and his voice grew deep. "Before now, before this, I didn't put too much planning into the future. I sort of allowed things to happen as they did, knowing the *gut* Lord has us under His watchful eye. But lately, well, I've been thinking about it a lot more too. And I wouldn't mind if each night ended like this, with us talking and . . ." He stood and leaned over the table more, and Joy leaned forward too, anticipating a kiss. But just as their lips touched, footsteps sounded on the back porch. Without hesitation they both fell back into their seats. Joy's heartbeat quickened, both from the kiss and the thought of being caught. Matthew's eyes widened and Joy's hand covered her face, attempting to hold back a giggle.

"Oops," he whispered.

The door opened, and Lovina walked in. She waved at Matthew and then pointed to the crumbs on the plate in front of him. "Oh, did you make lemon bars, Joy? I was craving them all day, and when you crave lemon bars, pie just doesn't fix it."

She hurried to the counter and opened the container, pulling out one bar. After taking a bite she eyed them. "I'm not interrupting something, am I?" One of her eyebrows rose.

"Not too much, and . . . I did tell Matthew that you like the idea of recipe boxes."

Lovina nodded. "Oh, and cookbook racks too. I was going to mention that. I've been asked if we carry them many times. You know, just simple wooden racks to hold someone's cookbook off the counter." She shrugged and turned to the sink to wash her hands. "I don't know why, but they'd sell well. Personally, I know where the best recipes are in a book by the amount of dried food on their pages."

Matthew squeezed Joy's hand, and her lips

pressed into a tight smile. Yes, many more nights like this without having to worry about family members coming in and out and interrupting their kisses. But until then Joy would enjoy every moment. And she could see in Matthew's eyes that he would too.

He pulled his hand back and stood. "See you in the morning then? After the delivery, at my house?"

"*Ja.* I'll see you there."

She walked him to the front door, wondering again how she'd been so blessed. She wouldn't question it, only be thankful for it. And even as she watched Matthew walk away, she felt complete. She wanted nothing more than to see what the weeks and months had in store for them both. Surely things would only get better from here.

Lemon Bars

Crust
2 cups all-purpose flour
1/2 cup confectioners' sugar, divided
1 cup butter

Preheat oven to 325 degrees. Mix together flour, 1/4 cup of the confectioners' sugar, and butter. Press into bottom of 9 by 9-inch pan. Bake for 20 minutes.

Filling
2 cups sugar
1/4 cup all-purpose flour
1/4 cup fresh lemon juice
4 eggs, beaten

In a large bowl, mix sugar, flour, and lemon juice. Add beaten eggs; mix well. Pour over hot crust. Bake for 25 minutes. Remove from oven and dust with remaining confectioners' sugar. Cool completely before cutting.

FOURTEEN

If you always wait for the right time,
you might never begin.
AMISH PROVERB

Joy paused in front of the small house, and a dull ache bowed her shoulders. Matthew was right. This was the house they were using for the television show. She took a deep breath and blew it out, thankful that she'd come alone. She should make the delivery and get on with her day without it becoming too much of a fuss.

Her hand tightened on the handle of the wagon. Six quilts were wrapped neatly and stacked. She'd walked by this house hundreds of times without really paying attention to it. It was the color of oatmeal with a small peaked roof covering the porch. Two tan, plastic chairs sat on either side of the white door. If she didn't know it was being used by a television show, she wouldn't think twice about it. It didn't look much different from any of the other houses on this street.

Her flip-flops patted the ground as she walked to the front and knocked on the screen door frame. She waited a few minutes and then opened the screen door to knock louder. Her fist paused midair. A sign was taped to the door.

Deliveries: Please go to . . . It listed an address a few blocks away. Joy was familiar with that area. Before buying the warehouse for Me, Myself, and Pie, Lovina had considered buying an old theater on that street. There were more warehouses there too. Were the television people using one of them to store supplies? She wasn't quite sure how such things worked.

It took no more than ten minutes to walk to the address. And their presence was easy to spot. Metal fencing had been erected around a large warehouse. Small trailers, like ones used for camping, had been set up in the back of the warehouse, behind the fencing. Vehicles were parked out front — both cars and delivery trucks. A security guard manned the entrance. Joy couldn't help but smile seeing him standing so erect and serious. Did they really think their Amish neighbors would try to break in and bother their things? She chuckled at the idea.

Joy took tentative steps toward the security guard. "I have a delivery. I went to the other —"

The man's brown eyes had fixed on her and narrowed. "Name?"

"Joy Miller. I work over at Pinecraft Fabric and Quilts. I'm not sure my name would be on the list though, since I never told it to the woman who bought these quilts."

He scanned the paper on the clipboard in front of him. "I'm sorry, Miss Miller, your name isn't on the list."

Didn't I tell you that would be the case? She held in the words, considering the minutes ticking down. Her empty stomach rumbled. She was going to miss the birthday breakfast.

His face folded into a scowl, and he looked again.

"I imagine my name won't be there as many times as you look." She tried not to get ruffled. "You see, a nice lady came by yesterday and bought these quilts. She gave me another address, but a sign there said deliveries must be made here."

"Quilts?" He eyed the wagon suspiciously. "And do you know the woman's name?"

She pulled out the business card and eyed

143

it, but the woman had used one of the cards from the fabric shop. "I'm sorry. She didn't leave her name. She was pretty. She wasn't Amish. I think she had brown hair, maybe with some blond in it. Or was it red? She did use her credit card, but I don't remember much more about her."

"I'm sorry, miss." The scowl softened. "I'm sure you're telling the truth. I've just been told not to allow anyone entrance unless their name is on the list. If you give me your phone number I can check —"

"Sir, I don't have a phone and —"

"Charlie." A voice interrupted her words. A man's voice, one that she recognized. "She's all right. Let her in."

She glanced up and recognized the *Englischer* she'd helped that first night, the same man who'd approached her at the bus stop. He walked over to where she stood and paused, gazing down at her wagon. "I didn't know about a quilt delivery, but it sounds legit to me." He chuckled and waved her in. "I assume this is for the set?"

The security guard stepped aside, but he still didn't look pleased. "If I can add your name." He held his pen up.

"She's fine, Charlie, I promise." The man walked toward the open warehouse door. He wore jeans and a pressed white shirt.

Still gone was the ball cap of the first night. He walked as if he ran the place, and she had no doubt he did.

She pulled the wagon behind her and followed the man. "Thank you, uh . . . I'm sorry. I don't know your name."

"My name is Steven Spielberg," he said, "and this is my lot."

"It's nice to meet you, Steven, but if I can just drop off —"

Laughter spilled from his lips, interrupting her words. "No, no. It was just a joke. Steven Spielberg is the most famous director in the world. Someone I aspire to be like, but I suppose I'm not being funny if you can't follow along." He gazed at her. "I honestly can't believe you haven't heard of him."

"Has he visited Pinecraft before? I really only get to know some of the regular *Englischers* who visit the fabric shop. And speaking of that, I do need to get going." She looked down at the quilts. "If you'll just tell me where to put these."

He paused and turned to her. "*Englischers?* Like from England?"

"*Ne,* not from England. It's just a name, a reference." She bit her lips. "It's what we call people who aren't Amish. I don't mean to be disrespectful, I promise. It's just a

145

common term."

"Interesting." He tapped his temple as if making a mental note. "I'm Rowan Grant. I'm the director here. I'm actually glad you stopped by. I'd love you to take an insider's look at our set."

"An insider?" She cringed at that. Being Amish was a faith, a community, not a club. But how could he understand that? "Yes, I suppose I am."

She jutted out her chin. "But I don't have much time," she said more directly this time. "There's a birthday breakfast —"

"It'll only take a minute." He took the handle of the wagon and quickly pulled it inside the large warehouse door. She had no choice but to follow. *Mem* would not be pleased if she returned without the wagon.

Joy walked into the warehouse, and her mouth dropped open.

"This is our open set. It's where we'll be filming the television show."

The set looked exactly like the living room of many Amish homes in Pinecraft. There were side walls and a back wall, but the front was open. It was as if someone had cut up an Amish home and partially put it back together here. The back wall was painted white. There was a gold sofa with a diamond pattern situated next to a white

146

sofa with a brown throw over the back. An old brown recliner had tufted cushions and a ruffled skirt.

A side table had coffee rings, and a Bible and devotional book sat there. White curtains hung in the windows, and there were two prints of birds that could have been calendar pages at one time. Joy tilted her head, and a strange sensation came over her. It was almost as if she'd been in this home before, which she knew wasn't possible since it wasn't a real home.

The kitchen looked similar to others in Pinecraft too. It had smoky-gray and tan linoleum, a gold refrigerator, and a narrow oven positioned next to it. Large canisters sat on the white Formica countertops. She chuckled seeing that the lower cabinets and upper cabinets were mismatched. The lower cabinets were a dark walnut color and the upper ones a light oak. It was just like her Amish neighbors to pick up sets at the thrift stores or as cast-offs when someone was getting a remodel. Sitting on the counter was a basket of clothespins and a basket of laundry as if the woman of the home was just getting ready to head outside to hang clothes on the line.

"Amazing," she whispered, looking around.

"Glad you approve."

"It looks just like the inside of many an Amish home."

"Yes, I know. I have a good set design team. They know how to research. They may or may not have been in the area for a month taking a look at some of the houses for sale."

A shiver moved up her arms as he said that. The Amish here were used to being watched. People were always curious. But to learn someone was watching that closely gave her an odd sensation. Had someone been watching her work while pretending to shop in Pinecraft Fabric and Quilts? Or maybe watching her and Matthew at the park as they talked across the table?

A chill moved down the back of Joy's neck, and something inside told her she needed to leave this warehouse and not look back. Yet the man still held the wagon's handle, and more than that, the happy look on his face gave her pause. He didn't seem as though he was out to mock the Amish. He appeared to honestly care about how he was to portray them.

She looked around, eyeing the lights, the cameras, and the numerous pieces of the set. It was a strange and new world, yet she had to admit it was a bit fascinating. *They are really putting all this work into a story about us? About our ways and our faith?*

Elizabeth's words, spoken at the sewing frolic, filled her mind. *The* gut *Lord uses many ways to share His story.* Was God a part of this? Would He really use *Englischers* to help others understand why they chose to live plain and chose to escape the trappings of the world?

"So you really think it looks good?" The man's voice interrupted her thoughts. "I want to make sure it's realistic."

"It's a wonderful job. You've done well." She smiled and then quickly hid it. She didn't want to act too friendly. Didn't want this director to think running into each other would be a regular occurrence.

"I'm glad you like it. And I know our set designer will make good use of these quilts. I believe you said you work at the quilt shop."

Joy felt the anxiety start at the back of her knees and climb upward like stinging fire ants. The thought of him coming to her workplace or stopping her on the street again pushed worries to the forefront of her mind.

"Yes, but I don't work there every day. It's really only a part-time thing. I enjoy helping Elizabeth out. She's my boss, and she's older. Sometimes I do take on extra shifts . . ." *Quiet, Joy,* she chided herself. *Stop blabbering so.* "I mean, I'm not there much. Not often at all, and —"

Her words were interrupted by women's voices. They entered the set and looked around. One was tall and slender, and she was wearing an Amish *kapp* and dress. The other was shorter and chubby, and she was snapping shots of the taller woman with her cell phone.

"I just want to see how these colors show up in a photo," the shorter woman said. She looked around. "Seriously, could they have come up with more shabby furniture? I mean, do people's homes really —"

Rowan — whatever kind of name that was — glanced at Joy and winced as if embarrassed by their words. "Alicia, Georgia, head over here. I'd like you to meet someone." He waved to them.

The woman in the Amish clothes glanced over her shoulder, causing her *kapp* to slip slightly. Seeing her face, Joy recognized her immediately. It was the woman she'd met a few days ago at the bus stop. She'd introduced herself as Alicia. But she looked completely different without makeup, in an Amish dress, and with her hair pinned up. She also didn't look right. Joy folded her

150

arms over her chest and cocked her head.

Rowan leaned closer. "So you don't approve?"

"Uh, what do you mean?"

"I can tell by the way you're looking at Alicia. You don't approve?"

"It's, well, I think . . ." She pressed her lips together, unsure how to respond. The *Englisch* woman wore the traditional clothing of the Old Order Amish — a long-sleeved dress, covered by a black apron that fell just below her knees. There was a problem though. The dress was Old Amish from Ohio, and the *kapp* was like those worn in Pennsylvania.

Then she noticed the woman's shoes. She eyed the low-heeled pumps and tried to stifle a laugh. "Oh, I hope you fix that before they begin filming."

"Fix what?"

"I'm so sorry." She covered her mouth with her hand and then removed it again. "I really don't want to get involved. I was just making a delivery." She reached down and placed a hand on the quilts. "If you can tell me where to put these, I will be going now."

"I can handle those." He picked up the pile of quilts, set them on a large crate behind a camera, and then turned back to her. She grabbed the handle of the empty wagon. Then she turned and took a few steps toward the exit, pulling the wagon behind her.

"Wait!" Rowan's voice was soft, yet commanding.

She stopped in her steps and turned. "What?"

He widened his stance, planting himself, and then he crossed his arms over his chest. "I know you don't want to get involved, but my name is going to be on those credits. I want to know . . . what didn't we get right?"

She looked to the two women, who were half paying attention and half staring at the phone with intensity.

"Eight ten!" the woman he'd called Georgia called out. "So close." She pulled the phone closer to her face. "But look, you got the biggest photo on the page. They must really like your Amish getup."

Joy turned back to the man. "It's just, well, anyone who's Amish will know they aren't really Amish. It's the subtle things."

He straightened his shoulders. "If it's the phones, they're going to put them away."

"It's not just the phones. It's more than that. Their clothes are all wrong. They're wearing *kapp*s from the Lancaster area, but their dresses are what's worn in Ohio. And that woman has a wedding ring —"

152

"But she plays a widow."

"Yes, but we don't wear wedding rings . . . or any jewelry for that matter."

Georgia glanced up from her phone. "Not even wedding rings?" Her brow furrowed. "I thought I read somewhere they did." She turned to Alicia and shrugged. "You know Rowan just called me five days ago when the original costume designer had to back out. I did my best. I suppose you're going to have to lose that bling too."

Joy shook her head. "And the *kapp* —"

"Is that what you call their hats?" Rowan asked.

"Yes, it is." She sighed and stepped forward, untying the woman's *kapp* strings. "First, we don't tie *kapp* strings; they just hang down. Unless you're a toddler or unless you're cooking — then you move them to the back."

Rowan tilted his head expectantly. "Is there anything else?"

"Well, her hands and face aren't right."

"Hands and face?"

"There's shiny polish on her nails and makeup —"

Rowan nodded. "Let me guess — you don't do that."

"No."

"But I'm not wearing makeup. At all."

Alicia stepped forward, stretching out her hands as if offering a plea. "I washed my face and —"

"Your eyebrows. They're shaped and plucked. And that lip gloss has a shine. And there must be a tint to your moisturizer. I can see it."

The actress's mouth dropped open. "Lip gloss? I can't even wear lip gloss?" She turned to the director with pleading eyes.

He sighed and ran his fingers through his hair. Then he motioned to a guy setting up cameras with a curve of his finger. The man sauntered over. "Listen. We're not going to be able to shoot today. This young woman has informed me of some serious issues with wardrobe."

The cameraman gaped. "Are you kidding me? Do you know how much it'll cost if we lose a day?"

"Yes, of course. But do you know how much it'll cost if our show becomes the laughingstock of the network?" His voice was tight, and from the look in his gaze, Joy could tell he was holding back.

The other man eyed her and narrowed his own gaze. Her hands tightened into fists, and she pulled them tight against her. She hadn't meant to cause any problems. *You just should have kept your mouth shut.*

"I'm sorry if I caused any trouble. I'd best be going."

Rowan nodded to her, and she turned and hurried off. She couldn't get out of that building fast enough. She also realized how naive Elizabeth had been. How could a television show share the real reason for their plain lifestyle if they couldn't even figure out that married Amish women didn't wear wedding rings? Obviously it was easy to build a set. Anyone could walk through an Amish home and re-create that, but unless one was raised in an Amish community, it was hard to understand the minor details and unwritten rules.

She hurriedly escaped out the tall door with the wagon clattering behind her. Joy sensed their eyes on her back, but she refused to turn or acknowledge how her minimal disapproval had messed up their grand plans. She hadn't meant to discourage them, but the man seemed to honestly want to know her thoughts. She was just glad she didn't have to reveal *all* her thoughts, because as she strode away the overlying thought was humor and disbelief. How did an *Englischer* expect to put on a dress and portray a lifestyle she'd never spent a day living? It was like a chicken putting on a fur coat and expecting to be accepted among the rabbits. What was under the costume made all the difference.

Being Amish was more than a way of dress and living. Their outward display was rooted in internal values and traditions. What the worldly people had left behind a century ago, her people still embraced: family, community, and sharing their life and work. It had to matter on the inside before anyone could portray it on the outside. No matter how nice Alicia seemed to be, there was a haunting look in her eyes that was hard to miss. More than that, the woman walked as if she carried a team of horses on her shoulders. Seeing that caused Joy's heart to ache, but it didn't cause her steps to slow. She had to get to the Slagels' house before too many questions were asked. And before she started wondering too hard about the problems of the *Englischers.*

Many Hands Make Light Work

In nineteenth-century rural America, social rituals grew up around tasks which could be accomplished quickly and efficiently by many hands. With the help of lots of friends and neighbors, a man could raise a small barn in one long day of work. Women had their equivalent in the quilting bee, where several women got together for the day to do the tedious, time-consuming work of finishing a quilt top made by one of them. Working together, they stitched through the three layers and added the finishing touches. Sometimes these quiltings were held simultaneously with the barn raisings, with a grand joyous feast ending the day of hard work and great pride. "The finishing of this quilt made a gala day for the neighborhood. It was unrolled and cut out with much excitement . . . It was truly a beautiful thing . . . an expression of the life of its occupants, a fit covering for those who made it."*

* Ellen H. Rollings, *New England Bygones* (Philadelphia: Lippincott, 1883), 238.

FIFTEEN

Kindness when given away keeps
coming back.
AMISH PROVERB

Matthew waited by the window, watching for Joy's approach. The aroma of caramel cinnamon rolls filled the kitchen. *Dat* sat at the table with his open Bible before him. The *Budget* sat next to it. *Dat* always took great care in reading both. Being a bishop was part sharing God's truth and part understanding the needs of the congregation he was chosen by God to serve.

Matthew turned back to his parents. "We can go ahead and eat if you'd like. I know *Dat* has to get going soon —"

"*Ne.*" *Mem* poured herself another cup of coffee. "I don't mind waiting. I enjoy Joy's company, and I'm thankful she's coming. So sorry she had to work so early though."

Dat pushed his glasses farther up his nose.

158

"Is the quilt shop open this early?"

Matthew crossed his arms and leaned against the window frame. "*Ne.* She said she had to make a delivery. Someone bought six quilts."

"Six quilts?" The spoon *Mem* had been stirring her coffee with clattered to the table. "Who would buy six quilts?"

Matthew shrugged. "I'm not sure." Worry folded his eyebrows. "I didn't think much of it."

Mem rubbed her brow. "*Ne* Amish person would buy six quilts. It had to be an *Englischer.*"

"The television show." His *dat* cleared his throat and it almost sounded like a low growl. "There has been a lot of talk about all the money they're spending around town. Buying up *gut* items to be used as props. Isn't it like the *Englisch* to waste like that?"

"Maybe you should have gone with her," his *mem* added. "You never know what they are up to over there."

Matthew's brow furrowed. He'd offered to go with Joy, but she'd quickly dismissed him. Had she known more about the delivery than she'd let on? Had it been to wherever they were filming the TV show? Something deep in his gut told him it had been. There wasn't any other explanation.

He moved to the table and sat down, wondering if he should go look for her. *Mem* slipped into the seat beside him. *Dat* removed his reading glasses and leaned forward.

"You need to encourage Joy not to get too involved. First the *Englischers* flood the village with their money, and next they'll be asking for helpers. I'm sure the wages will be well above what people usually get around here."

Dat glanced at Matthew and then back at *Mem,* who gave a nod. "Anywhere those TV people are doesn't seem like the type of place a young, single woman should spend her time. You don't know the type of influences . . ." Her voice trailed off.

"Joy is wise," Matthew stated, but his face flushed a little. Even as he said the words he remembered how she was singled out by the *Englischer.* He remembered how she'd helped the man, keeping it a secret from him. *What is she trying to hide?*

"She's a sweet girl. No one has a negative word to say about her," *Dat* stated, and from the look in the older man's eyes Matthew could finish the sentence for him — *yet.*

"She works hard and is so talented. You should see her hand-stitching — as neat and straight as if done by a machine," *Mem* stated, as if that proved her character.

A knock sounded at the back door, and Matthew rose. Joy stood there with a soft smile and a paper-wrapped package in her hand. "I'm so sorry. My delivery took me longer than I expected." She peeked around, catching sight of his *mem.* "Happy birthday! I hope I'm not too late."

Mem glanced over her shoulder, sending her *kapp* askew. "Oh, *danke.* I'm just glad you've come. You do like cinnamon rolls, don't you?"

Joy fiddled with the strings of her *kapp,* waiting to be let in.

Matthew opened his mouth to ask about the delivery but changed his mind. This was something they could talk about later, away from his parents. They liked her, and he didn't want to give them any reason not to. Matthew stepped aside, and she hurried inside.

Without hesitation Joy sank down onto the chair next to *Mem.* She placed the wrapped package on the table. "I hope you haven't opened your gifts yet."

A smile blossomed over his *mem*'s face. "*Ne,* I haven't. I told Matthew I wanted to wait."

Understanding his cue, he hurried to the

garage and took the small box off the shelf. He'd stained it and then given it a lacquer coating to make it shine. But his favorite part was what was inside, not only for *Mem* but for Joy too. It was a surprise neither of them expected.

He paused for a moment just outside the door, questioning if the time was right to include Joy's gift. He knew he wanted to marry Joy, but something inside nearly gave him pause. Should he ask her about this morning's delivery? Should he warn her about getting too involved with the *Englischers*? She seemed so impressionable.

In the end he decided his minor worries weren't enough to stop him from sharing the truth. He loved Joy, and he knew his parents believed her to be a wise choice for a bride. With the surprise inside the box, the days would be counting down until he confessed his love before the community. Until he made her his wife.

He entered the house, holding the recipe box behind his back. Matthew nodded his chin toward *Mem.* "Go ahead and open Joy's present first."

Mem didn't hesitate. She picked up the package from the table and opened it, pulling out two dish towels. A quilt pattern was sewn on the bottom of the towels in vibrant colors. On the top Joy had stitched one of *Mem*'s favorite sayings: "Kindness when given away keeps coming back."

"They're the colors from your flower garden," Joy gushed. "You do have some of the loveliest flowers."

"These dish towels are beautiful. What a thoughtful gift, Joy."

Joy turned to Matthew. "All right, your turn." Eagerness filled her eyes.

Matthew pulled his hand around and placed the recipe box on the table in front of *Mem*.

Mem's hands moved to her mouth, and she let out the smallest squeal. "So this is what you've been doing out there, *ja*?"

"Isn't it wonderful?" Joy jumped in before Matthew had a chance to comment. "I was talking to Lovina about it, and she'd love to sell them at her pie shop. She wants to order twenty to start, and she thinks they'll sell fast —"

"Twenty?" A chuckle spilled from his *dat*'s mouth. "When would you have time to make twenty recipe boxes?"

The hair on the back of Matthew's neck bristled, but he held back a scowl. *Dat* was one of the kindest men he knew . . . and also one of the most opinionated. "Well, they wouldn't have to be as intricate as

Mem's. It might take me a while —"

"Still, you have a job already." *Dat* closed his Bible and pushed it to the side. Then he leaned back in his chair and folded his arms over his chest. He always took that stance when trying to make his point. "You don't want to waste time on recipe boxes when you have more than enough construction work."

Tension wrapped around Matthew's chest like a vise. He felt Joy's gaze on him, but he couldn't look at her. He knew his father meant well, but *Dat* had never understood his love for woodworking. To *Dat* it was a hobby — something that should be done in one's spare time. And like most Amish men, *Dat* thought there was little spare time with all the work required to care for a family.

Instead of commenting, Matthew turned to his *mem.* "Open the box — there's more of your gift inside."

Mem opened the box and gasped. "Recipes! Where did they come from?"

"Well, you'll just have to look." He leaned forward and started to flip through them. "Some are from your sisters and some from cousins. I wrote to a lot of them, but I also asked Aunt Marilyn to help me spread the word, and she outdid herself. And . . ." He picked up one recipe card and turned it over. "You'll see on the backs that many people sent birthday wishes too."

"Look at this — the corn casserole from Rosemary Eash. She's my cousin on my mother's side," *Mem* explained to Joy. "Ground Beef Supper from Shari Weaver, who shares the same wedding anniversary we do, just off by a year. Sourdough cinnamon rolls and maple drop cookies from my sister, Edna." *Mem* clapped her hands together with glee. "Oh, I've asked for this cookie recipe a dozen times. I'm so happy she finally took the time to write it down." *Mem* flipped through more of the recipes and then came to an envelope and paused. "I recognize this handwriting." Her eyes darted to Matthew. "What is this? Who sent it?"

"Aunt Edna sent it, of course. I asked her to." He touched his *mem*'s shoulder. "You know what it is. You know why it was sent."

Mem glanced over at Joy, and tears filled her eyes. *Mem*'s hand covered her mouth, and Matthew was almost certain sobs would soon follow. After all, *Mem* had wanted this for him nearly as much as he'd wanted it.

Joy eyed him curiously. "Is it a special recipe? It must be extra special to get that type of response."

Mem lowered her hand. Her smile doubled

165

in size, and she reached over and gave Joy a tight hug. "Oh, I am so excited."

Laughter spilled from Joy's lips. "I . . . I'm so sorry. I don't understand." She sucked in a breath as *Mem* released her. "Is it a special recipe you've been wanting? Or recipes?"

Mem glanced up at him again. "Should I tell her or should you?"

He moved around the table and sat down next to *Dat. Dat*'s frown had disappeared, and his smile was nearly as big as his wife's. Matthew's relationship with Joy was something they both agreed on.

Matthew chuckled. "Go ahead, *Mem*."

"*Ja,* they are recipes, all right. My *mem*'s favorite. Family recipes she passed down to each of her daughters and daughters-in-law. An envelope of these recipes is given to every bride in our family on her wedding day. These recipes aren't anything special to most families, but they are meaningful to us."

"But I don't understand." Joy looked from his *mem* to Matthew, and then back to his *mem* again. "If you already received these on your wedding day, why did you get them again?"

Mem's eyes twinkled. "Oh, dear girl. They're not for me. They're for you. If I'm not mistaken, Matthew asked my sister to send them so I could give them to you. Not today, of course. But from the look of love on my son's face, very soon."

Joy gasped, and she turned to look at Matthew. "They're for me? On my wedding day?"

"It's just something I've been thinking about." He loved seeing the brightness of her face. "There is a lot to talk about, many plans to make, but I wanted you to know, Joy." He looked to his mother's and father's faces, and both seemed pleased. "I asked my aunt to send those recipes so you'd know I hope to marry you soon. Maybe not as soon as your two sisters, but hopefully not too long after."

He leaned forward, focusing on Joy's face. Tears rimmed her lower lids, and her lower lip trembled. Her mouth opened slightly but no words emerged.

"That's, uh, if you wish for the same thing."

A broad, luminous smile spread across her face. "*Ja,* of course I wish for the same thing. I can't imagine wishing for anything more."

Dat nodded in agreement. "And I can't think of a more upright young woman for my son. You'll be a delight to have in our family when the time is right, Joy. All my children have made wise choices so far."

Joy clasped her hands together, and more tears filled her eyes. She quickly dabbed them away. "I don't know why I'm crying. It's just . . . well . . ." She reached over and placed her hand in his *mem*'s. "I feel like I've stolen all the attention from your day."

"Not at all." *Mem* clucked her tongue. "Don't let that bother you. It's a gift to me. *You* are a gift to me. I've prayed for my son his whole life. I've also prayed for the special lady who would someday be his bride. I can't think of a more perfect choice —"

The ringing of Matthew's cell phone interrupted *Mem*'s words. He pulled it from his pocket and looked at the number. "Oh, it's Mose. He must be wondering where I am. I should answer this."

"*Ja,* of course." Joy patted his hand. "Go on to work. I'll just stay and help your *mem* clean up."

He nodded and walked to the door as both women offered him a wave. As he exited, he could hear *Mem* telling Joy about how the tradition started. He knew the story well. Grandma, when told that her cancer had spread, had set to work on writing out as many recipe cards as she could. It was her way to pass on something special to future family members.

Matthew's heart felt full as he sauntered down the front porch steps. He had no doubt *Mem* would do a fine job protecting that envelope of recipes until his wedding day. The more time he spent with Joy, the more he hoped the day would be sooner rather than later. He was older than most bachelors were when they married, but he had waited for a reason. He didn't want to marry just anyone. He wanted to find the right one to share his life with. Now that he had, Matthew didn't know how long he wanted to wait. He needed Joy by his side — for her smile and for the daily joy she brought into his life. Mostly he needed someone who believed in him and someone he could believe in. A happy marriage wasn't simply built on love, he knew, but on sharing dreams and living them out one day at a time.

Soft Caramel Cinnamon Rolls

1 3-ounce box cook-and-serve vanilla pudding
2 cups milk
1/2 cup butter
2 packets yeast
2 teaspoons sugar
1/2 cup warm water
2 eggs, beaten
1/2 teaspoon salt
1 tablespoon vegetable oil
6 cups bread flour
butter
brown sugar
ground cinnamon

Cook pudding and milk according to package directions. Add butter and let set until lukewarm. Meanwhile, dissolve yeast and sugar in warm water until foamy. Combine pudding mixture with eggs, salt, oil, and yeast mixture. Mix well. Gradually add enough flour to make a soft and somewhat sticky dough. Knead well. Place back in bowl and cover with towel. Let rise 45 minutes. Roll out onto clean countertop. Spread with generous amount of melted butter and cover with brown sugar and cinnamon. Roll up and cut into 1 1/2-inch pieces. Place in greased baking pans. Bake for 15 to 20 minutes, until golden brown. Frost with caramel icing.

Caramel Icing
1/2 cup butter
1 cup brown sugar
1/4 cup milk
2 cups confectioners' sugar

In a small saucepan, bring butter, sugar, and milk to a boil. Cook over medium heat for two minutes. Cool and then stir in confectioners' sugar.

Sixteen

You can tell when you're on the right
track — it's usually uphill.
AMISH PROVERB

The sewing machine hummed in Pinecraft
Fabric and Quilts as Joy worked on aprons
to sell in Lovina's pie shop. One thing she
enjoyed about working with Elizabeth was
that when all her work was done around the
shop and there weren't any customers, Joy
had time to sew.

Yet there was no joy in her work today.
Instead a darkness hung over her, blocking
out the light from the front windows that
dared to shine through. She'd hardly slept
last night. Happiness mixed with despair.
Happiness over Matthew's gift — a promise
of their future — mixed with the reality of
the needs at home.

Just as she had been getting ready for bed
last night, Faith had entered their room with

172

bloodshot, puffy eyes. She'd gone with *Mem* to *Dat*'s doctor appointment, and they'd gotten an estimate for the cost of *Dat*'s treatments. It was more money than they could imagine.

She never was great at math, but she had a lot of aprons to sew to even make a dent in the money they'd need for *Dat*'s therapy. She also planned on talking to her cousins to see if they'd be interested in taking any Made with Love aprons back with them to sell up north. They certainly sold well in Lovina's pie shop. Maybe they would in Ohio too. Anything would help.

But as she focused on sewing a straight seam, she resisted the urge to simply throw up her hands. What could selling a few measly aprons do to offset such a large bill?

The bell on the front door jingled, and Joy lifted her foot from the pedal. "Be right with you," she called, attempting a chirpy tone. Then she rose from the chair and turned. "It's a beautif—"

The words caught in her throat. Standing just inside the doorway was Rowan, the director she'd talked to on the set. The one who seemed to show up everywhere. And the last person she wanted to see in the shop today. She already had enough worries without him showing up. She just hoped today wasn't a day Matthew decided to come to the shop and surprise her.

Rowan's smile brightened as he strode toward her. "Oh, good. I'm so glad I found you. I had to ask a few people where the fabric and quilt shop was. Thankfully, the third person gave me good directions." He chuckled.

"There isn't anything wrong with the quilts, is there? If you want to exchange one . . ."

He wore a sweater over a white T-shirt and pushed up the sleeves as he talked. "No, it's nothing like that. I actually came looking for you."

"Me?" The hairs on the back of her neck stood on end. She rose from the chair and walked around it, gripping the top rung. Putting space between them. She'd helped the man once, and now he considered her his best friend. *Doesn't he have any Englischers to bother?*

"I need help." He raised an eyebrow. "Or rather the show needs help. It seems our costume designer, Georgia, doesn't know what she's doing. She's the first to admit it. Not that I blame her. I got online last night and . . . well, there are so many details. I had no idea there were so many Amish communities and that they all have different ways of doing things."

Joy cocked her head, wondering why this was suddenly such a big surprise to him. "I'm still not sure what you need, especially from me."

"Well, I was wondering if you know of any place where we could find some Amish dresses. If there is a store we can look at —"

"No." The word shot from her lips. "No, there's no store for that. At least not anywhere close to here."

His gaze narrowed, and he eyed her with disbelief. "There's no place we can shop for Amish clothes?"

"No, there isn't. All of our clothes are handmade. Each woman sews clothes for her family. Young women start sewing their own dresses while they are still in their teens."

"So there's no Walmart for Amish smocks?"

"*Ne.* I'm sorry. I wish I could help, but . . ."

"But you sew, right?" He pointed to the sewing machine. "Did you sew your dress?"

"Yes, of cour—"

"And could you sew some dresses for us?"

"Well, I have other things I'm working on — aprons I need to make and sell."

175

Rowan pulled out his wallet. "How about I order twenty aprons at double the going price? No, make that triple. And I'll triple whatever price you would have charged someone to make some dresses too."

Her eyes widened, and she sucked in a breath. Was this a real offer? He would do that — pay that?

"I don't know. There's no way I could sew that fast. I mean, if you already want to start filming —"

"Listen. I really need your help. You don't even have to sew all the dresses. If you find some friends to sew them — maybe even your sisters or cousins — I will pay you."

In her mind's eye she pictured that. She imagined herself going to the next sewing frolic and asking the women to sew dresses that would be worn by *Englisch* actresses. She remembered their reactions against the show. They would have no part of this. And why would they? This show — this man — was going to portray the Amish as he saw fit. Yes, he had gotten the set right, but if the wardrobe was any indication of what was to come, a lot of money was going to be spent and still the Amish would be a laughing-stock to the *Englisch* world.

Joy opened her mouth to tell him she wasn't interested when a second memory came to mind. It was Faith's tearstained face as she clutched Joy's hand the night before. After showing Joy the cost of *Dat*'s treatments, Faith had put the estimate aside and grabbed Joy's hands. "We need to pray now, Joy," she had said. "Pray that God will do a miracle and provide this money. Pray that even tomorrow there will be an unexpected blessing that will start us off strong."

An unexpected blessing. Joy eyed the man before her. He looked at her with a pleading gaze. Could he be the answer to Faith's eager request? She placed a hand over her heart and then returned to her seat. She had nodded, telling Faith she would pray, but truth be told she had worried instead. She'd lain awake considering how she could revise her apron pattern so she could make more aprons, faster. Yet here was a man standing before her offering more money for less work. Or more money for no work, if that was what she chose — just as long as she made sure he got what he needed.

"You don't mind if I don't sew them myself?"

"No, of course not. I also noticed how uncomfortable you were at the set. So if you'd rather have the actresses come here for fittings . . ."

Surprise arched her eyebrows. "Really?"

He leaned a bit closer. "I know not every-one in town is happy about us filming our show here. I don't want to cause any prob-lems."

Tears sprung to her eyes unexpectedly, and the darkness that had been hovering over her faded. The understanding look in this *Englischer*'s face — the soft smile on his lips — unnerved her. She'd believed in God for as long as she could remember. She'd first heard about Jesus and His ways on her mother's knee, but He had been a distant Lord who loved her. It didn't seem as though He was really involved in her life. But with this man walking in the door and offering what he did less than a day after Faith had prayed for help, it was . . . well, it was a miracle. Could God really use *Englischers* to bless her family?

Joy released the breath she'd been hold-ing.

"If you need some time to think about it . . ."

She held up a finger. "Uh, just give me a minute."

She never could have guessed this was how God would help them, but now the truth was as plain as day. Or as Elizabeth had said to her more than once, "You may not be able to see God with your physical eyes, but sometimes He does something big to show off."

Joy swallowed down her emotion. As she looked at the man's eyes she could almost picture God smiling at her, showing her He cared about *Dat* and about her too. "Yes, I think I . . . we . . . can do that. But the shop here might be too public a place." She nibbled on her lower lip, considering inviting them to her home. Should she ask her parents about it first? She tried to imagine their response. *Dat* was always kind and welcoming to *Englischers.* He wouldn't have a problem with it, she knew. *Mem* was unsure about the television show, but there had been a look of relief in her face when Faith and Joy had promised to help. Some of the other ladies might not understand why they would invite the television actresses into their home, but deep down Joy knew *Mem* would be accepting, thankful even, for this blessing of extra money that could go toward *Dat*'s treatments.

"Do you think the actresses could come by my parents' house later today? I'm off at three o'clock."

He nodded. "Yes. We can make it work. I have five main actresses. If we could get enough dresses to start, just one or two for each one . . ."

"I'll see what we can do." She took one of Elizabeth's business cards, wrote down her home address, and handed it to him. He took it, pulled out his phone and snapped a photo, and then handed it back. "I don't need this. I'd just lose it. I'm horrible about keeping track of papers. But I'll make sure my actresses are at your house later today."

"Yes. It sounds good. *Danke.* I mean, thank you." She considered inviting the actresses to stay and enjoy the Busy Day Casserole she'd seen her *mem* preparing this morning, but she changed her mind. That might be asking too much from her parents too soon.

She watched him go and considered taking her lunch break early so she could run down the street to Yoder's, where Faith worked, to tell her the news. Wouldn't her sister be surprised? Wouldn't she be excited to hear how fast God had answered their prayers?

Then, as she watched the man climb into his car, a new thought struck her, and Joy sucked in a breath. What would Matthew think? The excited beat of her heart from the provision of funds for *Dat*'s treatment slowed, and the dark clouds from earlier returned. Would Matthew understand? She still hadn't told him about *Dat*'s condition, and she knew how he felt about getting involved with the *Englischers.*

Will this hurt things between us? Joy folded her hands across her chest and then pulled in her arms. It was a risk she had to take, she supposed. Hopefully Matthew would understand. It didn't seem like a co-incidence to her that this director would show up at the store the day after Faith's prayer.

Lord, show me how to navigate these waters. I want to do what's right. I want to help. And . . . she didn't want to admit it, but she wanted Matthew's love too. He was her future.

Matthew seemed like everything she'd ever wanted in a husband. God surely wouldn't ask her to choose between her father and the man she loved, would He? Joy released a sigh. She supposed by this afternoon she'd find out.

Busy Day Casserole

1 1/2 cups cubed ham or ground beef
1 cup diced potatoes
1 cup diced carrots
1/2 cup cooked peas
1/2 cup cooked green beans
salt and ground black pepper to taste

Preheat oven to 350 degrees. If using ground beef, brown the meat in a skillet and then drain. Add the potatoes, carrots, and enough water to cover. Cook until crisp but still tender. Stir in peas and beans. Again add enough boiling water to cover. Into this stir 1 tablespoon flour mixed with water to make a paste. Place this mixture into a 9 by 13-inch casserole dish. Top with favorite biscuit dough, dropped by spoonfuls onto ham or ground beef mixture. Bake for 20 to 30 minutes. Biscuits should be golden brown.

Seventeen

Instead of putting others in their place,
put yourself in their place.
Amish Proverb

Alicia strode down the street with four other women by her side. She knew one of the other actresses, a young woman named Kristen, because they'd worked together on a television commercial when they were both cutting their teeth in Hollywood. The other three were older women. Julie would play her mother, Olivia the owner of a local restaurant, and Laura a meddling neighbor who always seemed to get her nose in everyone's business. Of course, the latter character would provide just the right bit of information to bring everyone together and resolve each episode's conflict at the end.

Alicia couldn't help but contrast Julie with her own mother. Despite the changes in the shooting, costumes, and schedule, Julie wasn't ruffled. Opposite of that, Alicia's mother reacted to everything. Things were either wonderful or horrible. There was rarely any middle ground.

Alicia supposed that's why she'd been drawn to Rowan in the first place. He'd been the stable one, the one who knew how to settle her emotions and roll with her punches. He'd been the solid foundation she'd always longed for as a young girl and still cried for when she drifted off to sleep alone.

"I don't know why we had to walk, and why they couldn't come to us," Olivia said.

"It's not too bad. Florida is beautiful," Alicia commented.

Olivia grunted. "This is what you call beautiful? It's hot as Hades today."

"Shh, you can't say those things around here." Julie patted Olivia's arm. "Look around. The streets are filled with Amish. You wouldn't want them to overhear you."

Laura sighed and fanned her face. "They're no holier than us, just because they look like they grew up on *Little House on the Prairie*." She pressed her fist into her hip. "Besides, all I wanted was a car to drive."

Olivia brushed a strand of golden, processed hair back from her forehead. "Honey, a car would stick out like a daisy on a rosebush. Sometimes part of the job is remembering that whatever we are asked to do, it's part of the job."

Alicia nodded, and up ahead she noticed a woman standing near an open gate. Along the road other Amish walked and rode bikes, but she would recognize Joy anywhere. Joy was tall and thin with golden brown hair that should be packaged into a dye bottle. She always stood erect and watched the world as if she was taking it all in.

In the two times Alicia had interacted with the young woman, she'd had no clear sense that Joy wanted to befriend her just to satisfy her own needs or wants. Something Alicia wasn't used to. Everyone in Hollywood strove to be seen and be known, and many times people tried to do that by attempting to foster a friendship with her. With Joy, what you saw was what you got.

Joy smiled as they neared. "Ladies, welcome. My *mem* and sister are both here. I hope you're hungry. My *mem* made three coffee cakes." Joy laughed and then hurried them toward the house. She turned her head and looked up and down the road before she opened the door. Was she worried about who saw them enter? Alicia had

185

heard rumors that many in the Amish community were not pleased they were here. But if there were any worries, Joy quickly brushed them away with a smile.

Alicia stepped inside and breathed in the aroma of cinnamon and cake. The living room was small but neat, and it opened up into a kitchen. When they had all entered the living room, an older man sat on a sofa, wearing an oxygen tank. He struggled to rise and then sat back down again. As the Amish woman welcomed the other ladies, Alicia strode over to the man.

"Oh, you must be Joy's father." She extended her hand, and he shook it. "I have to say, if your wife's coffee cake tastes as good as it smells, I have a big decision to make."

His eyes were bright, and he seemed pleased to be acknowledged. "Oh, what's that?"

"The problem is whether to have Joy measure my waist before or after I enjoy some cake. I have a feeling that if I have one piece I won't want to stop."

The man patted his thin stomach. "Oh, I'm supposed to be fattening myself up. I used to be as skinny as a beanpole before marriage. And as each of my five daughters has learned how to cook, I gained a few more pounds. Now they say I'm too thin again. I suppose I won't be able to win this one. But maybe since I just got this oxygen tank they'll feel sorry for me and give me two pieces."

They chatted for a little longer, yet even as Alicia talked, she also paid attention to the women chatting in the kitchen. She zeroed in on the cadence of the Amish words and their focus on their guests. If she had any worries that the actresses weren't welcome to this home, they quickly vanished.

They sat down to coffee cake first, and then each woman went into Joy's room to be discreetly measured for the dresses. Alicia paused as she stepped into the bedroom. It was as small as her closet back home, with two twin beds on metal frames. There was a quilt and a pillow on each bed. A table between the beds had a lamp and a few books. The closet door was open, and a few dresses were neatly hung.

Alicia packed more when she went away for the weekend than what was in that closet. An uneasiness stirred within as she realized she probably also spent more at Starbucks and on gourmet snacks than these women earned in a month.

When they were finished with the measurements, Alicia followed Joy to the kitchen. Julie was sipping on an orange punch as she chatted with Joy's mother. "It's so strange that you haven't heard of Alicia before. She's been on the cover of *People* a dozen times."

"And most of them were positive headlines," Olivia commented as she accepted another piece of cake. "But as my mother always said, 'A good reputation is more valuable than money.' Thankfully Alicia was one of the best-paid —"

A jab to Olivia's ribs by Kristen stopped the woman's words, and her eyes darted to the hallway for the first time, realizing Alicia was there.

Alicia's heart pounded as if each of the woman's accusatory words was being pounded into her chest with a hammer. *A good reputation.* She tried to forget that she didn't have one, but comments like these reminded her of her personal failure. A failure that made the headlines of most of the popular magazines.

"Good thing Hollywood is quick to forget. The latest scandal helps us forget the old ones, doesn't it?" Kristen said, attempting to sugarcoat the situation, but before she could continue, Joy's mother jumped in. She tapped the top of her *kapp* and then fixed her eyes on Olivia.

"We have a saying too, and I first heard it from my mother." The plump older woman cleared her throat. "Instead of putting others in their place, put yourself in their place." She pressed her hands on her apron and sighed. "It's hard to truly understand what someone else is going through unless you walk in their shoes."

Olivia's smile slipped from her face, and Alicia put a hand over her mouth to hide the smile. She never expected that. The woman's words touched her, especially considering that they'd just met.

Then the older Amish woman scanned the other shocked faces, pausing on each one. Finally, she turned her attention to Alicia. "I'm not sure why folks pay good money to read bad news. I just know it hurts plenty when it's you everyone's wagging their tongues about. And truly the only One we should be concerned about meddling in our business is our good Lord. Because His meddling isn't for the sake of harm, but always good."

Alicia nodded, although she wasn't sure if the woman's words made her feel better or worse. She knew the Amish believed God allowed both bad and good into one's life for His greater purposes, but what if you caused the greatest harm yourself?

She straightened her shoulders and strode into the kitchen, attempting to act as if Olivia's words hadn't just cut to her core. "If we're done, then I think we should get back to the set. Rowan asked that we try not to take too long."

The women thanked their host and gladly accepted the paper plates with coffee cake Joy's sister Faith passed out to each one.

As she stood just outside the front door in a summer dress, with a plate of coffee cake in hand, Alicia felt like a different woman living in a different time. She hadn't checked her cell phone once inside, and she hadn't missed it. Joy and her family paid attention in ways that most people Alicia knew didn't. They didn't just make small talk to pass the time until they moved on to the next thing. Instead, they seemed to really listen, really care.

Joy stood next to her with her hand resting on the door frame. "We'll do our best to get all the dresses done in a few days."

"A few days?" Kristen brushed her long, black hair over the back of her shoulder. "You can really get them done that fast?"

"Well, we don't sew them by hand." Joy pointed inside to the sewing machine in the living room. "The only things we sew by hand are quilts. And even then we do the piecing on the machine to save time."

"Thank you for helping." Alicia stepped closer to Joy. Then she turned to her mother. "And thank you for . . . your kind words."

As the others exited, Joy's mother patted Alicia's hands. "Remember, no matter what I've done, what you've done, Jesus wants you to know you can go to Him. I've never read a gossip magazine and I never will, but don't trust the words of others over the words of God."

Alicia nodded, and the words gave her a bit of peace even if they sounded impossible to follow. That's what her life was about, wasn't it? Pleasing others, being rated in movies. Being commented about at red-carpet events and being photographed looking less than her best on Starbucks runs. An actress's job was to be appraised and bid on one day and rejected and overlooked the next. Could she really trust what God said over what people did? And what exactly would God say about her? With the road Alicia had walked — especially in the last year — she didn't want to know.

"The cake was delicious. I can't wait to enjoy more tonight."

Joy's mother chuckled. "Good. And remember, when you get your dresses, if they

191

don't fit just right we can help you out."

The group of women left with a chorus of thanks, but the walk back to the set was quiet. Was Olivia worried she'd tell Rowan what she'd said? A few years ago she probably would have. But now Alicia didn't have the strength to get involved in an on-set feud. It's not as if anything she said wasn't the truth. Everyone, she supposed, wondered how things would turn out behind the scenes. Even though no one wanted to talk about the past, it had followed her and Rowan onto the set. Like an invisible gorilla, it sat in the middle of the room. She just hoped the beast would stay contained until their shooting was done. Not for her sake, but for Rowan's. She'd dragged his name through the mud with her the last time. And the last thing he needed was for her to do it again.

Streusel Coffee Cake

1 cup butter
1 1/2 cups sugar
3 eggs
1 teaspoon vanilla extract
3/4 cup buttermilk (or sour milk)
2 1/2 cups all-purpose flour
1/2 teaspoon baking soda
1/2 teaspoon baking powder
1/2 teaspoon salt

Streusel Topping
1 cup brown sugar
4 tablespoons all-purpose flour
2 teaspoons ground cinnamon
3 tablespoons butter, melted
1/2 cup chopped nuts (optional)

Preheat oven to 350 degrees. Cream butter and sugar; add eggs one at a time. Add vanilla and sour milk. Stir in dry ingredients. Put half of the dough in a greased 9 by 13-inch pan. Mix together streusel topping in a separate bowl. Sprinkle half of the streusel topping mix on the dough, then repeat layers. Bake for 1 hour.

EIGHTEEN

Bibles that are coming apart usually
belong to people who are not.
AMISH PROVERB

Alicia sat on the balcony and listened to the
waves rolling in. Seagulls cried out as they
dipped and rose on the ocean breezes,
almost dancing on the invisible currents.
The air was chilling today, and a slight mist
touched her face. Alicia wasn't sure if the
mist fell from the gray clouds above, which
had swept in last night and still lingered, or
if it blew off the expansive ocean beyond
her.

She pulled the plush blanket tight around
her and gazed out at the rising sun. She
needed to finish getting ready. Her car
would be here in less than fifteen minutes,
but she needed to clear her thoughts first.
She'd brought out her journal and a pen,
but for the last thirty minutes she hadn't

194

been able to figure out what to write. Then she knew. She had to write the truth, even though the words would be hard to get down.

I've read some of the commentaries about me being cast for this show. I've played both prisoners and spies, and I have a mean sweeping kick if I say so myself. The role itself doesn't bother me. My real personality is closer to this Amish woman's character than most of the roles I've played, but what's worrying me most is the internal struggle. The Amish live the way they do because they believe God has asked them to live separate from the world. So the basis of all they do is centered on God. Which means I have to think about Him.

For most of my life it's been easier not to think about Him. Because to think about Him means I know He's thinking about me. I hate to think of what God thinks of me — especially after all I've done. Good thing I'm an actress. This might be my biggest challenge yet. Acting as if my life is committed to God while at the same time not wanting to think about Him so much.

Matthew could tell there was a problem as soon as he arrived on the job site. Abraham stood near a stack of sheetrock. He turned and eyed Matthew with a look of concern.

"Please don't tell me the plumber called to cancel again." Matthew wiped his brow with his handkerchief and then stuck it back into his pocket. Last night's rain had made it extra muggy. "Today's not the day for problems. We really need him to finish the pipes before we get the sheetrock up."

"Oh, it's not that. I checked last night and the plumber will be here by noon. It's just that I went to Yoder's for breakfast."

"And . . ."

"Well, it's where Joy's sister works."

"*Ja,* I know that."

"Have you talked to Joy lately?"

The slightest smile touched Matthew's lips as he remembered the happiness on Joy's face when *Mem* described the recipes she was keeping for her. He looked back to Abraham. "I talked to Joy yesterday. She stopped by our house for *Mem*'s breakfast. It was her birthday."

Abraham tucked one hand into his jeans pocket. "And you haven't talked to her since then?"

Matthew's brow furrowed. Why was Abraham leading him like this? Why wasn't he just coming out with whatever he had to say? "When do you suppose I've talked to her?" His voice grew sharp. "We were working late last night, and then after breakfast I came right here."

Abraham shrugged. "Maybe you should."

"Can you please just tell me what's going on?" Whatever it was, it didn't seem like good news.

Abraham hesitated. "It seems Joy has a second job, working for that television program. Faith wasn't working at Yoder's today because Joy got her a job too. They're supposedly sewing dresses for the actresses."

Abraham's words felt like a punch to his gut. "She's . . . she's sewing dresses for the television show?" He pressed his fingertips to his temples, wondering why she would do that. Hadn't they talked about the television show? Hadn't she agreed they should stay as far away from them as possible? Or had he just imagined that conversation? "Well, maybe Joy is doing the sewing through the fabric shop. It only makes sense."

"It's not through the shop. She's working directly for them. Faith asked one of her coworkers if she wanted extra sewing work too."

Emotion grew in Matthew's throat. He

197

tried to clear it away, but it did little good.

"Not only that, but people are saying you and your *dat* must approve of the television show. That he must have changed his mind. We all know a woman you were courting wouldn't do such a thing if the bishop didn't approve."

Sudden anger boiled up in Matthew. If this was true, he had to talk to Joy. Didn't she understand that her actions impacted not only her and her family, but him and his family too?

Matthew was also angry with himself. He'd watched Joy from afar for so long. He'd tried to make sure she was of fine character and moral standing. He knew how often little things one overlooked in courtship often became big things in marriage. What had he missed? "So you're certain she's working for the television show?"

"*Ja,* one of the waitresses at Yoder's said Faith asked her to cover her shift this morning. And then one of the Millers' neighbors said there was a whole group of *Englischers* there yesterday."

"Doing what?"

"They didn't know, but everyone assumes they were getting fitted for dresses. I thought you would know though. Because out of all people, I was certain Joy would have talked to you."

Matthew lifted his face and resisted the urge to shout at the beamed ceiling overhead. A vein throbbed in his neck, and he clenched his fists.

"I actually asked her to forgive me for being angry the other day," Matthew mumbled to himself. "I assumed it was that *Englischer* who was trying to pull her in. I'd never have guessed she'd walk through those doors so easily. I thought I was overreacting, but it turns out I was right."

"Excuse me?" Abraham removed his hat and scratched his head. "It sounds like you didn't know about this."

"I didn't. Do you think I'd be here if I did?"

"Well, I was surprised to see you show up. I thought it would take longer."

"What?"

"Some of the men from the community were going over to talk to your *dat* about it, to see why he changed his mind. I thought it would be a while before I saw you, since I assumed you'd be in the middle of that conversation. It's not every day that someone like Joy is so boldly going against the bishop's wishes, especially when she's dating his son."

Matthew blew out a heavy breath, and he

looked at all the unfinished work around him. *Should I go see* Dat*? Should I tell him I had no idea?*

Matthew pictured his father's disapproving look. Mainly because it was the same one he'd seen last night. After dinner, while *Mem* was cleaning the kitchen, his father followed him into his workshop and noticed the small pieces of wood Matthew was preparing for recipe boxes.

"What are those?"

"Oh, something I'm working on the side."

"Are those for the recipe boxes for that pie shop?"

Matthew hadn't denied it. "*Ja.* Just something I'm doing in my spare time."

Dat's eyebrows had lifted. "Hobbies are called hobbies for a reason. There's *ne* use giving up well-paying work, especially when you're considering taking on a wife. I hope you do not let these take too much time — or let your work suffer." Matthew had nodded, acting as if he agreed, but deep down he was thankful at least Joy understood. At least Joy believed in his dreams.

But now he questioned all he knew about her. Had she really taken a job with the television show without even talking to him about it? His teeth clamped down, and rage seethed below the surface. Her decision not only made him look bad, but it made his *dat* look bad too.

Matthew picked up his tool bag and slung it over his shoulder. "I'll be back. Hopefully before lunch."

Abraham's eyes widened. "Where are you headed?"

"Do you really need to ask?"

"Most likely to see Joy, but I'm not certain that's a *gut* idea." Abraham took a step closer and paused. "Maybe you should wait. Work a while."

Matthew squared his shoulders. "Why?"

Abraham shrugged. "I'm just surprised, that's all. In all the years I've worked for you, I've never seen you lose your temper."

"I'm not going to lose my temper."

"I might believe that if I didn't see the vein about to pop through the skin on your neck."

"I just want to talk to Joy, that's all."

"Oh." The word fell from Abraham's lips.

"What does that mean? *Oh.*"

"Well, if you were headed to her house, she probably won't be there. That's another thing I've yet to tell you." Abraham lowered his gaze as if afraid to meet Matthew's eye as he spoke. "I knew what they were talking about is true because I saw Joy this morning."

"On the way to the fabric store?"

"*Ne.* Heading the opposite direction. She was walking toward the television show's warehouse, and she was carrying a dress on a hanger. If you want to find her, you might want to go there."

Matthew put down his tool bag. The last thing he wanted to do was make a scene. If he did, then people would be pointing fingers and saying more than they already were.

"So . . . you're not going."

"*Ne.*" He picked up a hammer and swung it around in his hand. "I think anything I have to say will hurt the situation, not help it."

Abraham stroked his chin. "*Ja,* well, I have two comments then."

"What's that?"

"Well, first, I'd recommend that you do what most Amish do around here . . . get the advice of the bishop before you do anything rash."

"*Ja.*" He lowered his hammer, feeling the weight in his hand. "And what's the second comment?"

"Do you mind if I go work on the other side of the room? I've seen you swing a hammer when you're upset, and it can get pretty intense."

Matthew didn't want to laugh, but he did. He then closed his eyes and told himself to remain calm. As his *mem* had taught him, his reaction was just as important as another person's wrong actions. Maybe even more since he was the bishop's son.

Matthew opened his eyes, blew out a deep breath, and looked at his friend. "You can work over there if you want, but I promise I'll calm down. I know high emotions never help when building a house."

Abraham tentatively walked to the area he'd been working on before.

Matthew cleared his throat. "*Danke* for telling me. I'm glad to have a friend who's willing to tell it as it is."

"I figured you'd want to hear it from me rather than someone else."

Matthew reached for his pouch of nails. "Oh, I'm sure I'll hear it from others. Of that I have no doubt. A lot of caring people in this community like to watch out for their own." He opened the pouch and pulled out a handful of nails. "Sometimes too well."

He'd talk to Joy. He'd talk to her soon, but first he needed to clear his thoughts. He was starting to realize Joy wasn't the woman he thought she was. Had he made a horrible mistake? How could someone so wonderful make such poor decisions? As much as his heart ached, at least he was discovering this now. But what did it mean — for them, for their relationship? He didn't want to think about that now. Not yet. He'd focus on one conversation at a time without worrying that everything he'd dreamed for his future was blowing away like sawdust on the wind.

NINETEEN

We are not bound to win;
we are bound to be true.

AMISH PROVERB

Joy was holding her breath as she waited for Alicia to exit the dressing room. But there was a slight smile on the *Englisch* woman's face when she walked out wearing the coral dress and *kapp*.

"You're not going to believe this, but I'm as excited about this dress as I was for my last Golden Globes gown." She did a slight twirl. "I can't believe you actually made it to flatter me and sewed it overnight. Unbelievable." Alicia smoothed her dress with her hands. "I hope you didn't cancel any special plans with your boyfriend. You do have one, don't you?"

Heat rose to Joy's cheeks. "Yes, I suppose you can say that." Warmth filled her chest at the memory of how Matthew had looked at her yesterday morning. Love was evident in his eyes. Even more so, she treasured the thoughtfulness of tucking those recipes from his grandmother into his *mem*'s recipe box. The loving gesture brought much happiness, but the thoughts of being here — at the set — brought worry.

Last night she walked over to his house after dinner, but no one answered the door. She'd considered walking over to his job site, but it was all the way across town. She hadn't wanted to take the time to go without being sure he was there. He and his *dat* could have taken his *mem* out for a birthday dinner for all she knew.

So instead Joy had hurried home, back to the many dresses she had to sew. And as she walked with quickened steps, she'd thanked God for the unexpected way He had provided money for *Dat*'s treatments. Surely when she explained, Matthew would agree that she'd made the right decision. After all, what could be more important than her father's health?

"The dress fits me perfectly." Alicia's words interrupted her thoughts. The *Englisch* actress pressed her hands into her hips. "Seriously, I have no idea how you sewed this in such a short amount of time."

"My mother helped. She has five daughters, after all. She's gotten pretty good about sewing dresses." Joy bit her lip. "I, uh, do have a question though." She smiled. "What are the Golden Globes?"

Alicia chuckled and then broke into a full belly laugh. "Oh, Joy, you're so refreshing to be around. Do you know about the Oscars?"

"Well, I have a cousin named Oscar."

Alicia laughed again, wiping tears from her eyes. "That's good enough then."

"I brought something else too." Joy moved to a table, where she picked up a box. It was an old ice cream tub that she'd washed out and decorated with contact paper. Many of her friends made similar boxes to store their *kapp*s. "I have a new *kapp* for you too. The one you have is from Lancaster."

"A new *kapp.*" Alicia pressed her palms together and smiled. "I'm sure I'll turn all the eyes of the Amish bachelors in this one." She placed it on her head. "Speaking of which, I'm certain your boyfriend is the man I saw you with at the bus stop. Are you . . . serious?" She grinned.

Joy knew she'd been able to change the subject the first time but not again.

"We're starting to be." She cut her eyes in Alicia's direction. Heat rose to her cheeks again, and she quickly looked away. "We are courting, and there has been talk of marriage."

"Talk of marriage is always good."

"Have you ever thought of marriage, Alicia?" Joy turned to her new friend.

Alicia's eyes darted away, but not before Joy noted a mix of pain and shame in her gaze. "I've been married."

"Really? Oh, I'm so sorry I asked. I didn't know."

Alicia turned back and offered a sad smile. "You might be the only one in the United States who doesn't know. Well, you and your Amish friends." She looked at herself in the mirror, tilting her head as if meeting a stranger. Or perhaps seeing herself in a different way. "The man I married . . . he's a great man. I highly recommend marriage." She shook her head and shrugged. "But that doesn't really matter now, does it?"

Joy wasn't sure how to respond. "I . . . I'm glad you like your dress."

Alicia nodded and then looked at the clock. "Oh, I need to get to the set. We're doing a run-through. I hope to see you tomorrow."

She pushed aside the curtain and took a shortcut. As she did, Joy looked beyond the curtain area to the doorway. Rowan stood there. He wore a puzzled expression, and she knew he'd overheard the conversation. *Does he know about her marriage?* Joy assumed so. Alicia said everyone did. It must be hard to have everyone know all your failings. To have it in the papers. She assumed that's what Olivia had been alluding to yesterday when they'd come to the fittings.

Joy made up her mind then and there not to ask any more about Alicia's marriage. It wasn't her place to know. She'd simply work to be the *Englisch* woman's friend.

"The first dress is done," she called out to Rowan. "I thought I'd see how it fits."

He inhaled a deep breath and approached. A forced smile filled his face. "Joy, I can't thank you enough. Your help with this . . . it means so much." He chuckled, but she also noticed a distant sadness in his eyes. "It seems as if you're always coming to my rescue. If it wasn't for your help finding our destination that first night, who knows where we would have ended up?" He paused and crossed his arms over his chest. "If you'd like I can write you a check for the dresses —"

She held up her hand, pausing his words. "No. Please wait until the other dresses are done. I wouldn't feel right getting paid for work I haven't done."

"Very well then, but there is something I

will insist on. We're doing a run-through of the first episode, and I need you to stay and watch."

"Really?" She pursed her lips and thought about all the work that waited at home. But curiosity caused her to want to stay. More than that, her sister Grace would arrive back in Pinecraft tomorrow, and Joy would never hear the end of it if she missed out on this run-through. Grace wrote for the *Budget,* and even if many people didn't agree with the filming, all of them would want to know the details.

Joy followed Rowan to the living room set. Alicia was sitting on the sofa, chatting with Julie, who, Joy now knew, played her *mem.* Rowan sat down in a high director's chair and offered the chair next to him to Joy.

Joy sat down, still not believing she was really here. Not believing that the first steps to a real television show were happening.

"Go ahead with the run-through, picking up where we left off earlier," Rowan called to them.

Julie cleared her throat. She sat and wrapped her arm around Alicia's shoulders, pulling her close. "Sadie, I'm so sorry you have to face this terrible loss, but know that I truly believe God has brought you to Pinecraft for it to heal. I hope the train ride wasn't too long."

Alicia sighed. "No. I enjoyed the quiet. Time to think. And if I never have to look at another Amish bachelor, it'll be fine with me."

A knock sounded. Julie pulled back her arm and then moved to the door. "Never look at a bachelor? I suppose, but maybe . . ." She sighed. "Did I tell you we have a new neighbor next door?"

The door opened, and a tall, handsome man walked in. He wore Amish clothes and had a brown beard. Joy lifted her eyebrows, hoping this man wasn't supposed to be the bachelor the mother was talking about. Heat climbed her neck. It was worse than she thought. All of it. She jabbed her thumbnail between her front teeth, telling herself to keep her mouth shut. This was of no concern to her.

Alicia, as Sadie, looked up from the couch and eyed him. "A new neighbor . . ."

The man stepped forward and extended his hand to her. "I'm Samuel." Alicia allowed him to shake her hand and didn't release it right away.

Joy couldn't stand it any longer. She stood and turned to Rowan. "Um, there's a problem. Well, more than one . . ."

"Cut!" he called.

Like puppets whose strings had been released, the actors released their poses and relaxed.

"A problem?" He turned to her. Annoyance was clear on his face. She told herself again just to forget it, just to let them do their show, but she couldn't let this slide.

"Yes, a problem. And yes, more than one." She sucked in a deep breath and released it. "I just don't know where to start."

"Start with the biggest problem first."

"The biggest problem? Well, Amish bachelors don't wear beards. Men wear beards only after they're married. Unless you meant for him to be a widower. Then he would wear a beard. My sister Hope will soon be married to a widower. When they first met she thought he was married. It was confusing to say the least —"

Rowan held up his hand, halting her words. "And what else?"

"Well, there isn't really a train that comes from Ohio. Most folks ride the Pioneer Trails bus. Although one of my cousins is taking a cruise ship, but that is very rare."

"And?" He looked to Alicia, motioning her to approach.

"And the *mem* . . . well, she was just too affectionate. Mothers snuggle their little children, but you don't really see that type of outward affection between adults in the Amish community."

"You don't?" Alicia's eyebrows peaked. "That's surprising."

"And I don't want to point out every problem, but that bachelor wouldn't just walk in the door like that. And he wouldn't offer his hand. More than that, well, the women would be doing something. They'd be darning socks or snapping beans. No Amish women would just sit there on the sofa in the middle of the day carrying on a conversation."

"What about sewing clothes?" Rowan asked. "They could sit there sewing."

"But the show starts in spring, right? Many of the Amish try to complete their sewing for the year by the time they plant a garden. It's hard to sit inside to sew when it's getting warm outside. Of course, since we're in Florida, I'm not sure if that matters." She shrugged. "I suppose you could have them sewing. Or cutting out boys' pants. Boys are always harder to sew for because there are pants and shirts. That is, if your character has a young brother. How many siblings does she have?"

"Only one sister — an older sister."

Laughter spilled out, and Joy eyed him. "You know you're writing about an Amish family, right? I'd allude to many more siblings, even if they live up north. A couple with only two children isn't very common. Not unheard of, but not common." The words had poured out of Joy's mouth, and when she was through she released a heavy breath. She knew in the grand scheme of things most of the little details didn't matter, but with all of them together — and the beard — it was impossible for her not to speak up.

Alicia appeared slightly annoyed, but she tried not to let it show. She turned to Rowan. "Do you mind if I ask Georgia to fix my hair while you're working out these details? There's a bobby pin poking me right behind my ear."

"I don't mind at all." Rowan lifted his hand. "Everyone, take five. This will be just a few minutes."

The actors and camera people moved toward a table of snacks. They all looked over the fresh fruit and nuts, but none of them seemed impressed. *Set out some whoopie pies, and that'll be a different story,* Joy wanted to say.

Without the others listening in, Rowan turned to her. "The more I do this, the more I realize I'm in over my head." He stroked his jaw and looked up at the lighting, deep in thought. Then his eyes moved back to her. "I assumed since the Amish speak English, it would be easy to figure out. I didn't really think of it as a different culture, but I was wrong."

Joy bit her lip. She glanced up at him. "I, uh, don't know if I should mention this, but back in Ohio we spoke to each other mostly in Pennsylvania Dutch. We still slip into that language when we don't want *Englischers* to know what we're talking about."

He scratched his head, and he wore a lost, faraway look in his eyes. Joy almost felt sorry for him. "Pennsylvania Dutch . . . of course."

He stared at the set a brief moment before his eyes brightened and he looked to her.

"I'd like to hire you. As a consultant. It's a paid position, of course, and I don't want it to take too much time away from the fabric shop. It's just that we need someone on set in the mornings to check everything over. Sort of like we did today."

Nothing about the idea appealed to Joy. She thought of the disappointed looks she received yesterday when she'd pointed out the problems with the wardrobe. And then today when she mentioned the long list of things that needed to be changed. Joy also thought about how awkward she felt with

215

all these cameras around. And then there was Matthew to consider and how his *dat* felt about the television show. She had opened her mouth to decline the offer when something stopped her.

One thing about his offer sounded appealing after all. *Mem* and *Dat* needed the money. They would never ask for it, of course, but she knew they wouldn't turn it away. The money from the dresses would help, but that was just a start.

"You said it's a paid position? Just to point out things like I did right then?"

He perked up. "Yes, I'll pay you well. Maybe three hours every morning."

"Every morning?"

"We try to keep the number of shooting days down as much as we can." A smile grew on his face. "And I understand some days just aren't possible. Like Sundays."

"I'm still not sure . . ."

She tried to imagine what her *mem* and *dat* would say. They had both been fine with her sewing dresses. And *Mem* seemed to have a weight off her shoulders knowing that two of her daughters were doing what they could to help with therapy costs.

But what about Matthew? Would he understand if she explained? He was a caring and compassionate person. Surely he'd understand if she explained *Dat*'s needs.

"Of course, we'll work around your schedule."

She moved back to her chair and sat down, trying to wrap her mind around what he was really asking her. "So let me understand this. You are going to pay me to come here and tell you what you are doing wrong?"

He offered a small smile and nodded. "Yes. That's what I'm saying."

"My parents raised a wise girl. I don't think I could say no to that. I'll have to check with my boss, Elizabeth, though. To see if she can cover for me. I think next week I was scheduled to work one morning shift."

"Sure. No problem." He slid his fingers into his pocket and pulled out a small card, handing it to her. "My cell phone number is on here. Go ahead and give me a . . ."

"Caught yourself, didn't you?"

"I suppose you don't have a cell phone, do you?"

"No, but I can come by tomorrow at eight o'clock if that will work for you."

"Yes. Thank you. I'll see you then."

As she strode off the set, Joy immediately wondered what she'd done. What would her parents think of this? What would Matthew?

She smiled thinking about him, and she knew he'd understand if she explained. Her parents needed money for her *dat*'s treatments. This opportunity was an answer to prayer. Surely he would understand that.

TWENTY

Children's ears may be closed to advice,
but their eyes are open to examples.
AMISH PROVERB

Matthew paced the walkway in front of the quilt shop. He'd worked at his construction job for less than an hour before he couldn't handle it anymore. He had to talk to Joy. He had to find out if what Abraham told him was true. Had she truly started working for the television show? Worse, had she done so without first talking to him about it?

He didn't feel as if she needed his permission, but they should have at least discussed this. They were looking ahead to marriage, after all. What affected one person affected the other. And the community knew their connection too. Abraham said everyone assumed the bishop had changed his mind after they heard Joy had gone to work there.

Didn't she understand how it made him and his family look in the eyes of the community?

He balled his hands into fists at his sides and then released them. Deep down he hoped Abraham was wrong. He wished it was just a misunderstanding. As in the game of grapevine, the story often changed when it moved from person to person. Matthew decided he wouldn't believe this news until he heard it from Joy herself.

He paused for a moment in front of the glass door and wondered if he should step inside again and ask Elizabeth if she had heard from Joy. Matthew had gone to Joy's home first, and they said she'd been planning on going to the fabric store after making a delivery. Her *mem* hadn't mentioned her daughter was delivering a dress to the television set, and he didn't ask. And when he'd arrived at the fabric shop, Elizabeth said she was late. This didn't seem like Joy, and Matthew decided to give her just a few more minutes. If she didn't arrive soon, then he'd walk in the direction of the TV show's location.

Beyond the sidewalk, cars and trucks moved up and down the street, filling the air with exhaust and fumes. Above, the bright golden sun blanketed him with oppressive heat, and Matthew wondered how his life had ended up the way it had. He'd come to Florida to be with his family, and he'd thought he'd found the woman he wanted to marry, but now he questioned that. *I should have stayed in Indiana. I should have stayed in a regular Amish community.* Yet even as he told himself those things, he ached over the idea of trying to love someone other than Joy.

The problem with living outside the box in a place like Pinecraft was that people often thought outside the box too. He couldn't think of one Amish woman he knew up north who'd go against the bishop's wishes so boldly. None who'd been baptized into the church, of course.

An older man rode by on a three-wheeled bicycle, and he curiously eyed Matthew as he passed. *I just need to go back to work. I'm wasting time.* The words barely crossed his mind when up ahead he saw a woman hurrying down the street. It was Joy, and her steps slowed as she saw him. She paused on the sidewalk about twenty feet away and then clasped her hands in front of her.

"Matthew. I was looking for you."

"You were looking for me?"

"*Ja.* I went to your house. Your *mem* said you were at a job site. I went there and . . .

well, you get the idea."

"And why were you looking for me?"

"Well, since you are here I assume you know. I . . . I need to talk to you . . . I want to talk to you about a new opportunity."

She twisted one *kapp* string around her finger, and her eyes met his briefly before looking away.

"Opportunity?" He took a step closer and nearly reached out to touch her, but from the uneasiness in her gaze he was certain she'd pull away.

Joy crossed her arms over her chest. "Well, at your job site I saw Abraham, and he said that he heard . . . about the opportunity . . . and he talked to you." She ran a hand down her neck and glanced up at him. "So, I know you've heard." She shrugged. "Everyone has heard."

"I want to hear it from you, Joy." Matthew didn't mean for his voice to sound harsh, but it did. He attempted to soften his tone. "Do you have time to talk? We can go someplace."

Joy took a step toward him tentatively. She glanced through the glass door, and so did he. Elizabeth was sitting at the counter. She seemed to be completely occupied with embroidering, but Matthew guessed otherwise. He had no doubt the older woman was paying close attention to them — especially to how he was handling the whole situation.

"I can talk to Elizabeth. I'm not sure if she had plans already. It's my day to work, but I don't see any customers and last night she agreed to fill in for me this morning while I went . . ." Her brow furrowed and grew into deep lines of guilt.

"We can go to my parents' house. Or Big Olaf's," he offered.

"Ice cream sounds nice, even before lunch. Let me go talk to Elizabeth." She hurried inside, but he didn't follow. He couldn't hear her words, but Joy talked with her hands and motioned to him. Something she said made Elizabeth laugh. He assumed it had something to do with the TV show, and that just made him madder. His anger, which had been simmering just beneath the surface, was starting to break through the cracks. *Does she think this is a joke? Does she think it's just a game? Is she making fun of me — of how seriously I'm taking this?*

Joy hurried out a moment later, and she wore the slightest smile on her face. Yet the smile faded when she saw him, and soon they were walking down the street side by side.

She fell in step with him. Her shorter

strides had to stretch to keep up with his longer ones, but she didn't complain. "So I assume since you talked to Abraham you know about my new job?"

He paused and looked down at her. "So you did get a job?"

"I did, and you won't believe what it means to us — not to just me, but to my sister Faith, *Mem,* and *Dat* too. We didn't know what we were going to do —"

Matthew held up a finger, and she stopped talking. He could nearly taste the anger in his mouth. Anger because she was taking this so lightly. Anger with himself for getting so wrapped up in her. "I just have one question. Before all else." He spoke through partially clenched teeth.

"*Ja?*"

"I thought you were at church last Sunday."

"*Ja,* I was. Remember, we had Sunday supper with Noah and Lovina afterward?"

"I remember, but do you?" He threw up his hands and sighed. "My father talked about the television show. He asked the congregation not to get involved with it or any of those *Englischers.* They have impure motives. They want to use our way of life for their own gain."

"I know many people believe that —

224

including your *dat*. But . . . aren't you going to give me a chance to explain?" Tears formed in her eyes, but Matthew ignored them.

Her words choked out. "This job is an answer to prayer."

"An answer to prayer?" He shook his head, not knowing what to do, what to say. Two *Englisch* women walked by and gawked at them. His guess was they'd never seen an Amish couple argue before. He hadn't seen it too often either, not even *Dat* and *Mem*. Something inside Matthew told him to just walk away. Just forget that he'd fallen in love with Joy. Just forget that he'd spent more hours than he could count imagining a future with her.

She reached over and touched the sleeve of his shirt, and then her fingers moved to his hand. She grasped it and squeezed it. "*Ja*, an answer to prayer." She released a shuttering breath. "If we could just go and order some ice cream or a coffee I can explain everything."

Voices filled the air, and a group of young Amish bachelors walked toward them. They carried fishing poles, and he knew they were heading to Phillippi Creek. They paused when they saw them and slowly walked around them, like a river parting around a large rock. And that's just how Matthew felt at the moment — like a rock with too many thoughts and worries rushing over him. Rushes of pain and frustration.

As the young men passed, one leaned in to the other. "That's the woman I was talking about," he whispered.

"*Ja,* and that's the bishop's son," the other responded.

Hot anger surged through Matthew's veins. "Listen." Matthew pulled his hand out of hers. "Let's talk tomorrow. I need time to think. And when we talk, I'd like to go someplace where we have some privacy."

"But don't you want to know why I accepted the job?"

"Give me a few days, Joy. I have a lot going on in my mind. A lot to think about."

She didn't respond but simply nodded.

"I'll come by your house in a few days or by the quilt shop."

He turned away and strode off. His chest ached as if a trowel had been jerked out of his heart with a firm tug. Guilt strode alongside him, poking and prodding with every step. *You should have listened. You should have at least heard what she had to say.*

One part of him knew this, but the other part of him didn't care. She'd made him look like a fool. She'd made a mockery of all that their community held dear. *She doesn't understand. Our community is assaulted by everything on the outside, and now she's chosen to break it apart from within.*

He'd seen the external pressures his *dat* had to deal with. He knew how hard his father worked to protect their community, their way of life. It wasn't an easy fight. The temptations of the world were a strong pull, and young person after young person walked away from their Amish ways, ignoring everything their ancestors believed to be true.

"Children's ears may be closed to advice, but their eyes are open to examples," Matthew whispered as he crossed the street. His father had spoken those words more than once in a sermon. He'd just assumed that since Joy sat in church, nestled among her *mem* and sisters every week, she believed the same things he did.

What if everyone made up their own rules? What if everyone decided they knew what was best? Then their Amish community would crumble. Conformity to their plain living and simple lifestyle was what kept them together. If Joy chose her own way, made her own plans now, it was a forewarning of what was to come later.

Matthew walked to the house where he'd been working but didn't stop there. As much as he needed to finish that job — get the income — he wouldn't be able to focus his mind on work today. He continued walking and soon found himself at home. More than anything he wanted to be in the workshop, shaping the wood with his hands. The wood seemed to have a life of its own. It begged to be made useful. The creation cried for a creator — this is something his *dat* didn't understand.

Joy understood. She believed in him. He only wished she believed in their community, their way of life, as strongly.

Maybe it's better I discover this about her now, before I commit my life to someone who too easily lets the world draw her away.

Maybe discovering the truth about Joy was worth the very breaking of his heart.

TWENTY-ONE

One thing you can learn by watching the clock is that it passes time by keeping its hand busy.

AMISH PROVERB

The day was rainy with a cold wind, and Joy rubbed her arms, attempting to manufacture some heat as she hurried home. She hadn't known many days like this since living in Pinecraft. The wind bit through the thin, white cotton sweater she wore over her dress and apron. She pulled the sweater tighter around her and then crossed her arms over her chest and sighed. Her mood was as gloomy as the sky above, and she wished she could just get into bed, curl into a ball, and sleep the day away.

She'd been working with Rowan on the set for a week, and still she hadn't heard from Matthew. He hadn't even given her a chance to explain about her father's current medical needs or what she'd been doing to try to help. She hadn't seen him around town either. Not that she'd been out much. Between sewing the rest of the dresses, working a few hours at Pinecraft Fabric and Quilts, and acting as a consultant on the set, there wasn't any extra time. She'd even missed Matthew at church yesterday. When she asked his *mem* about him, the older woman had simply offered a sad smile. "Matthew is feeling under the weather today," she'd stated.

Now it was Monday, and Joy already felt as if she'd worked enough for the whole week. The week's script had been delivered to her the night before. *Dat* had frowned at the idea of her reading through it on a Sunday night, but Faith had offered to do the dishes for her. Faith, more than anyone, understood what this extra income would be providing.

Joy had stayed up late reading it and making notes. Then she'd gotten up extra early to meet with Rowan to go over her script suggestions. After they'd nailed down the changes, the crew and actors showed up, and they set about the day's work.

Focusing on every little detail of the script was exhausting, and the environment on set was something Joy had never experienced.

Everything from how people dressed to how they talked to her was new and interesting. The interaction between actors and actresses was especially eye-opening. The way the cast and crew spoke sharply to each other, flirted, and even ignored each other at times was difficult to watch. Some days it seemed to her that more drama was happening off the set than on it.

The sun was just sinking over the horizon when she entered the house. *Mem* was in the kitchen, and the aroma of pumpkin spice cake greeted her. Joy paused her steps, and her shoulders stiffened. Pumpkin spice cake was *Mem*'s go-to favorite dessert when they had company.

Who is it this time?

"*Mem,* are we having people over tonight?" She moved to the stove top and lifted a lid. Homemade spaghetti sauce simmered — another one of *Mem*'s go-to meals for company. Joy returned the lid abruptly and it clattered into place.

If *Mem* noticed Joy's frustration, she didn't show it as she pulled out lettuce, tomatoes, and cucumbers from the refrigerator for a salad.

"Jake and Martha Houston are here from Walnut Creek. They're stopping by for dinner. Will you be home tonight?" The last

231

sentence was both a question and a request. From the quick glance in her direction, Joy knew *Mem* was weighing how much to press.

"I'm not sure. I might need to work late." Joy hadn't planned on working late, but there was sewing to do, and she could do it over at the fabric store. There was always sewing to do, and right now it sounded better than trying to keep up small talk with *Mem*'s friends.

"But our friends are here from Ohio. They're only down for a few days. Their eldest daughter, Barbara-Ellen, is expecting a baby, and they have to get back by the end of the week. They were hoping you'd be here. I think Jake wants to hear more about this program."

Joy scratched the point where her forehead met her hairline, pretending she didn't understand. "Program?"

"*Ja,* the television program you're working on. They stopped by earlier to let me know they were in town. Your new job came up in conversation."

Joy sighed. *I bet it did.* She imagined they'd even heard about it up north before they'd arrived. What happened in Pinecraft didn't stay in Pinecraft after all. At least not for long.

"Oh, I understand now." Joy forced a smile. "Jake wants to learn more details so he can write it all up in the *Budget*. He's been a scribe for quite a while, hasn't he?"

Mem sighed. "People are curious, that's all. It's not like this is something that happens every day."

"But maybe I should wait and share it with Grace. It's not her fault she came down with the flu and couldn't come home for another week."

Mem offered a wavering smile. "This is not a contest, Joy. This dinner is as much for you as it is for them. You've been so busy working that you haven't been around to enjoy a *gut* family meal and friends."

Joy nodded. She lifted the lid again and leaned in, breathing deep. The spaghetti sauce did smell good.

"*Ja*, of course. I'll go freshen up. But" — she pointed her finger into the air — "just know I'm going to save the very best stories for my sister."

"Well, that is thoughtful of you!" a voice called from down the hall. Then a blonde woman in a dark blue dress and white *kapp* hurried toward her. Grace was the prettiest of the sisters — all of them knew this to be true — but she had such a fun, sweet personality that no one minded.

233

"Grace!" Joy extended her hands. "You're home!"

"*Ja,* and I'm so glad you're going to give me the inside scoop on everything that's happening with the television show. I'm not sure why *Mem* was trying to mislead you." Grace stepped back and eyed Joy and then nodded her approval. "I did ask *Mem* to keep my arrival a surprise, but I had to give in. I just couldn't wait until supper to let you know I'm here."

Mem chuckled. "*Ja,* and that's another reason why I wanted you at home tonight. Your sister surprised us all."

Grace touched her stomach. "It turned out not to be the flu, just a bad reaction to take-out Chinese food. I wasn't used to it. Once I started feeling better, I climbed on the next bus. Thankfully there was an empty seat."

Joy pulled her sister in tighter. "It's so *gut* to see you. I feel as if you've been away longer than a few months."

"*Ja,* everyone from up north says hello, but I've missed so much around here. I've heard my sister's fallen in love and gotten a new job. Are things going well?"

Joy shrugged. "With the job, *ja,* but not so much with the love." She looked away, urging herself not to cry. "Matthew doesn't

234

understand about the job, and he won't even let me explain."

Grace took both of Joy's hands in hers. "I know he'll come around. And if he doesn't, then it's his loss. You're the most wonderful woman I know."

Joy bit her lower lip, and a tear trailed down her face. "That's kind of you to say. And I do have a lot to tell you."

"Go wash up and then you can start. I've heard so much about this Amish television show. It seems you're a topic of conversation in every house I visited . . . and I can't wait to hear the truth. I've never known anyone to work with Hollywood stars before."

Joy wiped her face and shrugged. "They're people just like us. That's one thing I've discovered. They laugh, they cry, and they try to pretend they haven't a care in the world when deep inside everything's falling apart."

Joy gave her sister one more hug and then hurried to her room. She was talking about Alicia, but she was also talking about herself. For just as wonderful as finding love was, even worse was knowing you made a bad mistake and lost it.

Joy wished she'd never seen love in Matthew's gaze. For now she knew what she had truly lost.

Alicia settled into the booth and scanned the restaurant to see if she'd been spotted. Working in Sarasota was so different from being in Los Angeles. In LA, paparazzi waited outside all the popular restaurants and clubs, waiting to see which celebrity guests would arrive. Here, a ponytail and sunglasses were enough to keep her mostly unnoticed. She spotted Rowan at the door and waved him over. He smiled as he walked her direction, and goose bumps rose on Alicia's arms.

"Thanks for inviting me to dinner." He slid into the booth across from her, picked up his water glass, and took a long drink. "What's the occasion?"

She'd given him the view of the ocean behind her, but instead of watching the waves, his eyes focused on her.

"Does there have to be an occasion? You eat dinner every night, I eat dinner every night, and we're in the same hotel."

"And . . ." He leaned closer.

She chuckled. "And I just wanted to congratulate you on a great first week. I've been on enough sets to know that's not always the case."

"Thanks. I think it's gone well too. I

haven't heard too many complaints."

She brushed her hair over her shoulder. "Yes, and that's because of the Amish woman. I still think everyone's trying to be on their best behavior."

"Maybe we should hire one for every set. Or you could just keep your costume and I could take you along with me."

Alicia smiled at that thought, and she also remembered traveling with Rowan wherever he worked. The memories brought a mix of both joy and sadness. Alicia didn't want to think of that now though. "Joy does have a calming presence to her, doesn't she?"

The waiter came and they ordered salads, and then they discussed the show's direction and what Rowan hoped to see in the future.

"Next week we're going to be filming on the beach. The permits came through."

"Oh!" Alicia clapped her hands together. "Will I get to wear a bikini? I haven't had a chance to work on my tan since I've been here."

"Oh, *ja*." He emphasized the Amish word for yes. "We'll have Georgia find one that complements your *kapp*."

Alicia puckered her lips and placed one hand on the back of her head, as if pretending to touch a *kapp* and pose from side to side.

Rowan's smile broadened. "Well, that's one way to get attention for the show. I'm sure all the tabloids would love to see photos of that."

Alicia nodded, and a warmth spread over her. She enjoyed bantering like this. She missed being with Rowan, and the last couple of weeks were a bright spot in the last year of heartache.

Rowan picked up the menu. "So do you know what you're going to order?"

She didn't need the menu to know she wanted the enchilada stack that she'd already had twice this week. And while she didn't want to bring a dark cloud over the evening, there was something she wanted to talk to her estranged husband about too. Something she'd wanted to say since the day after she'd left Prague a year ago. Something she'd had on the tip of her tongue every day since.

"I'm going to get the enchiladas again, and I want you to know how very sorry I am."

"Sorry for choosing Mexican food again?" He shrugged. "I'm not bothered by it if Mexican is your thing."

"Rowan. You know I'm not talking about

238

Mexican food." The edges of her words were sharp. "I did something horrible. Something I can never forgive myself for. I hurt you so deeply. It was something you didn't . . ." The tears came then, and she covered her face with her hands. "I've wanted to die knowing what I did. If I could go back and change it, if I could turn back time . . ."

"Ali. Look at me." His words were gentle, much gentler than she expected. That made her cry even harder. She didn't deserve his kindness. She didn't deserve to be here.

The waiter came up, and Rowan ordered for both of them. Then he sat silently, waiting for her to compose herself. She wiped her eyes with her cloth napkin and then finally looked up.

Rowan had tears in his eyes too. His face was red, as if he were about to cry. "I know you're sorry. I've known that." He swallowed hard and looked away, as if trying to get composure.

"How . . . how do you know? I've been too scared to talk to you."

"I've watched you. Just like you've been keeping track of me, I've been keeping track of you. Just like the Amish proverb says, 'You know a woman's heart by the life that she lives.' "

"That's an Amish proverb?" She chuckled

despite her tears. "You seriously just quoted an Amish proverb to me?"

Rowan wiped at his eyes too and laughed. "No, I completely made it up, but it sounds like something Joy would say, doesn't it?"

"*Ja.*" Alicia laughed. "I mean, yes, it does." She let her shoulders drop, and the boulders of pain and shame she'd been carrying around over the last year seemed to tumble off them. "So you forgive me? For what I've done?"

Rowan nodded. "It still hurts. I too am missing all we lost, but I do forgive you. I've messed up too much in my life not to."

Their salads arrived. Looking down at hers, the last thing Alicia wanted to do was eat. Too many emotions were surging within her — thankfulness mixed with all the painful memories. She picked up her fork and moved a tomato from side to side, and then she got up the nerve to ask the question she'd wanted to ask since arriving in Florida. "So where does that leave us?"

Rowan's eyebrows shot up, and she could tell the question surprised him. He took a few bites of his salad, as if he was trying to find the right words.

"I don't want you to get your hopes up," he finally said. "I don't mean to sound harsh, but I've been making a lot of changes in my life. I'm a different person. I can't let myself . . . well, let's just say I can't let myself be put in a place where I put you in front of other things anymore."

Good thing he didn't want to sound harsh.

"Like work?" She picked up a crouton and tossed it into her mouth. Confusion filled her mind, and her sadness morphed into anger. Was this what he'd planned all along? To draw her in, treat her with kindness, trick her into apologizing, and then cast her away? To get back at her for hurting him?

"No, like God."

"God?" The word sputtered out, and Alicia almost choked on her crouton.

"You know I was raised by my grandparents, and faith was a big part of their lives."

She tried not to smirk, but it was hard. "Yes, and I also know you left all that behind when you moved to Hollywood. If you told me once, you told me a hundred times."

"It's true, but it's also true that it's often during our darkest times that we truly understand what matters most. When I had nowhere else to turn, I rediscovered God. Actually, He'd been waiting there all long." He took another long drink of water and then focused on her eyes. "I hated what happened to us, but if it hadn't happened I'd still be feeling lost and empty inside. I know that doesn't make sense, but I forgave you a long time ago."

"No, it doesn't make sense. Well, not completely, but I'm glad you're happy." The slightest amount of tears came again, and she told herself not to cry. She shouldn't be sad. She should be happy that he'd forgiven her. That should help her go on with her life, right? But even though she was happy to see Rowan was doing so well, she felt betrayed. In a strange way, she'd almost rather have him be mad at her than this. Being mad would prove that he cared, but he was saying the pain she brought him made him realize what he really cared about . . . and it wasn't her.

"Listen." Alicia pushed back her plate. "I'm not feeling well. My head is pounding. And I'm not very hungry after all." She stood. "But I'm glad we had a chance to have this talk. I'm glad I know where everything stands." And then she strode away.

Her footsteps quickened, and her heart did too as she left Rowan sitting there. She was thankful that he'd found some sense of healing. But how could she — a frail human with more issues than she knew what to do with — ever compete with God for his love? She couldn't, which meant she'd continue to be alone. All she had left now were the memories of what they used to have — and what they used to be — together.

Pumpkin Spice Cake

1/2 cup solid vegetable shortening
1 1/4 cups sugar
2 eggs, beaten
1 1/4 cups all-purpose flour, sifted
2 1/2 teaspoons baking powder
1/2 teaspoon baking soda
1 teaspoon salt
2 teaspoons ground cinnamon
1/2 teaspoon ground ginger
1/2 teaspoon ground nutmeg
1 cup pumpkin puree
3/4 cup milk
1/2 cup chopped nuts

Cream shortening, gradually adding sugar until light and fluffy. Blend in beaten eggs. Add pumpkin puree and milk; stir and set aside. Sift together the dry ingredients, then add to the pumpkin mixture, stirring well. Stir in chopped nuts. Bake in greased 9-inch layer pans at 350 degrees for 30 minutes.

TWENTY-TWO

If at first you don't succeed,
there will be plenty of advice.

AMISH PROVERB

It was Friday afternoon, and Joy released a sigh of relief when the last of the filming was done for the week. She'd stayed throughout the day and watched the takes just to make sure they got everything right, but after two weeks of guiding the actors she'd had to point out very few mistakes. There had even been some moments when she'd forgotten they were *Englischers* playing parts. It seemed as if they were just Amish friends and she was getting a peek into their lives.

As she was gathering up her belongings to head out, Rowan strode toward her with an envelope. "I'm sorry it took so long to get this to you. I've had to deal with accounting and all that."

Joy took the envelope. *"Danke."*

Rowan cocked his eyebrow. "I know I should know what that means by now, but . . ."

"Thank you," she translated.

"Thank *you,* Joy. This show wouldn't be the same without you. I hope you understand that."

She nodded, remembering her first impression of Rowan. He'd been tired and frustrated that first night when he'd been lost and she'd helped him, but over the weeks she'd discovered how gentle he was. Even when things went wrong, he didn't yell or get upset, unlike some of the others on the set.

She strode out of the warehouse studio and walked straight to the bank. "Thank You, Lord, for providing." Once she got there, she found the lobby was empty. She stepped up to the counter and noticed a new face. It belonged to a young Mennonite man with an inviting smile.

"How can I help you today?"

"I'd like to deposit this check into my father's account. He's John Miller. It should be under John and Anna Miller."

He tapped away in the computer. "Yes, I see it." He took the envelope from her hands and opened it. His eyes widened slightly.

"Do you want to deposit all of it in there?"

"*Ja,* I do."

"Good. I can do that. I just need you to sign your name." He slid the check toward her, and for the first time she saw the amount. Joy sucked in a breath. She couldn't believe it. There must be some mistake. She looked into the envelope and found a slip of paper where the amount was broken down by tasks and hours. There was money for the dresses and money for her consultation. The amount she was paid each day to be on set was more than she usually made in a month working in Elizabeth's shop. Her heartbeat quickened, and the idea of her father's therapy became a reality before her eyes. *It could happen. It really could happen.*

"I take it by the way all the color has drained from your face that you hadn't actually looked at the check before now?"

"*Ne.*"

"The TV show must pay more than you expected. Is the filming going well, Joy?"

She looked at the check more closely and then eyed the man again. The check was made out to her, but even if he knew a Joy Miller was working for the TV show, how was he so sure she was that Joy Miller? How did he know the check was from the TV show? It was from a company she'd never heard of. Was everyone in town really watching her that closely — even people who weren't Amish? Did they all believe she was being prideful and doing her own thing despite what the bishop thought? That's what Matthew believed. Most likely that's what everyone else in town believed too.

Anxiety tightened the muscles in her neck and crawled down the back of her arms. Grace said everyone in town — and beyond — had been talking about the television show and about her. She'd thought that was an exaggeration. Now she realized it wasn't.

"I . . . I believe the filming's going well. Thank you for asking." Her voice quavered, and she thought of Elizabeth's words from yesterday. Joy had stopped by to check her schedule, and the older woman had taken time to encourage her and to pray.

"If you've gone to the Lord, and you believe you're doing the right thing, then trust in that," Elizabeth had said. "Sometimes it takes some people longer to come around, but if they're open to God's voice they eventually will."

Matthew's face filled her mind. She also thought of the bishop's order not to get involved with the *Englischers*. *I don't have anything to be ashamed of. This is a blessing.*

It's a way of provision.

"So it's a lot more money than you expected?" the man asked.

"I never asked what I would be paid, but I am thankful, especially with my *dat*'s medical bills."

"You don't have to explain, and you don't have to worry. Your banking is always confidential with us."

"Danke." She took the receipt from his hand. "That's *gut* to know."

Joy was sure the man's eyes stayed on her as she walked away. Would he really keep her personal business to himself?

"It doesn't matter," she mumbled as she left. "I know what I'm doing and why." And then, as the warm breeze outside caused her hem to flutter, Joy sent up a prayer. *Help me focus on Your opinion of me, God. It's the one that matters.*

Joy quickened her steps as she walked, eager to talk to Faith. Just a few more weeks like this and they'd have enough to provide for their *dat*'s first treatment. She never imagined it would happen so quickly, but she was thankful. No matter what anyone thought, God's plan for her to work with the television show was clear.

Joy poked the needle into the fabric. It was

Saturday, her day off, and it felt good just to sit and not think about a script, a wardrobe, or the million little details the Amish tended to and paid attention to. Things that the outside world never noticed or cared about.

Yesterday she was surprised when Alicia had sought her out, asking if Joy was open to spending any time together. Alicia commented that she'd love to spend a day as an Amish woman, sewing and cooking. Inwardly, Joy had laughed. In a typical Amish woman's life, very few days were set aside just for sewing and cooking, but Joy didn't tell the actress that. She liked the idea of relaxing in this way and spending time with Alicia.

Alicia had shown up right after lunch, wearing a long skirt and T-shirt and with her hair up. The rest of the family was out of the house for the afternoon, and the two women sat at the kitchen table, looking through *Mem*'s cookbooks and deciding what they were going to make.

"I learned how to cook and sew when I was younger — well, just a little." Alicia flipped through the pages. "I took home economics in eighth grade, and I know enough to impress my Hollywood friends when I host dinner parties." She sighed. "At least when I used to host them. Did you have home ec in your Amish school? You did go to one, didn't you?"

Joy paused at the recipe for Healthy Chocolate Chip Granola and put down a sticky note.

"*Ja . . .* I mean, yes. I did go to an Amish school, but we didn't have home economics. *Mem* taught me. I can remember sitting next to her during sewing frolics even as a toddler. Three of my sisters would be outside playing with the other kids, and my sister Lovina would be in the kitchen with the other girls her age. But I was always at *Mem*'s side, and I started sewing as soon as I could."

"Lovina . . . is she the one who owns the pie shop? Oh my word, I've never tasted such wonderful pie. Do you think she'd bring me a pie sometime?"

"I bet she would. Do you have a favorite?"

"A favorite? I'm not sure. I usually don't eat sweets. Wardrobe would have a fit if I gained too much weight, you know, but pie like that is worth an extra hour in the gym!" Alicia laughed, but the laughter didn't meet her eyes. There was something wrong, something sad inside this beautiful woman. Something Alicia especially tried to hide when she was on the set. Would Alicia ever

251

trust Joy enough to open up?

They were quiet for a while, each in their own thoughts, as they looked through the recipes. Then Joy turned to her friend. "So what movies or shows have you been in before?"

"Have you heard of *The Lockup*?"

"Can't say I have."

"Oh, yeah. You Amish people don't watch television, do you? Whoa. That's so crazy. I mean, I never thought of that before. You've never watched *Little House on the Prairie* or *Gilmore Girls*. Seriously, that's weird that people in the United States have no idea who Kim Kardashian is."

"Oh, I know who she is. I do shop at the grocery store and see the headlines. I just have no idea what she does."

Laughter spilled from Alicia's lips. "Uh, and the rest of the world asks the same question. No one really knows what she does."

"So did you play a prisoner in that television show?"

"Yeah, an undercover prisoner. I'd pretend to get arrested and get locked up. It was my job to solve the crimes from the inside."

"Was that hard — pretending to be a criminal?"

"Not really." Alicia flipped another page

of the cookbook and then shrugged. "I visited some real prisons . . . you know, to get into character. And I discovered that those on the inside aren't much different from those on the outside. We all want to be loved. We all seek to find value and worth. And we all want money and power. We just go about getting it in different ways."

Joy smiled and nodded, not knowing what to say. Things weren't like that in the Amish community — or at least with the Amish she knew — but she didn't want to bring that up. She didn't want to sound prideful. Sound like her community was better.

Alicia licked her lips at a photo of chocolate cake, and then she laughed again. "Wait. Listen to who I'm talking to. I forgot about your *kapp* for a moment. I suppose people don't sin like that in your group."

"Oh, people sin all right. I have sinned more times than I'd like to admit, but from a young age we are taught to put others before ourselves. To work together. To be humble."

"I can't even imagine. My old man was long gone even before I can remember, and my mom . . . well, she was often more interested in her newest boyfriend than in caring for me and my sister." Alicia reached into her purse and pulled out her cell phone, checking her messages. "You don't mind, do you?"

Joy forced a smile. "I'm fine. I know you have important things to keep track of."

After reading through some messages and clicking on some photos, Alicia put her phone back into her purse and turned to Joy, picking up where they'd left off. "I really can't imagine it. Having a family dinner with a mom and dad, sisters and brothers around the table. I used to think the movies just lied about stuff like that, because no one I know in Hollywood lives like that. Well, until I came here."

"You know what I'm thinking? You need to do some research, to get into character. How about you stay for dinner tonight at our place?"

"Really?"

"*Ja.*"

"And your folks won't mind?"

Joy paused for a minute, and she tried to picture *Mem*'s reaction. *Mem* would be surprised, but she'd be welcoming. Neither *Mem* nor *Dat* would ever turn a stranger away from their table.

"They wouldn't mind at all, especially if we're cooking."

"Oh, can we make this Shepherd's Pie?

I've never had it, but it sounds very Amish to me."

Joy laughed. "*Ja,* that's easy to make."

Alicia looked to Joy and her smiled faded just slightly. "I wish Rowan could see this — you and me sitting here, enjoying each other's company like old friends. I'm not sure he'd believe it."

"Oh really? Why?"

Pink touched Alicia's cheeks. "Well, this is not how I usually spent my Saturday afternoons back in LA."

Joy rose and moved to the pantry, checking to see if they had enough potatoes. If not they'd have to walk down to Yoder's Produce. "If you'd like you could call and invite Rowan."

"No." The word shot from Alicia's mouth.

Joy turned in surprise. "I see. You don't like that idea?"

"That sounded bad, didn't it? The truth is that Rowan and I . . . well, we had some issues in the past. It's best to just keep things work-related."

Joy nodded. "*Ja,* I understand. Men . . . they do cause all types of issues, don't they?"

Joy put the bag of potatoes on the counter and then took two knives from a drawer. "Ready to start making some Shepherd's

Pie? I'm going to get you started on that while I work on this granola. It sounds like the perfect thing to take to the set on Monday."

Alicia's eyes widened. "You're going to turn dinner over to me?"

"*Ja,* of course. You want to impress my parents, right?"

"If I don't poison your parents, it'll be a good day."

"Well, you don't have to worry about that. I promise." Joy couldn't help but laugh, and even as she pulled the other ingredients from a cupboard, a smile filled her face. For most of her life she'd been aware of the differences between her and the *Englisch.* It was quite refreshing to now focus on the similarities. Alicia was an *Englisch* movie and television star, and she was a simple Amish woman. They couldn't be more different on the outside, but on the inside they couldn't be more alike. They each wanted to be loved and appreciated.

As Joy expected, both *Mem* and *Dat* were welcoming when it came to having Alicia for dinner. And they were especially pleased to discover that Alicia had done most of the cooking.

Before the food was served, *Dat* bowed his head, and everyone followed. Silent prayers were familiar and comforting to Joy. When she lifted her face, she noticed a smile on Alicia's face.

"So what happens with this television picture? Is there a certain time when it shows?" *Mem* asked after they'd finished serving up the plates. "I'm sorry, I don't understand how it works."

Joy attempted to hide her smile. She had to give it to her *mem.* She was trying. It wasn't easy to talk about something you've never seen before.

"It's a television series. It'll play every Monday night, starting in the spring." Alicia took a big bite of her casserole and smiled. Her eyes widened as she looked to Joy. She nodded, excited about her accomplishment.

"But it's November now. Can you really make a show by the spring?"

"I can't, but Rowan — the director — he's pulled together a great team."

"So you'll be around a while?" *Mem* asked. "When I asked Joy that question, she said she didn't really know how long you'd be here."

"We'll be there through Christmas . . . at least that's the plan. Then we'll go home, and when the show airs, we'll see how the ratings are. Only then will we know whether the network will renew."

Heads bobbed around the table, but Joy knew her family didn't understand words like *network* and *ratings.*

"So have you been in other television shows?" *Dat* asked.

"Oh, yeah. Quite a few. The last two have been a cop show and a prison drama. They were pretty intense roles. I was ready to break out of the mold they were putting me in. And . . ." She let out a low sigh.

"And?" *Dat* asked, urging her on.

"And I'm tired of the darkness of it all, you know? Thinking about crimes and prisons all the time. I was ready for something lighter, happier. So when my agent pitched me a sweet family show, I was hooked."

Mem reached over and patted Alicia's hand. "We're glad to have you here."

"Thank you . . ." Alicia's voice broke, and she looked away. "I'm so sorry. I didn't mean to cry. It's just that I've never been so welcomed by a family like yours before."

"I'm glad you're here at our table." *Dat* appeared to have more color in his cheeks tonight. "The Bible says the *gut* Lord knows every person on this earth, and for some great reason He's connecting you with us here. It's not just a coincidence. It's part of a great plan."

Tears filled the corners of Alicia's eyes, and she nodded. Joy couldn't help but think back to the sewing circle and everyone who had so many worries about the television show coming to town. But now she knew they had a limited perspective. They had spoken from their fears, but thankfully God had seen beyond that. God spoke from His promises, and in the weeks to come Joy would need to remember that.

Healthy Chocolate Chip Granola

12 cups quick oats
2 cups wheat germ
2 cups sunflower seeds
2 cups flaked coconut
1 teaspoon salt
1 cup brown sugar
1 cup vegetable oil
1 cup honey
1 tablespoon vanilla extract
1 to 1 1/2 cups raisins (optional)
1 to 1 1/2 cups chocolate morsels

Preheat oven to 350 degrees. In a large bowl, combine oats, wheat germ, sunflower seeds, coconut, salt, and sugar; mix well. In a small saucepan bring the oil and honey to a boil. Remove from heat. Stir in vanilla extract. Pour over dry mixture; stir to coat. Transfer to large baking pan or divide into two pans. Bake for 1 1/2 hours, stirring every 20 minutes. Remove from oven and let cool completely. Stir in chocolate morsels (and raisins if desired). Store in tight container.

Twenty-Three

Faith rests on God, receives from God,
responds to God, relies on God.
AMISH PROVERB

"What do you mean they quit?"

They were the first words Joy heard from
Rowan when she arrived Monday morning.
Worries weighed her down, yet she'd tried
not to let it show. She'd seen Matthew at
church, but he'd slipped out just as the
service ended, and she didn't get a chance
to talk to him. *Does he think he can ignore
me forever?* It had been two weeks, and it
appeared that he did. But now that Joy was
at work she had to focus on the needs and
problems here.

"What happened?" Joy asked Rowan. He
was with one of his assistants, Heidi.

The woman turned to her. "We had a
contract for craft services, but the woman
was in a car accident . . ."

"A contract is a contract," Rowan sputtered.

"Her leg is shattered." Heidi placed a hand on her hip. "Her arm is broken in three places. And she did most of the cooking herself."

Rowan crossed his arms over his chest. He looked more tired than he had on Friday. Had he had a long weekend? A hard one? Joy really didn't know what he did outside of work. Maybe the problem was he worked behind the scenes even when everyone else got a break.

"Well, hire someone then."

Heidi sighed. "I'm looking into it."

"I'm sorry, I don't remember what craft services are," Joy said.

"Is. It's the catering department," Heidi commented. "To make the most of the time on set, we bring food in."

Joy nodded, understanding.

"Just make sure the new service knows how to make pie," Alicia quipped. She stepped out of wardrobe wearing her Amish clothes, but her hair had yet to be pinned up.

"Pie?" Rowan's brow furrowed. Then his face brightened. He turned to Joy. "What about you?"

"What do you mean?"

"Would you be interested in cooking for us? In providing meals and snacks on set?"

"Oh, I'm not going to have time for that. With all the sewing, and now the consulting . . ." She hid her yawn. "I do need to sleep." She didn't tell him she hardly slept as it was.

"Well, what about your mom or an aunt? Someone who can make pie and whatever you Amish make? Surely the ladies you know are used to cooking for large families."

"My mother is a good cook." Joy cocked an eyebrow, trying to figure out how that could work. "I can ask her. But I don't know. She's pretty busy caring for my *dat.*"

"Can you ask?" He looked around at those assembling. "If we don't get food, we'll have a hungry mob on our hands."

"Yes, I can run home and ask, but even if she agrees, lunch will be the soonest we can get you anything."

Rowan turned to Heidi. "There's a bagel shop down the road. Run and pick something up for breakfast." Then he reached over and placed a hand on Joy's shoulder. "I know I'm already asking a lot from you, but if you can find some help I'll appreciate it."

"I'll do what I can."

Rowan smiled. "That's all I can ask, Joy.

263

That's all I can ask." He turned and then paused. "Oh, and let me get you some cash to use for today. I'm glad I kept some around. Like my grandpa always told me, you never know when you're going to need to dip into your rainy-day fund."

Joy opened the kitchen door and stepped inside. Her *mem* stirred a small pot on the stove top. Joy leaned in, breathed deeply, and smiled. "It smells *gut* in here. What do you have cooking?"

"Chocolate gravy to go with the biscuits left over from dinner. Last week the doctor said *Dat* is losing too much weight. I'm trying to plump him up." *Mem* smiled. "Not that you would know what we had for dinner last night, of course. Heard you come in just as I got into bed."

"I was going over this week's script with Rowan, the director." Joy didn't mention that she'd taken the long way home, hoping to see Matthew as she walked but finding only a quiet house with no one in sight.

"I know chocolate gravy isn't your favorite, but I can put some butter and jam on a biscuit for you if you'd like."

"*Ja*, I'd like that. *Danke, Mem.*" She moved to the table and sat down, wondering how long it would take before *Mem* asked what she was doing home in the middle of the morning.

Mem eyed her. "You sure are quiet today. Is everything going well?"

"At work? It mostly is. It's a whole new world, really, but I'm getting used to it."

"So they're letting you off early for lunch today?" A bird chirped outside the window, and *Mem* cracked the window open so they could hear it better.

"I don't get lunch off today. In fact, I need to get right back. I hurried over because there's something I need to talk to you about. The woman they hired to provide meals for the set was injured in a car accident."

"Oh *ne,*" *Mem* gasped. "Is she okay?"

"She's going to be okay, but it puts us in a real bind. They need someone to provide the food. I was wondering if you'd be interested."

"Me?" *Mem* placed a hand on her chest, looking pleased. "What's required?"

"A light breakfast, lunch, a snack, and a light dinner. It's only thirty or forty people."

"Only! You make it sound easy."

"*Mem,* how many barn raisings and weddings have you helped with? Forty people *is* a small gathering."

"*Ja,* but that's one event. Not three meals

265

and a snack every day. I'm not sure I could do that much work."

"I'm sure you can find friends to help. You know everyone in Pinecraft and lots of people who are here for the season. I'm certain you could find some helpers. They pay well."

Joy didn't mention her *dat*'s doctor bills, and she didn't have to. She could tell from the new interest in her *mem*'s eyes that she was considering the very same thing. Had *Dat* and *Mem* checked their savings account yet? Joy was sure they hadn't. She was sure if they found that large sum of money in their account they would have said something.

Mem put down her spoon and then turned off the burner. "I suppose I could ask a few people."

"That would be wonderful. And before that . . ."

"Let me guess. You need dinner for tonight?"

"We actually need lunch . . . in three hours."

"For forty people?" *Mem*'s voice rose an octave. "It will be a lot of work." She looked at the clock. "And I only have three hours."

Joy offered a forced smile. "Maybe Faith can help? Grace? I believe Faith should be home soon from Yoder's."

"*Ja,* and Grace is visiting a friend. But I'll need to run to the store, and . . . where will I get money for all that food?"

Joy reached into her pocket and pulled out some large bills. *Mem*'s eyes widened. "This is for the food, and the rest for your trouble."

"*Ne,* that's too much."

"*Mem,* you have to understand. This is a different world. Today the pay is more because it's unexpected, but . . ."

"It's a godsend, that's what it is." *Mem* turned from the stove, the chocolate gravy now forgotten. "Do you have a minute to go over a menu?"

"*Ja,* of course . . . and I'll also stop by and order some pies from Lovina. I know you won't have time to worry about baking today."

"Make sure you ask for the apple cream pie. It's new to the menu and delicious. Even *Dat* ate two pieces last night."

Joy smiled and nodded, and inside she praised God. Not long ago she had no idea how *Dat*'s medical needs would be taken care of. Now she knew. God had brought the most unlikely situation their way to provide for what her family needed most.

Apple Cream Pie

1 unbaked pastry pie shell
3 cups finely cut apples
1 cup light brown sugar
2/3 cup heavy whipping cream
1/4 teaspoon salt
1 heaping tablespoon all-purpose flour
1/2 teaspoon ground cinnamon

Preheat oven to 450 degrees. Mix together apples, sugar, cream, salt, and flour in a large bowl. Spoon into unbaked pie shell. Sprinkle cinnamon over top. Bake for 15 minutes; reduce heat to 325 degrees and bake for 30 to 40 minutes longer. Serve chilled.

TWENTY-FOUR

Remember that if the outlook may not be
bright at times, the uplook always is.

AMISH PROVERB

The gaggle of women entered the building.
Some Joy knew and some she didn't, but
she knew Rowan had told the security guard
to take all their names from *Mem* and then
let them in.

Mem walked to where Joy stood by the
tables that were always ready for meals. "Do
we just set up here?"

"*Ja, Mem.* Just put it down anywhere."

Joy hurried toward an older woman and
helped her with the large casserole dish she
was carrying. "*Ja,* place the food right on
these tables," she repeated.

The woman set down the casserole. It was
hot and bubbling and smelled delicious.

"You must be Joy. I'm Adeline, and most
of us are from Ephrata, Pennsylvania. We

269

met your *mem* at Yoder's Produce. We were supposed to have a sisters' sewing circle today, but this sounded like a lot more fun."

Joy smiled. Wasn't that just like *Mem* to rope them in? There was so much conflict of late within the community that *Mem* had been smart to ask outsiders for help. And these women seemed pleased. Even as they placed their dishes on the table, they scanned the set. They took in the television crew and the lights, and their eyes settled on the Amish living room set. Alicia sat on the sofa in her Amish dress, reading over tomorrow's script.

Adeline stepped closer to Joy and pointed to Alicia. "Is that woman Amish or *Englisch*? It's hard to tell. She's not an actress, is she?"

Joy lifted her chin and smiled, pleased by the woman's comments. If this woman couldn't tell Alicia was *Englisch,* then she knew she'd done her job well.

"She's one of the actors. And a dear friend," Joy added. "She's going to love all this food. It smells so wonderful, although I'm sure I'm going to get some complaints."

Adeline's face fell. "Complaints? Why?"

Joy chuckled. "Oh, because wardrobe has already had me take her dress out once. I suppose she's been eating too well around Pinecraft. Georgia — the wardrobe designer

— is almost ready to ban Alicia from ordering in from Me, Myself, and Pie. Alicia loves it, of course. She was determined to try every pie on the menu, and from what I hear she's getting close."

The woman hung on every word, and Joy knew she was giving them plenty of news to tell when they returned home. Yet for the first time, it didn't bother her. They'd talk about the cameras and the set, so they might as well talk about the people too. These were real people with real needs. For so long she simply thought of the Amish relationship with the *Englischers* as "us versus them," but the more time she spent on the set, the more she thought differently about friendships and the need for all people from all backgrounds to know God.

The women had barely set the food on the table when the crew gathered around, ready to dig in as if they were soldiers who'd just gotten off a march. Georgia didn't wait to be served. She picked up two steaming biscuits and slathered them with butter and jam. With elated voices, everyone else eagerly let the ladies pile paper plates with their requests for fried chicken, potato salad, zucchini casserole, homemade bread, chocolate chip cookies, and pie. *Mem* had brought a fresh fruit salad, and her bowl was empty within minutes.

Joy watched her *mem* scooping up healthy portions of casserole onto paper plates. If Joy lived a hundred more years, she'd never forget the transformation of her mother right before her eyes. She appeared twenty years younger. Her smile was bright. Her eyes twinkled. For the first time Joy realized how much her father's illness had taken its toll on *Mem.* How nice it was to sit back and watch her work.

Joy couldn't help but smile as she watched everyone eat too.

"This is amazing," one of the cameramen declared, licking his fingertips.

"Are they coming back for dinner?" one of the men asked, dabbing his mouth with a white paper napkin.

"Yes, we'll be back," *Mem* piped up, and a cheer rose.

"You're still eating?" Rowan asked, walking up to his assistant.

"Is there still food on the table?" Heidi asked.

"Yes."

"Then I'm still eating."

Joy walked up to both of them. Alicia was there too. "You know they're bringing more food tonight and tomorrow, right?"

Alicia wrinkled her nose and grinned.

"Yes, and I can't wait to see what it is."

Mem approached Kristen with two paper plates. "Would you like a piece of pie?"

The actress placed a hand on her flat stomach. "I can't remember the last time I ate pie. But if you want to cut one of those in half —"

"Oh, nonsense." *Mem* handed her the plate with the largest piece. "One piece of pie isn't that much. Besides, you need to plump up."

Joy laughed. "There is no such thing as small in my mother's portioning."

"No, honestly. I can't eat that much," Kristen said even as she took the plate from *Mem*'s hands. Her eyes widened as she took a bite. "This is amazing."

Mem winked. "I told you."

When they were nearly finished, Joy took a plate herself and stepped to the back of the line. Someone walked up behind her, and she turned to see Rowan.

"I think this is a hit. They're taking the job, right?"

Joy turned to her *mem.* "Are you sure? Do you think you can handle all this every day they're shooting?"

"I won't be able to do all the cooking, but I'd be happy to find people who can."

Joy leaned in close to her, whispering into

her ear. "But what will the bishop say?"

"The bishop. Oh, *ja . . .*" *Mem* nodded. "I already stopped by and talked to him and Jeanette."

"You did?"

"*Ja,* I told them about your *dat*'s therapy. He not only understood our need to make money, but he said he'd put in a special request for those in the church to help too. They'll be taking up a collection."

Hearing that, Joy's heartbeat quickened. She placed a hand over it. "And did he talk about me? Did you mention that's why I'm working here too?"

Mem's brow furrowed. "Why you're working here?"

"*Ja,* to earn money for *Dat*'s treatment. And that's why Faith was helping me sew." Joy didn't know whether to laugh or cry. "*Mem,* have you even looked in your bank account? We almost have enough for his first round of therapy."

Tears filled *Mem*'s eyes. She covered her mouth with her hands, and then she reached out and grasped both of Joy's shoulders. "I had *ne* idea, Joy. I really had *ne* idea."

"I'm just glad I could help, *Mem.*" Joy glanced up and noticed Alicia standing nearby. Had she overhead?

Mem moved back to the table and began

gathering up all the empty dishes. As she did, Alicia stepped closer.

She chuckled. "I've never seen the crew so excited about craft service meals."

"Yes, there's something to be said for good Amish cooking. What do you think, Alicia? Maybe sometime this week you can come help us make Shepherd's Pie for the whole group."

Rowan sidled up with a smirk. "Alicia doesn't cook, let alone Shepherd's Pie."

Alicia looked up at him. "There's so little you know about me lately. Isn't that right, Joy?" Alicia gripped Joy's arm. "I'm not the same person I was a year ago, Rowan. I *did* make Shepherd's Pie for Joy's whole family. It seems I'm becoming a little more like Joy every day."

Alicia bit her lip and tuned to Joy. "I've even started reading my Bible. I found one of those Gideon Bibles in the dresser of my hotel room. I want to thank you, Joy. Thank you for being here, and thank you for being such an example to me. I'm not sure how everything would have worked out on this set if it hadn't been for you."

"Well, thank you. I . . . I don't know what to say." Joy reached out and took Alicia's hand, and Joy could read more in her gaze.

"You have something you want to ask

me," Joy said. "I can see it in your eyes."

Alicia's eyes widened. "How did you know?"

"I sit in a director's chair." Joy chucked. "I'm getting good at reading people."

Alicia glanced at Rowan. "Uh, maybe we can talk about it later."

Rowan lifted his hand. "I get it. I understand. I'm not invited in this conversation." He sounded as if he was hurt. Or maybe he was angry. But what would he be angry about?

Seeing him go, Joy lifted her eyebrows as she turned to Alicia. "Well?"

"I was talking to some of the cast, and we were wondering if you'd want to do a Bible study with us at lunch. After we eat. Maybe starting tomorrow?"

"A Bible study?" Joy's eyes widened.

"*Ja.*" Alicia chuckled. "I mean, yes. Me, Georgia, Kristen . . . a few of the camera guys mentioned they might be interested too."

"It sounds interesting. Let me think about it. I like the idea of Bible reading together." She smiled. "It's the *leading* that has me nervous."

"Yes." Alicia nodded. "Of course."

Joy was about to ask more about Alicia's expectations when she heard footsteps beside her.

"Excuse me." A young Amish woman stepped up to Joy. Joy had seen her around town. *Mem* had obviously roped her in too. "I'm sorry to bother you, but Jeanette asked me to deliver this to you." She pulled out a small envelope from her apron pocket.

Joy swallowed hard. "Jeanette, the bishop's wife?"

"Ja." The young woman nodded. "She stopped me just outside the gate. She wanted to deliver it to you herself, but the security guard wouldn't let her in. Your *mem* had them put my name on the list, but not hers." The young woman smiled. "She was quite upset when I came upon her. She even offered to carry in one of the casseroles, but the security guard wasn't fooled."

"She . . . she was coming to bring this to me? *Danke.*" She took the envelope from the woman's hand.

Joy stepped over to Rowan and told him she'd be back shortly, and then she hurried into a back corner, hoping no one would follow. It wasn't until she'd stepped away that she realized she hadn't finished talking to Alicia about the Bible study, but she had plenty of time to do that later. Right now Joy had to know what Matthew's *mem* had sent. She opened the envelope and pulled out one thin sheet of paper.

Dear Joy,
Your *mem* stopped by this afternoon and told us she was going to be cooking for the television show. She also explained why the money is needed. Jacob and I feel so bad that we didn't help sooner. Of course, we didn't know.

Even though she didn't say so, I assume that's why you're working there too. I know my son doesn't know this, and I hope you'll tell him. He's angry, but I believe he will come around and understand. He wouldn't be so angry if he didn't love you so deeply. That's what I keep telling him.

That's not the point of my note, though. I'm writing to tell you Jacob and I will do what we can to get the community to help with the expenses for your *dat*'s therapy treatments. That's what a church and community are supposed to do — share together in all things, both *gut* and bad. With that promise, we also encourage you to step down from your job. A television show is *ne* place for a young woman such as you. Don't be tempted

278

by the world and all that it offers.

I'm having another sewing frolic tomorrow. It won't be the same without you. I hope to see you there.

Love, Jeanette

Joy didn't realize her hands were trembling until she attempted to fold the paper. Matthew was angry, but if she quit, all would be forgiven. And the church was going to help provide for *dat*'s treatments. It seemed almost too good to be true.

For a moment she tried to picture life as before. Before she'd started working on the set, she'd woken up slowly and had time to talk with *Mem* and *Dat* before heading over to Pinecraft Fabric and Quilts. She had time to attend sewing frolics and to be with Matthew. That old life was what she wanted most, wasn't it? To know *Dat*'s treatment would be covered and that she could go on with her romance? *To love and to be loved? To marry and live a simple Amish life?*

That's what she wanted before, but now . . . What had changed? She'd made new friendships with *Englischers*. And she saw that while she had been sewing with friends and working in a quilt shop, there were real people out in the world who needed hope and to hear about God's love. And now Alicia wanted to start a Bible study. She was opening up right before Joy's eyes. Her friend would be crushed. She'd close back up and resurrect those old walls if Joy walked away now.

"What am I going to do?" she whispered.

"Joy!" Rowan called her name. "We're getting ready to shoot. Are you almost done?"

She folded up the letter and tucked it into her apron pocket. She didn't have to decide this moment. She had tonight to think about that. Today she had a job to do.

Joy's knees trembled slightly as she hurried over to Rowan. She offered a smile that she hoped was as sweet as one of Lovina's peanut butter pies.

When she paused beside him, he eyed her suspiciously. "Ready to get started?"

"Yes, of course. Why wouldn't I be ready?"

"You just look a little pale, that's all."

Joy patted her cheek. Then she swept her hand around the room. "That's because you've been keeping me inside this set. I'm happy we'll be shooting outside the rest of the week."

"Yeah, me too," Rowan said, but he still looked worried.

Joy sat down in her director's chair next to his, knowing whatever decision she made, people would get hurt. If she stayed or if she went, someone wouldn't understand. Someone would feel abandoned.

Zucchini Casserole

2 cups cooked, sliced zucchini
1 cup milk
2 eggs, beaten
1/4 cup butter, melted
1 cup crushed crackers
1/2 teaspoon salt
1 tablespoon sugar
1/8 teaspoon ground black pepper
3/4 cup shredded cheddar cheese
1 small onion, chopped

Preheat oven to 375 degrees. Combine all ingredients together; place in a well-greased 8 by 8-inch casserole dish. Bake for 35 minutes or until golden brown.

TWENTY-FIVE

Faith without works won't work.
Faith with works will.

AMISH PROVERB

Joy woke up extra early to read her Bible and pray. Yet even as the minutes ticked by, she was afraid to get up. Afraid to get dressed. Afraid to make a decision. She lay gazing at the dust in the air as the morning sun brightened the bedside table and illuminated her Bible. As she looked at it, a Scripture verse she'd learned at school came to mind.

"The grass withers and the flowers fade, but the Word of God stands forever," Joy whispered.

She had a choice to make. She could get up, get dressed, and go to the sewing frolic at Jeanette Slagel's home. She could be accepted once again, and she could continue her relationship with Matthew. Or she could

get dressed and go to the set. She could finish the role she'd been given there and lead
the Bible study at lunch.

The Word of God stands forever.

She could surround herself with godly
Amish women who knew God's Word, knew
Him, and trusted Him. Or she could go
share His Word with those who were hungry
for it. Who didn't know His Word and who
didn't know Him.

She thought about Elizabeth. The woman
was eager to share the goodness of God with
anyone who came into the fabric store and
quilt shop.

"If God brings me a person who needs a
taste of God's Word, I'm not going to send
them away hungry," Elizabeth had said
more than once.

Joy also thought about what Alicia had
told Joy's family over Shepherd's Pie. She'd
taken on this project because she wanted
something wholesome and good in her life.
What was more wholesome or good than
God?

Tears filled Joy's eyes as she thought about
Matthew next. She had no doubt that she
was in love with him. He was the person —
the only person — she could imagine spending her life with, but to walk onto that set
today would mean walking away from him,

from their future.

"I trust You, God." The words came as a whisper. Even if she did become Matthew's wife, she'd always regret turning her back on those who needed to hear about God's love so desperately.

Joy rose and dressed in the good coral dress she always wore to the studio. She needed to trust God with this, even if it meant walking away from the only person she could picture sharing a future with. Tears fell down her cheeks, but there was no other way.

It had been a quiet morning on the set. Everyone was getting ready for a new scene, and in a strange way the once-dramatic cast members had started to act more like friends. A storm had blown into Sarasota, so instead of filming on the beach they'd set up a front porch set inside and worked on this different scene. The mock house front was an exact duplicate of the small house they were renting close to Phillippi Park. The carpenters had built the porch and landing on the studio set. But instead of the two plastic chairs, someone had mounted a porch swing. The result was charming.

Rowan was nowhere to be seen, so Joy

moved to her regular chair and waited.

"Hey, do you think you can help?" The voice was from right behind her, and Joy assumed the cameraman, Steven, was talking to one of the crew. She didn't turn.

"What is her name?" Steven was asking someone. Then as if remembering, he blurted it out. "Joy." His hand touched her shoulder, and she jumped.

Her heartbeat quickened as she turned. The man stood right behind her.

Heat flooded her cheeks. "I'm so sorry. I had no idea you were talking to me."

"I need your help with this scene. It just doesn't look right on camera."

"All right. But what do you need? I'm not sure how much I can help."

"All I need is for you to go sit on that porch set. An Amish bachelor has come to town, and he's supposed to meet Alicia — Sadie's — dad . . . or as you say, *dat.* I just need you to tell him her *dat* isn't home."

Joy looked at each of the cameramen. All eyes were on her and her face grew hotter still. *Just do it and you'll be done before you know it,* she told herself. She blew out a breath and hurried to the porch swing.

Then she looked around. "And what am I doing now that I'm here?"

"What do you mean?"

"I mean an Amish woman never just sits on the porch. We are always doing something. Even if we were waiting for a friend to visit we'd be writing a letter or mending."

"Okay." He pointed to the dress she'd planned on taking home to mend the hem. "Work on that."

A stagehand brought her the dress and a needle and thread as an assistant gave her the lines. Joy thought about mentioning she'd be carrying around a whole sewing basket, but she decided not to push it. It wasn't as if she was going to be in this television show.

She adjusted herself on the swing and started hemming. She'd seen a new actor on set and she assumed he was the man who would be playing the Amish bachelor. He'd come in this morning, and he didn't look very Amish to her. Still, when footsteps neared, her heart pounded. She could feel the blood moving through her veins from her heart to her limbs.

"Miss?" a voice asked. She looked up. He wasn't the new actor she expected, but she had seen this one exiting Yoder's Restaurant the day before. He had a tan face and light blond hair. His blue eyes nearly pierced her.

Joy sat silent, eyeing him, and then she

remembered why the character was talking to her, or at least why the cameraman said he'd come. Joy couldn't remember her lines completely, so she decided to wing it.

"If you're looking for my *dat,* he's not here. He's, uh, still in town. He should be back soon."

He pointed to the empty rocking chair. "Do you mind?"

"*Ne,* not at all."

He sat down, and his eyes dropped to her hands. For a moment he watched as she worked.

"Small, neat stitching, just like my *mem* does it."

"My *mem* too." She set her mending to the side, wondering what else to do or say.

"Cut!" Rowan's voice broke through. She hadn't even known he'd been out there or that they'd been filming. Then he hurried forward. "That was perfect. Just perfect. Tell the writers to capture that dialogue." Then he turned to an actress who was standing to the side. "Did you see that? Joy rocked the swing slowly. She talked slow. There was no rushing the words. Did you see her blush, and the way she caught her breath? And did you see the way he looked at her, both with interest and acceptance? That. I want that."

Joy cleared her throat, hearing those

words. She hadn't meant to blush or catch her breath. She was just surprised to see who the actor was, that's all.

"All right." The actress stepped forward. "I'll see what I can do . . . unless you want her to play the part."

The woman meant that as a joke, but Joy could tell from the look in Rowan's eyes that he was considering the idea.

"No, no. I'm not interested in that." She rose and hurried back to her chair. But Rowan beat her there.

"Are you sure you don't want to play that part? We already have the first scene. Your character is only going to show up once in a while."

"I honestly do not want to be an actress."

"I hear what you're saying, but if your mother says she doesn't mind, will you?"

Joy put her fists on her hips. "I know my mother. She's a good Amish woman. She is *not* going to let me be an actress."

"But if she said yes, then would you? Promise me that you would."

Joy jutted out her chin. "Yes, if my mother said so, then I suppose I would."

"Good. Just make sure you wear that coral dress. I want to keep the next scene consistent."

"But you haven't even asked her."

"I already did."

"What are you talking about?"

"When she brought food earlier. I mentioned I needed someone for a new character spot. I asked if I could cast you. It's just a very small part, Joy. There are only a few more scenes."

Joy's mouth dropped open. She looked to the new actress and the actor who played the bachelor. "So you were all in on this?" She looked to the cameraman. "You set me up?"

Alicia strode out and slid her arm through the crook of Joy's arm. "You're a visiting cousin — my visiting cousin. It'll be fun."

"I . . . I don't know what to say."

"Say you'll let us shoot two more scenes. Then we'll be done."

"Yes, fine. Let's get it over with." She picked up a copy of the script and scanned it. "But if the bishop says anything negative, he's going to have to talk to my mother about this."

If Joy's nerves weren't already shot over the idea of having to act in more scenes, sitting down with the small group of cast and crew for their first Bible study did the trick.

As soon as lunch was over and all the Amish women had gone, the group sat around a long plastic table someone had set up just outside the dressing room. Alicia, Georgia, and Kristen were there, in addition to some of the crew. Kristen sat down next to Alicia and then turned to her. "Oh, I hope this chair was open. You're not saving it for Rowan, are you?"

"No, Rowan's not coming. He's sitting outside today eating his lunch. I invited him, but he said he wasn't interested."

"Wasn't interested?" The cameraman, Steve, shook his head. "Rowan told me he became a Christian. I've even seen him reading his Bible a few times when I get here before everyone else."

"He's changed," one of the grips commented. "I've worked with him on other jobs, and he's a lot different."

"I think it's me," Alicia stated bluntly. "If I wasn't here, he would be."

Joy ran her finger over the cover of her Bible. "I don't know if that's true. Maybe he just . . ." She tried to think of an excuse, but there wasn't one.

"He's been colder to me lately. Ever since I mentioned the idea of a Bible study." Alicia opened the Bible in front of her — the one she'd taken from the nightstand in her hotel — and thumbed through it. "I'm sure he thinks this isn't for real. That I'm just trying to get his attention."

"It's his loss then." Kristen patted Alicia's hand. "We know you're not doing this just to impress him."

The others around the table nodded, but Joy didn't quite understand. What she did understand was that the others were waiting for her to start the Bible study. Without hesitating, she opened her Bible to Psalms.

"One psalm has meant a lot to me. Psalm 86. The psalms are actually songs, most of them written about twenty-five hundred years ago. Many were written by a man named David, and others were written by men whose names have been lost in time."

"Well, that sucks. Writing a great song that stands the test of time and no one remembers your name," Steven said.

"You shouldn't use the word *sucks* at a Bible study," Kristen chided as she fiddled with one of the bobby pins keeping her bun in place.

"This is a Bible study?" asked another of the grips. "I just thought we were getting more pie." He took a piece from the pie on the table in front of Joy.

"You get both." Joy met his eyes with a pleased smile. "Pie . . . and we're going to talk about God and the Bible. I don't think we need to use the term *study*."

"Yeah, it sounds like something old church ladies do, and Alicia is as far as you can get from an old church lady." Steven chuckled.

Surprisingly, Alicia ignored the comment and instead handed her Bible to Joy. "Can you find it for me? I'm not sure where to look."

"Sure. The Bible has sixty-six books — sort of like chapters — and Psalms is in the first part, which is called the Old Testament." Joy glanced around, and saw that she was losing her audience. "But the easiest way to find Psalms without looking at the table of contents is with this trick." She placed the Bible on the table in front of her. She stood it on its spine and placed her finger in the middle. And then she let the Bible fall open, half on either side. "This is Psalm 35. If we just flip a few more chapters later, we'll get to Psalm 86. Here, let me read the first verse: 'Bow down thine ear, O LORD, hear me: for I am poor and needy.' What do you think that means?"

"Bow down your ear?" one man asked. "Sounds like this David dude was asking God to lean down to listen to him."

Joy couldn't help but smile. She tried to imagine one of their ministers saying *dude,* but she couldn't. "Yes, that's wonderful. What else?"

Alicia leaned over her Bible, studying the words. "It says he was poor and needy, so he must be an ordinary person — not rich or anything."

"Maybe he's even homeless," Georgia commented.

"Do you think so?" Kristen scowled. "How would we still have his words? Homeless people didn't read and write back then. Maybe he just thought he was poor."

The way they were listening and interacting brought a surge of happiness to Joy. "Actually, David was a king. He had a palace made of gold, silver, and expensive wood. It just goes to show that it doesn't really matter what you have. You have nothing if you don't have God."

The conversation continued. Many commented about some of the richest people they knew who were miserable.

"A couple of the best actors I've worked with have committed suicide," Alicia said softly. Then she looked away.

An uneasy feeling settled in Joy's gut, and she dared to speak what everyone was thinking. "I imagine someone around this table has considered suicide, but I hope all of us know that is never the answer. The true answer is doing what David did. He turned to God. Finding hope is understanding our own need, understanding that even if we have everything, without God we have nothing. It's asking God to bow down and listen to us. And it's feeling free to say what we need to say to Him without being afraid."

No one around the table spoke, but she could tell they were considering her words.

They read the rest of the psalm, and when they were finished Alicia rose and left the table without a comment.

"What's got into her?" Kristen asked, watching her go.

Steven scratched his head. "Maybe she's still upset about Rowan."

"Or maybe she's thinking about a friend who committed suicide."

Joy nodded. "Reading God's Word has a way of digging up stuff. God's Word is often called a light, and sometimes when light shines into places that have been dark awhile, it's hard to face what's hidden there."

Kristen leaned forward and shut her Bible. "That's easy for you to talk about. You haven't lived the way many of us have, Joy." Her voice was curt, and Joy tried to ignore the sting it caused inside.

"I have junk hidden inside too," Joy managed to say. "Pride is a big one. Thinking that being good is good enough — that I

295

really don't need God. That's probably the biggest sin of all."

A few of the others nodded, but she could tell they didn't believe her. Yet the more time she spent at the set, the more she knew it to be true. She had a relationship with God, and knew better, and still tried to do things her own way. Wasn't that a greater sin?

Joy closed her own Bible and rose. "If any of you would like to meet again tomorrow, we can —"

"Wait! We're not done yet." Steven pulled off his baseball cap and pressed it to his chest. "It doesn't seem right ending without praying. Can I say something, Joy?"

"Of course you can." She sat back down, folded her hands, and lowered her head.

"Dear God, thank You for bringing Joy here to remind us what really matters in this life. Thank You for bending down Your ear to us. Uh, amen."

A chorus of amens echoed around the table, and they all went separate ways. Joy sat in her chair for a moment, content. She'd forgotten about her own upcoming scene until Georgia spoke.

"The next scene is a close-up, and Rowan wants to make sure we have some powder on your face. Follow me."

Joy followed, and with each step her nerves shimmied up her arms and down into her fingers, causing them to tremble. What had she gotten herself into this time? She wasn't looking forward to finding out.

It had been too easy to memorize lines. Too easy to play a part. Too easy to forget the bishop was against the television show. Too easy to accept the praise and accolades of a job well done, and that's what bothered her most. So when the rest of the cast and crew stayed at the set for dinner, Joy excused herself and hurried to the quilt shop. She knew it would be empty, and that's just what she needed — space to think, time to pray.

Fading sunlight filtered through the windows, yet the burden Joy carried seemed to darken the room with each breath. Was it just a month ago when she'd chatted with Elizabeth about how she appreciated being Amish? She'd always liked knowing exactly what was expected of her, but during the last few weeks those lines blurred. She'd dared to step out, and she knew one thing for certain — the line between black and white wasn't as clearly drawn as she'd expected.

Instead of unlocking the door and turning

over the sign in the window to Open, as she usually did when she entered these doors, Joy moved to the small room Elizabeth had once used as an office. These days Elizabeth had a bookkeeper take care of all the books off-site, but the older woman occasionally slipped in the back "to catch her breath," as she liked to say. Joy wasn't surprised to find a notebook and Bible on the desk. She sat down and looked at the book.

"What do You require of me?" she whispered, knowing God heard and trusting He would answer.

In her mind's eye, she saw a row of people — her parents, those in her community, the local ministers, and even the bishop. Her whole life she'd watched and listened to them all. Like Matthew, she'd been quick to learn the rules and consistently stick to them. Yet not once had she questioned whose rules they were. Were they really from God, for God?

Tears filled Joy's eyes, and she rested her elbows on the desk, leaning over it. "I wish the answers were more plain," she mumbled. "Why can't You just send me a letter and tell me what to do? Elizabeth says to listen to Your still, small voice, but how can I be sure? What if I make a mistake? What if I lose them . . . him . . . ?"

Emotion caught in her throat, and a tear tumbled down her cheek. The teardrop fell onto Elizabeth's open notebook and the words the older woman had written there, and Joy quickly brushed it off with her thumb. Her tear smeared a word that caught her eye. *Grace.* It was underlined three times. Joy couldn't help herself. She had to know what that word meant to Elizabeth. She leaned forward to read her friend's words.

Grace is knowing I can't do anything to make God love me more. Grace is knowing nothing I do will make God love me less.

Joy read the sentences again, realizing she didn't believe what they said. Not really deep down, where it counted. Yes, she'd always known God loved her, but did she honestly believe it was unconditional love? Did God love her if she worked on a television show? Did God love her if everyone in Pinecraft disapproved of her — especially Matthew?

Did He love her if she failed to share His love?

She leaned back in the chair and let those questions play through her mind. If her role in life was to show love, then was she making the right choice . . . choosing to love many? Choosing to hurt one?

Twenty-Six

True compassion brings action.

AMISH PROVERB

The next day's shooting wasn't as bad as she expected. Joy shot one scene with Alicia and another with her pretend father as they packed up their things and headed back to Ohio. They just needed her there long enough to introduce Alicia's new love interest in the show. Jonathan was the tall blond man who interacted with Joy in her first scene. Jonathan was both his real name and the name they used for the show.

"I grew up in Indiana. I was around Amish people all the time," Jonathan confessed as the whole cast and crew ate dinner together that evening.

"Oh, really? My aunt lives in Shipshewana," Joy commented. "She's my favorite aunt, and I gave her the first quilt I ever made." Joy chuckled. "I wonder if she kept

300

it. I'm sure she has it tucked away some-where around there. I must have been nine years old at the time. It was a good try even if it wasn't pretty."

Kristen eyed her curiously. "You made a quilt when you were nine years old? I feel like a slacker. I was excited when I sewed a button back on my shirt last month!"

Joy laughed and then turned to Jonathan. "My Aunt Martha is a wonderful person, and I love to visit her house. Her scrap closet especially."

"Her scrap closet?" he asked.

"Yes, when it comes to fabric she doesn't throw anything away. She collects all the scraps from the items she sews. She gathers scraps up from every sewing frolic she at-tends." In her mind's eye Joy remembered her aunt's sewing room, the numerous bins of fabrics separated by color and size of scraps. "She even uses tiny scraps to make fabric beads for the small girls in their fam-ily to string together."

Alicia seemed to be listening to the conver-sation but didn't comment. She pushed her food around on her plate, and Joy wondered what she was thinking about. Maybe the next scene? Was she just trying to be polite by sitting quietly as she listened?

"I have one of Aunt Martha's quilts on

my bed," Joy added. "I don't need it for warmth, but it's beautiful, and it reminds me that with God, nothing goes to waste. Every experience — good or bad — contributes to our lives. Sometimes we don't understand why things happen the way they do, but when all the scraps are stitched together they become a beautiful mosaic."

"I've always wanted to learn to do that." Alicia sighed. "It's so amazing that someone can take all these random pieces and put them together to create something beautiful."

Joy turned to her friend. "Quilting isn't hard. I can show you."

Alicia sat up straighter and pushed her paper plate to the side. "Show me?"

"Sure. I have one I'm piecing together out of scraps of fabric. It's supposed to be my sister's wedding quilt, but it will be for her first anniversary at the rate I'm going. If you'd like to come by sometime we can finish piecing it together."

Alicia's face was pink with excitement. "I would love that." She opened a hand and placed it over her heart. They sat there talking longer about the types of quilts and patterns until one by one the rest of those who'd been sitting near them got up and left.

"I never thought I'd be doing this — learning to cook, to quilt. It's almost as if I'm a whole new person."

"Don't be so dramatic." A voice carried from down the hall. Footsteps sounded, and Rowan rounded the corner and entered the kitchen area. He locked eyes with Alicia.

Alicia's brow furrowed. "And what is that supposed to mean — don't be so dramatic?"

Rowan looked tired. It had been a long day — a long few weeks — and it was starting to show. "You know what it means, Alicia. You're good at playing parts, stepping into roles. That's what makes you a good actress."

"You're saying that I'm doing all of this because of my role? Spending time with Joy, cooking, quilting?"

He closed his eyes and rubbed his temples with his fingertips, as if her question gave him a headache. "Of course. You don't really think you're going to return to LA and host a sewing frolic, do you? It's fun seeing you like this though. It's a softer side of Ali I haven't seen." He opened his eyes and focused on her again.

Ali?

Alicia's eyebrows folded at this nickname, and Joy could almost see the resolve slip from her face. Anger stirred within Joy.

303

Didn't Rowan see what he was doing to her — trying to shove her into a box? Trying to trample all the ways she was attempting to change? Trying to discourage all the ways she was trying to grow?

"Do you know what I love about quilt making?" Joy interrupted. "Taking old scraps, piecing them together. Making something new, something useful, something beautiful. I like to think that's what God does with all our lives, don't you? He sees the beauty in things we thought were just scraps, and He pieces them together in ways we can't imagine."

Rowan eyed Joy, overtly agitated. "You aren't buying into this are you, Joy? I've known Alicia a long time. We were married, together for five years."

Married? Joy gasped. Now it all made sense. How they seemed to know each other so well yet also tended to keep each other at arm's length.

"So basically what I'm saying, Joy, is that you can teach Alicia how to quilt, but don't think she's really changing into Betty Crocker. And you can teach her how to pray and read the Bible, but she'll never be a Mother Teresa. I'm tired of working with pretenders." His face contorted with anger, and then his eyes widened in surprise at his own words. Without another word he turned and stalked toward the door.

"That's not cool, Rowan!" Alicia's voice rose, calling after him. "Maybe I deserve to be treated like that, but Joy doesn't. Some Christian you are!" She pointed at him, but with his back turned he couldn't see her. "Sure, go ahead and walk away. You're good at that."

Joy reached over and touched Alicia's arm. "Don't let him get to you."

"That's easy for you to say. You don't know him — the power he has in this industry." Her face fell as if her briefest hopes had been extinguished. "You also don't know what I was like in LA — what I'm really like. I think you'd be shocked."

Joy nodded, and her mind thought about some of the tabloid headlines she'd read before. "Believe it or not, I have a good imagination. And I've been schooled at the checkout line." She reached over and took Alicia's hand. "But I also know who I see — who you really are. Rowan is right. You're a good actress, but I honestly feel your life in LA is where you've been playing a part." Joy released a long breath. "Don't let him do this to you. Don't let him — them — put you in a box anymore. God has so much planned for you. Great things you can't even imagine."

How many times had Elizabeth said that to her? More than she could count, and while she somehow believed it for Alicia, Joy couldn't picture that for herself. Not anymore.

Tears filled Alicia's eyes, but she quickly wiped them away. She jutted out her chin and focused on the door Rowan had just walked through. "I want to trust God. I want to change, and I'm trying. But I honestly would like to learn to quilt, no matter what my estranged husband says."

"Well then, I'd like to teach you. Would you like to come to my house tonight?"

"What about you coming to my place?"

"Your place?"

"I'm staying at a hotel overlooking the ocean. It's only a fifteen-minute drive. I have a rental car now. I'll drive you over and then take you home later. You can bring all your things."

"Are you sure?"

"*Ja.*" Alicia chuckled. "I mean, yes, I'm sure. I don't mind at all. It'll be fun. It's something to look forward to."

Joy's mind was filled with thoughts about quilting and about going to Alicia's hotel, so she didn't notice Matthew standing on her porch until she'd already walked through her front gate. He was wearing his work clothes, and he looked disheveled, as if he'd just run across town to make it before she got there. Matthew's lips were chapped, and his face was flushed. There was a weariness about him that Joy hadn't seen before. She thought about the time she'd spent with him in his shop. The joy she'd seen on his face then was gone.

His eyes widened when he saw her. One eyebrow cocked up saucily, along with the corners of his mouth. "Joy, it's so *gut* to see you." He took two steps to her and then paused. "You look wonderful. I . . . I've missed seeing you."

She nodded and bit her lower lip, not knowing what to say. "I've missed seeing you too, and I've missed our talks. How's work, and . . . Have you had time to work on those recipe boxes?" It felt silly to offer up small talk when she had so much she wanted to say, wanted to know. But that's all she could offer. The pain of his silence still pricked her heart.

"Ne." He lowered his head. "I've just been busy on my construction job. And even though I've tried not to think of you, it's been very hard not to. I've been so angry with you — angry about the choices you've made." He pulled off his straw hat and ran

his fingers through his hair. "And it was only last night that *Mem* told me what was happening, why you chose what you did. She explained about the treatments your *dat* needs — about his failing health. And as soon as she told me I realized you had tried to tell me those things."

His voice lowered. His face softened. "The day I went to the fabric shop, you wanted to go to Big Olaf's to talk. I thought talking would make things worse — that you'd just try to justify your actions. I thought I was doing the right thing. I believed by staying away from you, you'd realize you were wrong. That you'd quit."

"And now?" she asked.

"Now I know I've made a horrible mistake. I'm so —"

"Shh." She covered his lips with her fingertips. Touching him caused a warm sensation to run down the length of her arm. "You don't have to explain. I grew up this way. I know how things work. I understand what it means to shun someone — if not technically, at least make them feel like an outcast."

Emotion filled his eyes. "It's not what I wanted. I never wanted it to be like this."

"*Ne.* Of course you didn't."

"Joy, it hurts me to know I'm bringing you

pain," he said in a gruff voice. He swallowed hard.

Before she could stop herself, Joy stepped forward and offered him a hug. As she wrapped her arms around his neck, she could feel the thrum of his heartbeat for only a second. Was it breaking like hers?

"I'm thankful for this job — for the money my *dat* . . ." She couldn't say more. She couldn't pretend that was the only reason she was still on the set, but how could she explain?

Joy released her grasp. Matthew held on to her for a few seconds more before he let her step back.

"But things are different now." Matthew's face brightened. He stepped back too, to get a better view of her face. "*Mem* told me the church will be helping with your *dat*'s expenses now. I'm just so sorry you felt you had to carry that burden alone. Everything will be better, you'll see."

"Better?" Joy jerked her head back, suddenly knowing where this was going, knowing why Matthew was here.

Her eyes skittered down to his nervous fingers as he fiddled with the hat in his hand.

Joy released a sigh. "I never expected it to end like this."

"Who said it's ended? We have a second chance."

Her eyes met his, and although he said the words, she saw worry in his gaze. *Does he expect me to just walk away from my job so we can pick up where we left off?*

Matthew pulled back slightly, putting more room between them. His face was in the shadows, but she didn't need to see it to know he wasn't going to like hearing her say she wasn't leaving the set — not yet.

Joy took a deep breath and spoke the last words she wanted to say. "I think we should take a break for a while."

Matthew's eyes widened and he smirked. "Take a break? Did I hear you just say that? You sound like one of those *Englisch* couples. You're becoming just like them, aren't you? That's just what my father was afraid of."

"I'm learning a lot — about them, about myself, about God."

He turned away and shook his head, not believing her. "So you're not leaving, are you?"

Joy didn't need to answer. He already knew.

Footsteps sounded from the roadway behind them, and boys' voices carried. A small group of Amish teens walked from the river, carrying fishing poles. They walked by the front of the house, looking first to Matthew and then to her. One of the teens gave his friend a nudge. Then he stumbled on a rock in the road, righted himself, and quickly moved on down the street. The other teens followed, each glancing over their shoulders at her. Even in the murky light she spotted accusations in their gaze.

"So everyone really is talking about me, aren't they?"

One of the teens paused and looked back. He met her gaze and his brow furrowed, almost as if he wanted to ask her something. Joy tilted up her chin and waited.

"Hurry, Saul, or we're gonna miss dinner."

"*Ja,* everyone's talking, Joy. About you and about me. I can see in their faces that they all believe I'm a fool for still holding on to hope."

"I'm so sorry. I never meant —"

The sound of a car pulling up in front of the house interrupted her words. Joy turned and saw Alicia climb out of the driver's seat. Only then did she remember their plans for tonight.

Alicia was wearing a summer dress with thin straps, and her hair was braided and cascaded over one shoulder.

"Hi, Joy. Are you almost ready?" She strode up the sidewalk, and even though she was talking to Joy, Alicia eyed Matthew with curiosity.

Next to her, Matthew's breathing grew heavy. His chest rose and fell, and Joy knew he was working to maintain control. Did he assume it was Alicia's influence that was drawing her away? Joy placed a hand on his arm as if trying to calm him, but Matthew pulled away.

"Actually, do you mind if we put off quilting until another day, Alicia? Something's come up tonight."

"*Ja,* I mean yes." Alicia chuckled. "Oh my goodness, I can't keep those *ja*'s out of my vocabulary. I'm turning a little too Amish." Then Alicia turned back toward her car.

Joy smiled, unsure of how to respond.

"Oh." Alicia paused, turning back around. "Rowan sent a text message out to everyone, telling them not to come in until noon tomorrow. Can you tell your *mem* we won't be needing breakfast? And you don't need to be there either. Rowan has some type of Skype meeting with the network."

Joy nodded, even though she had no idea what Alicia was talking about. Skype? It made no sense.

"Thanks for letting me know. It'll give me

a chance to stop by the fabric store. I've been missing my friend Elizabeth."

Alicia gave a final wave and then drove off. It wasn't until the car was completely out of sight that Joy turned back to Matthew.

"I suppose I'll be leaving." His voice was sharp. "I don't think there is anything else for me to say here." He focused his gaze on her. "Unless you can think of anything."

She read the ache in his eyes and knew it mirrored her own.

Say you love me. Say you're not going to give up on me. All those words and more filled her mind, but she simply shook her head. "*Ne,* I suppose there isn't anything more. I'm sorry, Matthew. So sorry things turned out this way."

"Listen." Matthew held up his hands, a look of desperation replaced his anger. "We don't need to make things final today. Why don't we take a few days to think about things? When you're ready, why don't you come over, and we can talk again."

He leaned down, kissed her temple, and then strode away. He was so strong, so handsome. And so hurt. And she was the reason.

Joy rushed inside, ignoring her *mem,* Grace, and Faith, who were all in the kitchen. She couldn't look at them, couldn't talk to them. She hurried to her room instead and flung herself onto her bed. Then, as if a movie were playing through her mind at double speed, Joy thought about where she'd end up if she continued down this path. The television show would be filmed, and her *Englisch* friends would move back to their own lives. Matthew would move on too, finding the perfect Amish bride who would always listen to the bishop and never disagree. Who wouldn't shame him. And Joy would be alone.

Lord, what am I doing? Why am I doing this?

From the kitchen, Grace called her to come have dessert, but Joy didn't respond. The last thing she wanted was to look them in the face. They no doubt had all overheard what was happening on the front porch. There was no way she could pick up her fork and try to put any food in her mouth. It was hard to breathe. Her lungs felt as if they had been trampled by horses and then put back inside her to die a slow death. Her chest ached, and her mind felt as fuzzy as if she'd fallen asleep and was startled awake. She wanted this to be a bad dream, but it wasn't.

She'd hurt Matthew. She'd hurt his heart. She'd hurt his reputation, and he hadn't done anything to deserve that. Nothing at all.

Tears came next, heavy and hard, and suddenly Joy realized she had a choice. She didn't have to continue working with the show. They could go on without her.

God, can You bring in someone else to help Alicia? It doesn't have to be me.

Releasing a heavy breath, Joy sat up, knowing what she had to do. Knowing this was her story and that she had one more chance to turn it around. Knowing she didn't have to let true love walk away while she simply stood back and cried.

Alicia pushed up her sleeves and then moved to the bathroom sink in her hotel room. *Stitched together. Stitched together.* The words replayed in her mind.

She turned on the water, letting it run until it turned warm. Then, with a few pumps from the hand soap, she began washing her hands, moving up to her wrists. The water turned beige as it pooled in the sink. The stage makeup stripped away layer by layer until the red, angry scars appeared at her wrists. She'd hidden them from everyone. Only her manager and her makeup artist knew. The makeup artist had shown her how to apply the makeup herself. Even

Rowan didn't know how far she'd fallen six months ago.

Her manager, Reagan, knew because he'd been at her side as she'd woken up in the psych ward. Shame and pain flooded her, remembering the look of fear on his face. Not fear over losing her, but fear of her deeds being found out. Fear of the media picking up on the story. Fear that she wouldn't be able to come out ahead in America's eyes this time.

"Don't worry, sweetie. No one has to know about this," Reagan had said. Not "Are you okay?" Not "I'm so glad you made it." His words reflected the truth of their relationship. He was there to protect her image, to gloss over the pain that plagued her.

She lied to her psychiatrist after the attempt. She said it was her split from Rowan, the tabloids, and the pressure from Hollywood that had led to her attempt. She didn't mention the abortion. And when the psychiatrist had mentioned it after looking at her medical files, she claimed that the decision hadn't bothered her. That's what she was supposed to say, wasn't it?

What she hadn't told Joy was that there was a reason she didn't like the idea of God gazing down at her. Because He, too, knew what she'd done.

But since arriving back to her hotel room, she'd read about David — the guy who wrote those psalms — and Alicia realized he had messed up big-time too. He'd committed adultery. He'd committed murder, and yet he still turned to God.

Alicia dried her hands and arms with a fluffy, white cotton towel and then moved to the bed. The bedding was white, clean, perfect — a contrast to her ugly scars.

She adjusted the pillows against the headboard and then sat, leaning against them. Alicia thought about Joy's words during their Bible study. *David had a palace made of gold, silver, and expensive wood. It just goes to show that it doesn't really matter what you have. You have nothing if you don't have God.*

Alicia had discovered what it was like to have everything and feel like it was nothing. She also knew it wasn't just the alcohol that had caused her to sabotage her relationship with Rowan. During the weeks before her trip to Prague, he'd started talking about children and his desire for a family. The conversation had scared her.

After her abortion, she'd convinced herself that she wouldn't be a good mom and that she'd never have kids. To choose to have a child with Rowan would prove how wrong she'd been. A life growing inside her would remind her of the one she'd taken away. And so she'd done the only thing she knew to do — she committed the horrible sin that would push Rowan away from her. And it wasn't until he was gone that she realized how much she wanted him close. How much she loved him and needed him.

The room was still, quiet. Alicia focused on her own breathing. She looked at her scars again and thought of Jesus's scars, and for the first time in her life she believed. She believed He saw her and listened to her. She believed He loved her and wanted her to come near. She knew this because God had brought Joy into her life. God had brought a woman who modeled what is right and pure. A woman who talked about a God who liked to stitch together the torn and ragged scraps of each person's life.

And so for the first time in her life, she closed her eyes and prayed a simple, honest prayer. "Yes, Lord, I believe."

Stitched Together

The stitch is worked from right to left on double material. First baste carefully together the two materials; the basting may serve as a guide to the worker, and also keep the materials from slipping apart. A seam should be made far enough from the edge of the cloth to avoid the danger of raveling.*

* Mary Schenck Woolman, *A Sewing Course for Teachers* (Washington, DC: Frederik A. Fernald, 1915), 47.

TWENTY-SEVEN

How we sit with the broken speaks louder
than how we sit with the great.

AMISH PROVERB

"I'm sorry you're having a hard time, Joy,
but I've been praying for this." Elizabeth sat
at the sewing machine in Pinecraft Fabric
and Quilts. Her hands still held the strips of
fabric she'd been sewing. Joy imagined Elizabeth would be tired and overwhelmed
since Joy had spent so much time on the set
and not in the shop. But the older woman
had been sewing pot holders with a smile as
if nothing was wrong in the world.

Elizabeth's smile even grew when Joy
rushed in and shared what had been going
on — especially how she was now second-
guessing her decision to stay with the show.

"What have you been praying for, Elizabeth? That Matthew and I would decide not
to court? That I would find myself at odds

320

with the community? That I ruin my life?"

"*Ne,* sweet girl. I would never pray for those things. I've been praying that God would do whatever it takes to draw you closer to Him."

"But if you prayed that, surely you knew what would happen . . ." Joy bit her lower lip. "I mean, you can't just pray that and leave it up to God. After all, everyone knows not to pray for patience, or God will give us lots of opportunities to practice it. So if you pray that I'll need to depend on God, then . . . well, I'm not quite sure what I'm saying."

Elizabeth pushed back from the sewing machine. She patted the wooden chair next to her, motioning for Joy to sit down. "Are you asking if I knew difficulties would come to you because of my prayer?"

Joy shrugged. "*Ja,* I suppose I am."

"Joy, I wasn't praying for difficulties in your life, but sometimes that's what it takes for us to get to the end of ourselves and to the end of our strength. It's often how we learn to depend on Him." Elizabeth offered a soft smile. "I think every opportunity is both a gift and a challenge. The challenge is that you are stepping out into uncomfortable places, and you're discovering who opposes you as well as who believes in you.

But the gift is that you're discovering new parts of yourself and new parts of God."

Joy shifted her weight from side to side. "I suppose that's true, but I wish more people understood. I don't think it's fair that people say I'm just trying to be rebellious and go against the bishop. I didn't set out to make him or Matthew look bad. People have ne idea that my motivation was to help pay for my father's therapy." Joy pressed her lips together. She hadn't meant to share that much. She didn't need praise for what she was doing, but it hurt her that so many people seemed to be judging her.

"I've heard about what you're doing for your father. Jeanette came in and told me. She sounded proud of you even though she wished you didn't have to work." Elizabeth reached over and patted Joy's hand. "I don't think everyone is as upset as you think they are."

"Matthew is. We are no longer courting. Well, he told me to think about it, but we both know how it's going to end."

"*Ja,* I know." Elizabeth sighed. "And you know what else I know?"

"What's that?"

"Even more snowbirds are returning. The Grabers, over at the trailer park, have been busy getting everything ready."

Joy's mouth dropped open. "*Ja,* okay, and what does that have to do with this conversation?"

Elizabeth's light blue eyes sparkled with humor. "What I'm trying to say is that seasons come and seasons go. Circumstances change, people change. Just because things are this way for you and Matthew now doesn't mean they'll be this way forever. Who knows what the months ahead will bring?"

Joy nodded, offering a reserved smile. It made sense, but it was hard to believe when she had so much ache stacking up inside her chest.

"You know, Elizabeth, we've been friends for a while, and I wish I could be more like you. That I had more faith. That I trusted God more. I'm trying to do my best, but I feel as if I'm failing everyone."

"Oh, Joy, don't you understand? You get to know God better only when you cling to Him. And you cling to Him only when there is nowhere else to turn. We are all frail humans, but we act as if we can take on this world with our own wit and our own strength. We try for a while. Sometimes we do all right, but most of the time we make a big mess of things. And then, when we come to our senses, we realize we need God. It's then when we turn to Him — when we get to the end of ourselves. My dear girl, I've made many mistakes. The faith and trust I have now has come from times when I've made those mistakes and clung to God."

"So do you think I've made a mistake, Elizabeth? Was I wrong to take this job?"

"*Ne,* I don't. I think the mistake you made was thinking that everyone would understand. Sometimes when we feel as if we're following God, we get a lot of protests — especially from those closest to us."

Joy nodded. "*Ja,* Elizabeth. I understand." She sighed. "But I really have to run. I need to get to the set. They, uh, need me today. And then tomorrow . . ." Joy didn't say it, but she was seriously considering telling Rowan at the end of the day that she wouldn't be coming back. Both the love and the pain in Matthew's gaze wouldn't leave her.

"Are you busy tonight?" Elizabeth asked.

"Yesterday they said we'll be wrapping up early today. I'm hoping that's still the case."

"Would you like to come by my place for dinner? I'm having a dinner party. I'd like you to be my guest."

"A dinner party?" Joy couldn't help but chuckle. "That sounds like a fancy *Englisch* thing. When we invite people over we simply

324

call it supper."

"*Ja,* well it is what it is." There was an intense gaze in Elizabeth's eyes. One Joy didn't expect. "But you'll be there, won't you?"

Joy leaned forward and placed her hand on Elizabeth's. "*Ja,* I will." She squeezed and then released her hand. *What is really going on?* Elizabeth wouldn't invite Matthew without telling her, would she? She wouldn't try to fix things between them, right? As far as Joy could see, there was no fixing this. Maybe things would never be the way they used to be, even if she quit her job with the show now. With sunken shoulders, Joy turned toward the door.

"And one more thing." Elizabeth's voice called out, stopping her in her tracks.

Joy glanced over her shoulder. "*Ja,* what is it?"

"I don't want you to quit. Not today."

Joy touched her hand to her neck and turned slowly, surprised. "What do you mean?"

"I mean you're tired, you're uncertain, and you have a broken heart. It may seem like the logical choice to quit this job. After all, that will solve all your problems, or at least it will seem to. But wait until after tonight. Tonight is important, Joy. There is something I want you to see."

"I can do that."

"Promise me." Emotion filled Elizabeth's voice.

"*Ja,* I promise."

Joy walked out with a strange sensation tingling up and down her arms. How did Elizabeth know what she'd been thinking? How did the older woman know she'd decided to quit? It didn't make sense.

Then again it didn't make sense that Elizabeth had started praying for that warehouse even before it came up for sale and even before Lovina decided to open a pie shop. And she'd been praying for a community garden even before Hope embraced the idea of starting a garden behind the pie shop. It was strange that Elizabeth would be aware of such things unless . . . unless Joy took her words to heart.

"I've learned to cling to God," Elizabeth had said.

Joy walked with a quickened pace down to Gardenia Street, yet her mind was on another image. It was of her in their home up in Walnut Creek when she was just a young girl. She was always the first to rise. *Mem* never had to rouse her for chores. Instead, it was the gentle click from the front door latch that woke her — *Dat* going out to the barn to care for the animals.

She'd rise, tuck her blanket around her, and on cold days, sit by the fireplace and wait for *Dat* to return. He would, sometimes with ice crystals on his beard, and then after warming up by the fire, he'd sit in his favorite chair and pat his lap, inviting her into his arms.

With her body snuggled to his side, *Dat* would open his Bible and begin to read out loud. She guessed he did it more for her benefit than his, and he'd read in English. He'd often read the Lord's Prayer or one of the psalms. Sometimes he read stories of Jesus. She loved listening to those best.

And that's what she thought of when Elizabeth talked about clinging to God. It seemed the same to her as clinging to her father's lap. Because she was close to *Dat,* she heard him read, heard him talk to her *mem,* and heard his whispers when he spoke to her. Because she was close to *Dat* those mornings, she heard things her sisters didn't. They were still his little girls, of course, and they still had special relationships, but she got to know him more and hear him better because she was on his lap.

Something inside Joy made her want that with God too, but something else was fearful of it. What if she grew closer to God and then discovered He was different from what she thought? What if she found out things she didn't want to know? What if she grew close only to be disappointed? After all, she had a hard time picturing Him as she did her father. God seemed more stern than that — more focused on the rules. But maybe there was more to Him than she knew.

What would it take to find out?

Twenty-Eight

To grow old gracefully, you must start
when you are young.

AMISH PROVERB

Joy walked up to the small house. It was
gray with white trim, and it had a fancy
door, as if someone had salvaged the door
from a much nicer, bigger home and
brought it here. The lawn was mowed, but
the closer Joy got the more she noticed more
weeds. She didn't know why she expected
anything different though, since Elizabeth
was having a harder time getting around of
late. Joy made a mental note to talk to her
dat about that. Hope and Jonas would be in
town soon, and she knew her sister and
future brother-in-law would love to tackle
the yard. And Jonas's daughter, Emma,
would be right there to help.

Joy knocked once, her knuckles rapping
softly on the wood. Then she heard Eliza-

329

beth's soft voice calling to her, telling her to enter.

Joy had been to Elizabeth's house numerous times to talk with her boss, to drop off deposit slips, and to bring her fabric, but today the place looked different than she'd ever seen it.

A long table had been set up in the middle of the living room. A pressed white tablecloth hung nearly to the floor. Various chairs were positioned around the table — dining room chairs, lawn chairs, and an office chair. But the simplicity of the chairs was made up for by the grandness of the table. Joy's mouth circled into an O as she neared.

"Elizabeth, it's beautiful."

The older woman walked from the kitchen, wiping her hands on a dish towel. "My mother loved china, and she used to pick up pieces at yard sales. Nothing matches, but I think that's what makes it so special — mismatched items coming together on display."

Joy reached her hand forward and ran her finger along the rim of a white china dish with a pattern of pink roses around the rim. Eleven other place settings were on display, each unique yet beautiful. "This must be a special dinner party."

"Oh, it will be." Elizabeth pointed to the

kitchen. "Can you help me carry in the food?"

"Now? Don't you want to wait?" When they walked into the kitchen, Joy looked to the wall clock, noticing it was five minutes to six. "I'm sure the others will be here in the next few minutes."

"Oh, I'm not so sure about that." Elizabeth motioned to a small pan with sliced roast beef inside. "There are potatoes and corn in the oven too. Pot holders are in the drawer."

Joy placed the meat on the table, returned to the kitchen, and opened the oven door. There was a small bowl of mashed potatoes and two ears of corn already smothered in butter. Tension tightened Joy's gut. This wasn't nearly enough food. Had Elizabeth asked her to bring something and she'd forgotten? Or maybe Elizabeth had expected her to bring a dish without being asked. Joy used the pot holder and pulled out the potatoes.

"If you need me to, I'll run to Yoder's," she called to Elizabeth, who'd already taken a seat at the table. "I'll be happy to go pick up a few more sides."

"Nonsense. There's plenty. And I'm glad you're a few minutes early because my stomach has been rumbling for the last half hour."

Joy placed the potatoes and corn on the table, puzzled by the contented look on her older friend's face.

Joy looked toward the front window. "Shouldn't we wait for the others?"

"Sit down, Joy," Elizabeth stated plainly. "I'll explain after we pray."

Joy did as she was told. She sat down, scooted in, and folded her hands on her lap. Then in unison the two women bowed their heads in silent prayer.

Joy prayed for her friend, prayed that her mind wasn't slipping as their grandmother's had done five years ago. She also prayed that Elizabeth could stay steady on her feet. And finally, she prayed she'd be better at anticipating her friend's needs.

Elizabeth served Joy and then herself. "Eat up . . . and there is plenty for seconds."

"But what about the others?"

"Oh, they'll be coming, but not today."

Joy tilted her head and slowly cut her roast. She took a bite and chewed with intention, wondering what else to ask, what to say.

Elizabeth chuckled. "I can see you are troubled, but I've done this as an illustration."

"An illustration?"

"*Ja.* You see, when I was your age, I had a dream about a long table just like this. It was fancy, and I didn't understand it." Elizabeth took a bite of her potatoes and closed her eyes as she chewed. She smiled out of pure enjoyment. "When I was growing up Amish, one would never think of having dishes like these. It would be far too fancy. The only reason my *mem* started collecting them was because they were used and not in a set. Buying a piece for a few coins was practical, but I always guessed she enjoyed their beauty too."

"And the table in your dream. Was it filled with guests?"

"*Ne,* and that was the strange part." Elizabeth dabbed the corners of her mouth with her red paper napkin and sighed. "It was just me with all the food. The first time I dreamed it, I was excited — all that just for me. But the next time, I wished I had someone to share it with. And each time I dreamed it after that, all I could focus on were all those empty chairs."

"How many times did you have the dream?" Joy had nearly forgotten about her meal and was focused on her friend's face. "And why haven't you told me this before?"

"Oh, I've lived many years. There is too

much about me and my life to tell. And I probably had the dream five or six times before the first guest arrived."

Joy sat up straighter. She put down her fork. Her eyes focused on Elizabeth. "A guest? Was it your mother, finally able to eat a feast on all her china?"

"*Ne.* It wasn't. It was a neighbor, Wilma. She was *Englisch.* I used to go visit her when I was a child because she had a lot of pet birds. One would sit on my finger and mimic me. When I got older, Wilma had a lot of questions about my *kapp,* my dress, and our Amish ways. I tried to explain the best I could, but it was hard. I often didn't understand it all myself. Then one day I got tired of answering all her questions. I saved up my money and bought her a Bible. It was the first one she'd ever owned." Elizabeth's eyes flickered and her voice softened. She was still talking, but it was as if she were looking into the past as she spoke, rather than focusing on Joy, who was sitting right there in the room.

"After that, whenever I visited Wilma, I always saw that Bible sitting on her table. Once I saw her with a group of women, walking into a church. She seemed happier, and sometimes when I visited there were other friends there too. Nice Christian ladies."

Warmth filled Joy's chest. "She started to believe in Jesus, didn't she?"

"*Ja,* and that's what I started to figure out. That's what I believe the Lord was trying to tell me. Later, I read in His Word about the banqueting table Jesus is preparing for us. I've read many times how in heaven we'll be eating and feasting with God. Jesus said in one of His parables that we should go out into the roads and country lanes and urge people to come to the feast. There will never be more people than seats in God's kingdom. In fact, the opposite is true."

Joy glanced to the empty seat next to her and then the one after that. And the one after that. "And these seats." Her lips opened in realization. "The invites weren't your job, were they? They were mine."

A slow smile lifted Elizabeth lips and pushed up her cheeks. "God already knows who He wants sitting in these chairs. He has places for the men and women around us. He wants to guide them to Jesus so He can welcome them into heaven, but first we need to welcome them into our lives . . . or sometimes step into theirs. If we don't spend time with people in this community who need Jesus, there will be no relationship. Without a relationship there will be no reason for them to take time to listen as we talk about God and faith." Elizabeth sighed. "How will they come if they do not hear? And how will they hear if we do not go to them?"

Joy nodded and wiped tears from her eyes. She understood why Elizabeth hadn't wanted her to quit. She also understood why God had put her where she was. Her job wasn't over yet, and that job had nothing to do with the television show. Why had it taken her so long to see that?

Twenty-Nine

Be life long or short, its completeness
depends on what it was lived for.

AMISH PROVERB

Joy didn't waste any time inviting her
friends to the table — or at least inviting
Alicia to visit. The evening started out with
dinner for her family. They had a casserole
her *mem* called Sunday Dinner, and then
her parents and sisters went over to Hope's
garden behind the pie shop to finish making
plans for the upcoming weddings. Alicia had
shown up after that, excited for time together.

At the kitchen sink, Joy filled the coffeepot
and then poured the water into the machine
and turned it on. Thirty seconds later the
coffee began to drip.

"It's so much easier making coffee here
than back home. Back in Ohio, *Mem* would
put a coffeepot on our woodstove in the

337

kitchen."

"You cooked on a woodstove?"

"We had a gas stove too, but *Mem* preferred the wood one. I'd say most of the people from our church feel the same."

"I'm not sure I want to go to your church." Alicia chuckled. "I won't fit in. I . . ."

"What do you mean?"

"Well, unless I borrow clothes from wardrobe, I won't be dressed like anyone else. And then all the Amish I've met here are so gentle, so thoughtful. I'd be like a bull in a china shop." She stood and held the edges of her floral skirt and did a curtsy. "No one has ever accused me of being gentle or soft-spoken. In fact I'm pretty sure this is the only role I've ever played without carrying a gun."

"That's not what believing in God is all about, Alicia. It's not like you have to change everything in your life."

"Just my lifestyle, my language, my habits, and my clothing. Not much at all."

Joy chuckled. "Don't feel that you have to become Amish when you turn your life over to God. Jesus died for the sins of every person — not simply those who wear a *kapp* or grow a beard. I choose to remain Amish because I like our simple lifestyle. I like our focus on God and our families."

The smile that was typical on Alicia's face had disappeared. She quickly wiped her eyes and then looked down at her fingers. Her nails were cut short and without nail polish, just like an Amish woman's. Alicia squeezed her fingertips into her palms, obviously trying to hold her emotions at bay.

"What's wrong? Did I say something wrong?" Joy asked.

"I'd like to believe you, Joy. I really would. But you're so innocent. So unblemished. It's easy for me to believe God loves and accepts you. But me . . . well, that's another story."

"What do you mean?"

"I do believe there is a God. That's been a huge step, but I've done some things I regret. Lots of things, but two things I'm pretty sure God won't ever forgive me for." Alicia stood and paced to the window, staring out into the neatly manicured backyard. Her shoulders were squared and tight, and she reached her hand up and rubbed the back of her neck as if that would release the tension she felt inside.

Joy wanted to go to her. She wanted to say something to make her feel better. She also considered changing the subject. It was hard to see her friend struggling so. Yet

God's quiet Spirit inside told her to just sit still and wait. She didn't need to try to push out words to fill the empty spaces, because if she did, Alicia wouldn't have the chance to express her heart.

"I read through the Ten Commandments last night," Alicia finally said. "Someone had highlighted it in the Gideon Bible in my hotel room." She tilted her head as if thinking through the list in her mind. "I attended church a few times as a kid, so I sort of knew what they were, but I was shocked to discover I've broken every one."

Joy's mouth opened slightly, and she tried not to let out a gasp. *Every one? Dear God, what did Alicia do?*

Alicia turned slowly. "You Amish people are probably the only ones in America who don't know this — you know, with the tabloids and all — but Rowan and I split up because I had an affair with one of my costars. I won't go into details, but I was blasted by the media . . . and Rowan was crushed."

"I didn't know. I'm so sorry."

"I wish I could go back and do it over. Or rather *not* do it. Rowan and I had something good." Tears came then, and Alicia returned to the table, sitting across from Joy. "That's not the worst of it though, and when I tell you this you'll be one of the only people on the planet who will know, but ten years ago I . . . I had an abortion."

As Joy slowly took in that revelation, she ached with compassion for her friend. Alicia's face turned red, and the tears came harder now. She placed both hands over her face and hung her head. "I . . . I regret it. I'd just gotten my first role. I thought a child would ruin everything . . . and the doctor said my problems would be over if I did it . . . that everything would go back to normal. But it was a lie. Nothing but a lie."

"I'm so sorry you have to deal with such pain. Nothing can undo a decision like that, but I do know one thing."

"What's that?"

"I heard this from a visiting minister once. He told us about a man who was drinking and driving and hit an Amish buggy, seriously injuring a couple and killing their three children. When the man was in jail, the Amish father visited him. He was in a wheelchair. He'd come to offer the prisoner forgiveness, and he told him Jesus wanted to forgive him too. The man was full of pain and said he could never forgive himself."

"Yes." Alicia nodded. "I understand that."

"I'll never forget the minister's words. The Amish man told the driver if he believed his

341

sin was greater than Christ's sacrifice, he was basically saying, 'Thanks, but no thanks for what You've done, Jesus. What You did wasn't enough.' "

Alicia sucked in a breath. "Do you think that's true?"

"With everything in me. Yes, Alicia, you made horrible choices, but Jesus's sacrifice covers every one of them. *Every one.* He not only loves you, but He was there with you. He didn't want you to make those choices, but He wept when you did, because He loves you."

The sobs came louder then, and Alicia rested her arms on the tabletop and placed her face on her arms. She cried until Joy was sure there were no tears left to cry, and Joy knew she had only one more thing to ask. "Do you want to pray? Do you want to ask Jesus to forgive you? To make you new again?"

Alicia nodded, and hope swelled in Joy's chest. Then it slid down her arms and into her stomach, dancing like butterflies.

"All you have to do is silently pray and ask Him to take your sins away. Tell Him you have faith and believe."

Alicia lowered her head, and even though no words were emerging, Joy knew everything was changing deep inside.

Like a storm calming, Alicia's trembling body stilled. Joy could almost see the ripple of forgiveness radiating from Alicia's soul. After a few minutes, her friend lifted her head. Her makeup was smeared under her eyes from crying. Joy handed her a napkin, and Alicia attempted to wipe it away.

"You've never looked so beautiful," Joy whispered.

"Why, because I cried my makeup off? Maybe I'll turn out Amish after all."

"No, because I can see peace on your face."

"Yeah." She smiled. "I feel peace. To know all those bad things aren't mine to carry anymore — that Jesus took them away."

"And I want you to know something else too. Whenever you feel like remembering your past and feeling bad, instead you need to turn to the present — to what God is doing — and thank Him. Also, look into the future and see what He's got planned."

"He has a future for me planned?" Alicia asked.

"I know He does. He has one for us both," Joy admitted.

Sunday Casserole for 20

8 cups uncooked potatoes, cubed
2 cups uncooked elbow macaroni
2 cups frozen peas
2 cups cubed ham
1 pound grated mild cheese
8 cups milk
1 tablespoon salt
1/4 teaspoon ground black pepper (or more
  to taste)
1/2 cup grated onion

Combine all ingredients together and pour into a large roaster pan. Bake at 250 to 275 degrees for 3 1/2 hours. Makes 20 servings.

THIRTY

In school you're taught a lesson and then given a test. In life you're given a test that teaches you a lesson.

AMISH PROVERB

The last few days of work had gone by quickly. Joy enjoyed helping Rowan with new scenes, and she'd especially enjoyed the Bible study times after lunch, but with Saturday came the realization that she had to go talk with Matthew. She'd taken a few days to think about it as he asked, and she was certain he wasn't going to like what she had to say.

Even though it was nearing Thanksgiving, the weather was perfect, and the streets of Pinecraft were filled with Amish families on holiday. Joy spotted a man on a bicycle, pulling a small cart. The cart was black with two white wheels and a white wooden railing wrapped all the way around the rim. In it sat four toddlers, three girls, and a boy. The boy stood at the railing nearest to the bicycle, and his small, chubby hands gripped the side. His blond hair was long — past his ears and cut straight across his forehead. He wore a white button-up shirt and black pants. He was the sentry, she supposed, keeping an eye on their path. The three girls wore matching cornflower blue dresses and black *kapp*s tied under their chins in neat bows. They looked at her as they passed with solemn faces, and Joy remembered her own mother tying her *kapp* before she was old enough to let the *kapp* strings hang free. Could they see her tears even from a distance? Joy offered a smile and waved. One of them — the youngest — waved back.

She was giving up so much more than hopes of a marriage. What about children? She knew a man like Matthew would be a wonderful husband and father, and this one decision was setting the course of her life. But could she walk away from those who truly wanted to know about God? Yes, her desires here on earth were at stake, but so were the eternal souls of the friends she'd grown to care about.

As soon as the bicycle and wagon passed, two more children walked by with their mother. The boy wore a blue T-shirt and swimming trunks with the name Lightning McQueen on them. The girl wore a black-and-white jumper, and her hair was in a tight French braid. Other than the boy's haircut, one would never know they were Amish. They walked just ahead of their mother, who was in Amish dress. The children were ready for the beach, and she smiled thinking of them laughing and dancing in the waves.

She found Matthew at home. He was sitting on the front porch, and he didn't seem surprised to see her. He also didn't seem surprised by her tears as she told him about her dinner at Elizabeth's and her decision.

Matthew nodded once and then looked away. "So what you're saying is you're still not willing to quit the show?"

"It's not the show that's important to me. It's the people. Don't you see that? God has placed me in their lives for a reason. I can feel it deep down."

"Can you sit? Can we talk about this?" Matthew placed an arm around her shoulders and moved her inside to the living room. He led her to the sofa, and she sat down. He sat down on the other end of the couch with a wide space between them, a space that yawned like a wide chasm, one

Joy was sure would be impossible to cross.

She knew the rules. She understood why the bishop had asked the congregation not to get involved with the television crew — there were simply too many ways their community could possibly be exploited — but she also knew she had to stay with the show. She couldn't walk away from Alicia — from the others.

"I don't know what to say. I don't know if there is anything for us to talk about. We both heard your father's words at church. We know I can't choose both."

Why did her tears start again? She pulled out a handkerchief and dabbed her eyes. She wanted to be strong, but the pain was so great. *God, is this what You really want?* Because to her it made no sense to walk away from the man she wanted to spend her life with and walk toward new friends who may or may not change.

Of course that didn't matter, did it? The result wasn't up to her. It was up to God. All she had to do was be obedient.

"I just wish this were easier." Her words released with a heavy sigh.

"I don't understand why it needs to be hard. If you truly cared about me, about the community, then there would be *ne* question of what you would do. You could walk over there, tell them you quit, and every-thing would be fine — it would be *gut* again."

Out of nowhere came a hot surge of anger, bubbling up inside of her. "*Ne,* it wouldn't be fine. Why can't you see that?" She rose, balling her hands by her sides. "Do you think it's all right that we continue as we are — that we stay in our safe cocoons with people just like us while there is a world out there longing for God's hope?

"There are hurting people, Matthew. People who need to hear that God loves them. A hurting woman had given up on herself until she realized God had not given up on her and never will. She finally found someone she trusts — me — and I can't walk away from that."

"And what about my trust, Joy? What about the trust of the community? Those producers are making a spectacle of us. Can't you see that? I'll have to admit that at first I liked the attention of being an Amish person in a mostly *Englisch* community, but now I can't even work on someone's roof without people stopping to snap photos. Do we not have a right just to live a simple life without being under a spotlight?"

Joy paced across his living room and back, willing herself to calm. "You are wrong,

349

Matthew. The producers aren't here to make a spectacle of us. Have you ever thought that with all the bad happening in the world, viewers simply want to be reminded that good still exists and that people can live simple, godly lives? Maybe it's okay to share hope, to share joy with people who are tired of all the reports of shootings and kidnappings and war."

Matthew was silent then, but Joy could see from the hard look on his face that she wasn't winning him over. Maybe it was better this way. Maybe she needed to know how he really thought about their community and the world before marrying him. And maybe she was discovering a bit of herself too. A bit of her own heart.

Joy turned and moved to the front door. She paused but didn't turn around. She couldn't face him. She didn't want to see the anger and disappointment in his face. "I'm sorry things didn't turn out. I want you to know that I still think you're an amazing —"

"Stop." Matthew's voice cut off her words. "I can't hear that now, Joy. Please stop."

She nodded and then slipped out. Her flip-flops smacked the concrete on the walkway, and she quickened her pace. She didn't want to wait around to see if he'd come after her. She knew he wouldn't. Instead, she needed to get home as quickly as she could.

Yet with each step, fear roiled within her. What if this was her one shot at love? What if she never married? What if she never became a wife, a mother, all because of one decision? Was it worth it — worth taking the chance?

Her fear spawned a shot of adrenaline, and Joy began to run. She hadn't run like this since she was a girl, but she couldn't get home fast enough.

She rounded the block and raced to her house. She slowed slightly as she rushed up the porch steps and into the front door. *Mem* and Grace were in the kitchen talking. In the living room her *dat* was reading the *Budget.* They all looked up surprised as she passed, but she didn't pause.

Joy rushed to her room and threw herself onto her bed. The angry heat that had risen inside her turned cold, and then her body trembled. It was as if the ache that grew attempted to slip out through her skin. She rolled to her side and pulled her knees to her chest just as she had as a little girl whenever she was scared or afraid.

"O God." The words came out as a whisper. "I need You, I need You." She clenched her legs harder. "I can't do this without You. I don't want to do this without You. I've never needed You more."

A cry heaved from her chest, and Joy covered her mouth, worried that her *mem* and sister could hear it. Sure enough, a few seconds later there was a knock at her bedroom door.

"Joy, are you all right?" Grace's voice carried through the wood of the door. Her younger sister no doubt heard her sobs.

"I don't want to talk now if it . . . it's all right."

"*Ja,* of course."

The retreating footsteps told her Grace was respecting her wishes. Knowing that, Joy pressed her face farther into her pillow, wishing for the first time ever that Jesus was there and that she could snuggle into His arms and hear His whispered words. Words that told her everything was going to be all right.

I've never needed You more, God, she prayed again.

The amazing thing was that even as she lay there, she wondered if she'd ever truly needed God before now. Sure, she'd had some troubles growing up, but even then she was able to handle them herself. And for the problems she couldn't handle alone she'd had help — from her *mem,* her *dat,* her sisters.

But now she needed God, and she wanted Him like never before. It was a new feeling — a feeling of brokenness. And as much as it hurt, she knew Elizabeth was right. This was the exact place God wanted her to be.

Matthew paced in his shop, and he'd never felt so close to losing control. Something heated and tense within him wanted to pick up his stack of wood and hurl it piece by piece across the room. But what good would that do? His parents had arrived home not long after Joy left, and if he started throwing wood they would hear. They'd see the mess. His *dat* would try to talk to him, and the last thing he wanted was to talk to his *dat* right now.

He had to get out of there. He had to think. But where could he go? He couldn't even leave the house and walk down the street without being surrounded by people. He could go to the park and walk into the wooded area, but he'd have to pass a hundred people he knew to do it, and they'd all look at him with either pity or accusation. Pity that the woman he was courting had chosen to work on the television show instead of choosing him. And accusation

353

that he'd chosen her in the first place. After all this time, after all his waiting to find the right woman to marry, he'd chosen wrong.

He was angry with her and angry with himself for getting angry. He wasn't one to act like this. He knew he had to get control of himself, but his knees trembled and his gut tightened — proof that he was far from being in control.

Matthew tore his hat from his head and threw it to the floor. Then he picked it up and placed it firmly on his head, realizing he had to leave before he suffocated. Even his shop, his private sanctuary, was filled with thoughts of her. Shame heated his face even now, and he opened the side door of their garage and stormed out, riding on his wave of anger.

THIRTY-ONE

The yoke of God does not fit a stiff neck.
AMISH PROVERB

They were behind on filming, and since they'd had a few half days during the previous week, Rowan decided to finish the week's filming on Saturday.

Joy was thankful she'd told Rowan she'd be in late. By the time she quit crying after talking to Matthew and had washed her face, it was nearly noon. A heaviness weighed on her, remembering their exchange of words that morning.

She was also thankful no one was in the house when she was ready to leave, and she nearly got to the front door when she remembered Rowan had asked her to bring in her Bible to use as a prop. She returned to her room, retrieved it from the bookshelf, and then pressed it to her chest. She didn't want to know what Matthew would think of them using her actual Bible as a prop in their television show. No, she couldn't think of that.

She'd taken only a few weary steps when a piece of paper fluttered to the floor. It was a piece of notebook paper that had been torn and folded. Without having to look, Joy knew the words written on the page in neat, ten-year-old print:

"For this day is holy unto our LORD: neither be ye sorry; for the joy of the LORD is your strength" (Nehemiah 8:10).

She tucked the paper into the Bible and let those words replay in her mind: *For the joy of the Lord is your strength.* She'd liked the verse as a child because it had her name in it. That's why she'd chosen to memorize it all those years ago, but the more she thought about it the more it made sense. A person only needed strength when they were weak. And when one was weak it was hard to be joyful. It was almost impossible to make yourself joyful when everything was going wrong, but could God make that possible?

She thought of that phrase again. *Joy of the Lord.* Joy from Him.

As she exited the house, she breathed a

quick prayer. "Lord, I need joy, but at this moment joy seems very far away. I know joy comes from You, though, so please give me what I cannot give myself. Amen."

The prayer was simple, yet Joy knew it was important. It was one of the few times she'd turned to God instead of attempting to care for herself.

It was also important because she didn't want Alicia to know everything that was happening. Her friend had enough to worry about. It wasn't that she wanted to hide her problems, but rather that they would be too hard to explain. Unless one was raised in an Amish church and home, the disagreement between her and Matthew would make no sense.

The roadway was busier than it had been a few weeks ago, and Joy knew it was because more and more people were coming down for the season. Cold winds from the northern states blew many snowbirds to their warm, Southern nests.

Yet more Amish meant more awareness of the television show. And more awareness would be more talk, and more talk would mean people all over their town would be writing to their friends back home, telling about the *Englischers* who were trying to portray them on television. More than that, they'd all be sharing about the Amish woman who was helping the *Englischers.* She thought she'd gained attention when her quilt won a blue ribbon at the fair, but that would pale in comparison to this. It wasn't what she wanted to be known for.

Her stomach growled, and Joy realized how little she'd eaten the past few days. Yoder's Produce loomed ahead, and since she had plenty of time before she had to be at the studio, she decided to slip in and pick up a couple of pieces of fruit.

Joy grabbed an orange and a banana. On a whim she picked up a box of whoopie pies she knew Alicia and Georgia would enjoy. Joy stood in line behind an Amish woman she'd seen before. Joy believed she was here with a group from Ohio and was almost certain she'd been at the last sewing frolic.

"It's getting chilly out there, isn't it?" Joy rubbed her arms for emphasis.

"At least there's not snow like back home," the woman commented as she turned. She seemed to recognize Joy when she turned around, but then she quickly looked away.

"My sister's in Kentucky," Joy offered. "It's been a hard winter there. She's looking forward to coming down next week."

The woman's mouth pursed but she continued staring off to the side, ignoring Joy completely.

From somewhere in the store a baby cried. Behind Joy, the door opened and two *Englisch* women walked in on their lunch break. Joy had the urge to explain to the Amish woman ahead of her why she was working with the television production team, but then she changed her mind. She wasn't going to change this woman's opinion of her no matter how she tried.

With a heavy heart, she paid for her items when it was her turn at the cashier and then hurried toward the set. No longer hungry, she left the orange and banana on the picnic table outside Big Olaf's as she passed, hoping someone would enjoy them. She kept the box of whoopie pies but lost the joy of giving them.

She walked a few more minutes, and the warehouse lot loomed before her. A few Amish men mulled around outside, peering through the chain-link fence and trying to figure out what was happening. Charlie, the faithful security guard, stood by his post, and she waved at him. Joy didn't slow her steps as he stood, opened the gate, and waved her through.

There was finality in those steps. Once inside, stepping in front of the camera again, there would be no going back. All her life she took pride in being Amish. She took pride in her ability to make good choices and to excel at quilting. *Pride in your work puts joy in your day, Mem* had told her more than once. But from this moment on she could no longer take joy in those things. No, now her joy would simply have to come from the Lord. She was doing this for Him, and as long as she remembered that, as long as she continued to look ahead instead of looking over her shoulder, she'd be all right.

Abraham leaned against the wall. "I don't get you."

"What do you mean?"

Matthew had decided if he couldn't be alone he might as well work. He needed this job and needed the money, although not nearly as much as if he were still planning for a wife soon.

"A beautiful woman loves you. You can see it in her eyes. It's also clear that you love her too, so what's keeping you apart?"

"She made a choice."

"It's a television show." Abraham let his hand with the hammer drop to his side. "She's making sure they portray us the right way. I think people should be thanking her."

"She's doing more than that."

"Are you talking about the acting?"

"Of course I am."

"And how does that make her any different from those ladies who are over there cooking up all that food for them? And how are we any different, working on this cottage for *Englischers,* for that matter?"

"It's very different. I can't even see how you think it's the same. It's making a graven —"

"Don't you start with that 'making a graven image' business. Do you really think when the Israelites were in the desert, God was thinking about television shows being made thousands of years later? I'm *ne* minister or bishop, but my *mem* and *dat* read me the Bible. If I were to guess, that commandment is talking about making an idol and worshipping it instead of God."

"*Ja,* that's one man's opinion. The whole community thinks differently. Most Amish communities don't allow photographs. And that probably means they don't allow videotaping, since it's a series of pictures."

Abraham nodded and listened, but his face held humor, as if he wasn't buying Matthew's argument at all.

"What's so funny?"

"It's funny that you're not admitting what

the real issue is, and I wonder if you even see it."

"What do you mean?"

"I mean you're concerned more about what everyone thinks about you than you are about the woman you claim to love. Last time I looked, the Bible said something about being selfless. And you say you want to marry her? I have no doubt that if anyone tried to hurt my *mem,* my *dat* would stand up for her. He would die for her if he had to. But instead of being there for Joy, you've turned against her too. That's not love."

Matthew balled his hands into fists and held them at his sides. "How dare you say who I do or don't love!"

Abraham stood straight and shrugged, and his nonchalant attitude caused Matthew's heart to pound.

"Sure, you have warm feelings inside, but that's not love. I'm going to stand by what I just said."

"Oh, so what am I supposed to do, just be okay with her working for that show and being filmed? Should I be okay that she's shaming herself in the community's eyes?"

Abraham ran his finger around his collar and narrowed his gaze. "And shaming *you?* You forgot to mention that . . . and I think that's what this is really about. Her actions are shaming you."

Matthew had not been an angry man in his past. But the anger that ignited the first time he saw Joy talking to that *Englisch* man — with everyone at the bus stop watching — hadn't died out. It had simmered inside him, casting dark shadows on everything in his world.

"You don't know what you're talking about." Matthew spoke through clenched teeth. "I'm only thinking of her. What will it do to her to be around all those *Englischers*? How will people think of her from now on?"

"And how will they think of you? You don't have to admit that's what's driving you." Abraham pointed his finger into the air. "I can see it in your eyes. And I recognize it. For a while I saw it in my own reflection. The community . . . their opinions . . . it's a powerful thing, especially when you've been raised to conform, to obey, and to stand out only for the *gut* things, for right actions."

"You know what?" Matthew tossed his hammer onto the rough wood of the subfloor. I don't need your help anymore. And I don't need your opinions. Get your things, and I'll drop off money for your work later today. I don't need this right now."

Abraham pushed his hat back on his head.

"You remind me of my old dog Gus. He had a crooked back leg. Sometimes I bumped it — not on purpose, of course. But when I did, he snarled at me something fierce. Few times he even bit me. I know he didn't mean to. That dog used to follow me wherever I went. It's just that it hurt."

He picked up his tool belt and slung it over his shoulder. "I just hope you get it checked out. Took my dog to the vet and there was nothing he could do, but I still felt bad for him."

Matthew refused to respond, especially to someone who didn't even act Amish half the time. He didn't need Abraham around, not if he was going to talk to him that way.

He watched his former coworker leave and noticed a sadness on the man's face. The sadness wasn't over losing his job — Matthew could tell that. Maybe it was a look of pity more than sadness.

He feels sorry for me. And somehow even knowing that made him angry. Abraham was one of the most noncommittal Amish men he knew, and yet he dared to pity *him.*

Abraham walked out onto the road, but then he paused and turned. "I just have one question to ask you. One question that won't let go. You don't have to answer me — I don't need to know — but maybe it's something you need to think about."

"*Ja,* and what's that?" The words shot from Matthew's mouth.

"I was just wondering when everyone's opinion started mattering so much. And when you started thinking you had to be perfect — to make the perfect choice for a bride. It seems to me that you put a lot of pressure on yourself. Pressure that God never intended."

Abraham didn't wait for a response. Instead, he simply slunk away in his casual manner.

"And when did you decide it didn't matter?" Matthew whispered under his breath. Yet even as Abraham strode away, his words settled on Matthew like a heavy burden. A weight he couldn't shake away. Or maybe it was a weight that had been there a long time and was just coming to the surface.

Matthew turned over in bed. Bright moonlight filtered through the white curtains, but he knew it wasn't the moonlight that kept him awake. It was Abraham's words. The answer to Abraham's question didn't come immediately, yet as he stayed at work, sliding a new window into its casing, the answer came.

He'd been only five or six years old the

day his *dat* had been appointed bishop. He didn't think much of it at the time. Only years later did he understand how God's call had affected everything in their lives.

What he did remember was his grandfather's stern talk. They had just barely left the church service when his grandfather had sat out on the porch and put Matthew on his knee. "Do you understand that your *dat* is an important man now?"

Matthew had nodded.

"That means everyone will be watching him, and they will be guided by him. Everyone will be watching you too."

"Why?"

"You represent your *dat* and your family. When you look bad, it makes him look bad. And when he looks bad, God looks bad. Understand?"

Matthew had nodded. He'd understood, maybe too well. *Be good and reflect my father well. Be good and reflect God well.* He'd done that the best he could, but still he failed.

What will happen if I don't reflect Him well? It was a thought Matthew didn't want to answer. Just as God called his father to be bishop, he'd been called to be the perfect bishop's son. Isn't that what his grandfather meant? And if he did, was he right? For the first time in his life, Matthew wasn't sure.

Chocolate Whoopie Pies

1 1/2 cups shortening
3 cups sugar
3 egg yolks, beaten
3 teaspoons vanilla
1 1/2 cups buttermilk (or sour milk)
3 teaspoons baking soda
2 teaspoons salt
1 1/2 cups hot water
1 1/2 cups cocoa
6 cups flour

Filling

1 1/2 cups white shortening (not butter flavored)
5 tablespoons milk
3 cups powdered sugar
3 teaspoons vanilla
3 egg whites, beaten stiff

Preheat oven to 350 degrees. Cream together shortening and sugar. Add egg yolks and vanilla. Stir in buttermilk. Add baking soda, salt, hot water, cocoa, and flour. Beat well. Drop by tablespoonfuls onto greased cookie sheet and bake 12 minutes.

For the filling, cream shortening and milk. Add powdered sugar and vanilla; mix well. Beat in egg whites until filling is fluffy.

To assemble pies, spread a heaping spoonful of filling on flat side of half the cookies. Top with remaining cookies. Makes approximately 40 whoopie pies.*

* Sherry Gore, *Simply Delicious Amish Cooking* (Grand Rapids: Zondervan, 2013), 174–75.

THIRTY-TWO

Many light things make a heavy bundle.
AMISH PROVERB

Alicia was just getting ready to head home after work when she entered the wardrobe room and paused. Someone was in the chair by the sewing machine. Not just someone — Joy. Joy was blinking fast and her lips were compressed, as if there was a tidal wave of emotion building up inside that she was trying to hold in.

Alicia flipped on a switch, flooding the room with light. Joy covered her face and pulled back as if the white light from the overhead bulb burned her skin. Her fingers shook, and Alicia expected a sound, a cry, to emerge. But none did.

"Joy, are you okay?" She rushed to her friend and kneeled at her side. When Alicia placed a hand on Joy's knee, it was moist. *Tears.* Alicia's heart cinched down as if the woman's pain had seeped through her skin. It was a feeling she hadn't felt in a while — compassion. In LA she hadn't been shielded from the pain of others, yet she thought they pretty much got what they deserved. Here, with Joy, it was different. Whatever hurt her friend must be serious. And Alicia honestly wished at the moment that she could carry some of Joy's pain.

Alicia swallowed down the emotion. "Is it your dad?"

"No. He's fine. It's just . . ." Joy pulled a handkerchief from her shirt pocket and wiped her face. "It's just that Matthew and I are no longer courting."

"You broke up?"

"Yes, I suppose that's what I did."

"What? You broke things off? But you told me you love him. You told me he's the man you want to spend the rest of your life with."

"He is. It's just . . . his father is the bishop, and there are standards. It's the whole community, really. They disapprove of . . ." Joy paused, as if trying to find the right words. "They disapprove of *me.*"

Anger shot down the back of Alicia's neck and through her arms. She stood, fists at her sides. She wanted to hit someone. She wanted to march over to the bishop's house and give him and his community a piece of her mind. "Who in the world could disapprove of you?" She spat the words out. "They are fools. They are . . ."

She wanted to use stronger language, but she refrained. The old Alicia would have used every curse word she knew. The old Alicia would have marched over there, kicked down their pretty white picket fences, and made a scene.

You're not that person anymore. You're a new creation.

Ever since she'd prayed the other night and turned everything over to God, she felt a new light and peace deep inside. Yet she was having a hard time changing her old habits.

Alicia spun around and moved to the window. When she'd parked at the set it had been sunny. Now the rain was falling in big, heavy drops. "I don't know how anyone can disapprove of you, Joy," she finally said.

"It's hard to explain. Most people would not understand unless they were Amish. I've just . . . well, I tend to push the rules. Their rules anyway. And they're not all right with that. It's not just them. It seems these days all the young people are trying to figure out what being Amish really means. Everyone's weighing what's important inside and out."

"But what does Matthew think? Surely he

doesn't just let people treat you that way. I haven't talked to him, but I can't imagine him standing back and letting this happen to you."

"It's our community. It's how things work."

"None of this makes sense. I know plenty of people whose parents despise the person they're with, and it's horrible to watch." Alicia spat. "It makes me think maybe this Christianity thing isn't worth it — that it's all full of judgment. Maybe it's not something I want. I mean, everyone I know who is living without God treats people this way. What's the difference?"

Joy's tears came again. She shook her head, and Alicia could see that the Amish woman was processing her words. Alicia didn't completely mean what she'd said. She did believe in Christianity because she knew Jesus Christ had transformed her heart. What she didn't like was how some Christians treated each other. Weren't the Amish supposed to be full of love and forgiveness, or was that some type of act?

Alicia cupped her left hand and made a fist, and then she smacked it with her right hand like a boxer prepping for a fight. "Want me to talk to Matthew, knock some sense into him? I totally can."

"N-no, don't do that. I n-never wanted to bring you into this. I-I didn't want you to see me like this or find out what happened. I was planning on coming to work and acting fine, but after the scenes were done, I just broke down. I'm not sure if I can go home tonight. My sisters are going to be able to see everything all over my face. They know me too well."

"I wouldn't know about that," Alicia mumbled under her breath. She almost spilled out that she and her sister rarely talked and the only time they connected was near Christmas, when they'd meet up for lunch to exchange expensive gifts — gifts that said more about their own success than it did about their consideration for the other person.

Instead, Alicia kept her mouth shut because she didn't want to take the conversation away from Joy, away from what she was experiencing.

My, aren't I becoming thoughtful?

She could almost imagine Rowan's voice, mocking her for acting like someone she wasn't, but then she pushed that out of her mind too.

After a long, intense silence, Alicia moved to the props closet. "It's raining outside. I'm pretty sure I saw an umbrella in here.

When I find it I'll walk you home. I'll even sacrifice and stay to eat whatever dessert your mother made, just to get your sisters' attention off of you."

"You will? What an amazing sacrifice." Even as Joy wilted back against the cushioned chair, a hint of a smile touched her lips. But instead of getting up, she closed her eyes, and a pensive look crossed her face as if she were riding swells of memories.

Alicia found the umbrella and sat down. Seeing the pain reflected on Joy's face caused a few of her own memories to resurface.

"I remember being in Amish country once before. My grandmother — my mother's mom — came one summer and took me to meet her parents in Pennsylvania. We drove through country roads most of the way, and at times I was certain we'd end up lost. But then a little town would pop up, and my grandma seemed to know just where she was.

"One day there was this huge mountain range, and at a curve in the road a billboard rose up. Beware Lest You Forget the Lord, it said. Not much farther, I saw a buggy with a bearded man in the seat. I asked my grandma if we'd traveled back in time to the days of Laura Ingalls. She laughed.

"The man had a straw hat with a brim, like the hats I've seen around Pinecraft. He wore suspenders before they were hipster, and a woman wearing a bonnet sat beside him. The more we drove, the more buggies we saw. When we passed one of them, four children looked at me."

"Maybe it was me, except I never was in Pennsylvania as a child." Joy offered a sad smile. "I remember watching cars zoom past as we quietly plodded along."

Alicia sighed. "Sometimes, when I couldn't sleep, I'd pretend I was one of those children, living in one of those Amish farms we passed — farmhouses made of stone, at least in that place — and with hand pumps out front. I'd pretend I had a mom who was going to make me a big breakfast and a dad who would be up with the dawn to milk the cows. I'd imagine we lived near the creek by the covered bridge and that the next day we'd go and stick our feet in the water as we watched the boys jump off the bridge into the creek. I'd forget for a time that my dad had a new wife and my mom drank too much."

"It sounds like you had a nice time with your grandma though."

"Yeah, I did. She loved God too, and she liked to talk about Him as she drove." Alicia chuckled. "Although I didn't think she knew what she was talking about at the time because she also smoked cigarettes. Even though my mom drank, she never touched a cigarette, and in my childish mind smoking was worse than drinking, so I thought my grandma must not really know what she was talking about."

"It's strange how we try to make sense of the world as kids, isn't it?"

"Yes," Alicia whispered. "And it's also strange how God brings everything back full circle. For most of my life I assumed that trip was just a random occurrence. But now I know differently."

"What do you mean?" Joy sat erect, intent on Alicia's every word.

"Well, look at us. We're here and you're now my best friend. I think God was giving me a glimpse of what was to come. How much I'd need you, how much we'd need each other, and how you'd point me to Him."

Joy knew Alicia was trying to get her mind off her pain when she insisted the perfect way to spend a Sunday afternoon was to go to the beach.

Alicia picked her up, and as they drove, Alicia told stories about some of the most

377

awkward scenes she'd ever filmed. It felt good to laugh, good to get away from the eight square blocks that made up Pinecraft.

Siesta Key Beach was filled with young people playing volleyball, families romping in the sand, and couples cuddled on beach blankets.

Alicia wore a modest bathing suit with a cover-up, and her hair was knotted in a bun. She also wore large-rimmed sunglasses, and Joy understood. She wanted to go unnoticed. She wanted to enjoy the day without throngs of people interrupting their fun.

"Those sunglasses hide your face pretty well," Joy commented, "but perhaps the best disguise is that you're hanging out with an Amish woman."

Joy looked around at the people watching them. "You know, you're right, Joy. You're getting more attention with your dress, *kapp,* and flip-flops than I'm getting. I should take you with me whenever I travel." She laughed.

They found a place near the water and laid out an old quilt Joy brought. The salty scent of the ocean mixed with the aroma of barbecuing hot dogs. The crashing of the waves sounded like a loud roar.

Alicia kicked off her sandals and sat on the quilt. "Is the water cold here this time of year? I see some kids are swimming, but my guess is that I'll turn blue if I try."

"I'm not sure." Joy shrugged. "I haven't gone swimming here before. I know many Amish who have, but I don't own a suit." She sadly smiled, remembering how worried she'd been over not being appropriate in a swimsuit, so just not swimming seemed like a better choice. That seemed like such a minor thing now compared to what she'd done.

"Well, you've walked in the water then. Did your feet get cold?"

The sun was bright overhead, and Joy shielded her face with her hand. "No, I haven't walked in the water either."

Alicia gasped. "Wait, let me get this straight. You've lived here for a couple years and you haven't put your feet into the ocean?"

"No. I haven't. I'm content watching everyone."

"Oh, no you don't." Alicia stood and reached out her hand. "C'mon."

"I'm fine just sitting and watching." Joy scooted back, out of her friend's reach. "Please enjoy yourself. I might try to find some shells to take home to my soon-to-be niece, Emma, in a little bit."

Alicia pouted. "I'm only going to enjoy

379

myself if you come in the water too." She reached over and grabbed Joy's arms and tugged hard. "I'm not going to insist that you swim in your dress if that's what you're worried about. I just think you should put your feet into the water."

"Fine." Joy sighed, letting Alicia pull her up. "But only my feet, and only for a few minutes."

With her teeth clenched and her hands balled to her sides, Joy stepped into the waves. The water was warm as bathwater. She didn't expect that. Water had been cold all her life up north — in the creek on their property, from the pump by the garden, and from the small lake only a short buggy ride from their home. That seemed like a different life, the life of slow-plodding horses, of expansive fields, and of sifting through her Aunt Martha's fabric closet. Some folks called her aunt a hoarder, but Joy appreciated her. Martha didn't let anything go to waste. She liked to refer to herself as a collector. *Oh, what would all my friends up north think of this now, me walking in the ocean in November!*

For a moment, instead of the waves of water, Joy imagined the fields back home, a green sea that rippled with the breeze. She thought of the life she imagined with Matthew up there. The life she could have had. The life that would never be.

"I'm ready to get out." Joy turned and hurried back to her quilt. Alicia eyed her but continued to dance in the waves. How could it be that where Alicia found freedom, she found bondage?

O Lord, show me, too, how to be free.

Thirty-Three

No matter what, no matter where,
it's always home if love is there.
AMISH PROVERB

Joy rushed home during the lunch break at the studio, eager to see her father. They'd celebrated a simple Thanksgiving, and then her parents had been gone a few days days while he was in Orlando for treatments, and she missed them. Her sister Hope wasn't able to arrive from Kentucky as she had planned, and the house seemed emptier without *Dat.* Thankfully, other Amish women had taken over the cooking for the studio while *Mem* was gone, but she guessed *Mem* would soon be back in the swing of things.

Joy entered the house, passing through the kitchen and rushing by the stacks of borrowed dishes on their table — things they'd be using in a couple of weeks for Hope and

Lovina's double wedding. Soon there would be food to buy and prepare and guests to welcome from up north, but all those tasks paled in comparison to *Dat*'s health.

Dat's wrinkled face brightened as she entered the living room. "It was a hard few days at the hospital, but things are better now," he called to her. "It's *gut* to be home. *Gut* to see you."

He patted the sofa beside him, and she sat down. The most recent edition of the *Budget* was open and spread over the arm-rest. She picked up the paper and folded it, placing it on the table next to the lamp.

"I want to thank you, Joy, for all you've done." *Dat*'s voice was low, soft. "I know how much you have sacrificed. And I want you to know that although I'm thankful, I worry you've made the wrong choice."

"*Dat*, what do you mean?"

"Even with the best results these treatments will extend my life by only a few years. I'm afraid what you've given up — your relationship with Matthew — will impact your future for much longer."

"Oh, *Dat*, don't you see? I wanted to do this for you, and God's been changing me in the process too."

He ran a hand down his beard. "What do you mean?"

"If this hadn't happened, and if I hadn't worked on the set, I would have continued to believe life was about how well I performed, instead of understanding that I need to lean on God day by day."

Mem entered the living room, and from the soft smile on her face, Joy knew she'd overheard the conversation.

"It's *gut* to be home. It's *gut* to see brightness to your eyes once again." *Mem* glanced around. "I remember when we first moved here. I didn't believe this place would ever feel as welcoming as our Ohio home, but you know what? It does."

Joy looked around at the simple sofa with the crocheted afghan over its back, the two recliners, and the small tables. *Mem*'s touches were all around the room — her basket of yarn, her hurricane lamp on the table, and her small hutch with china. Joy's eyes darted to the stitched sampler on the wall. She'd made it years before from a kit she'd received as a Christmas gift. It had an Amish couple, their small house, and flowers. The saying on it read, "No matter what, no matter where, it's always home if love is there."

The stitching wasn't perfect, but she knew why *Mem* had hung it. This wasn't their home in Ohio, but as long as there was love and family, it was home. And Joy knew right now the best way she could show her father love was by not asking too many questions.

Instead she needed to wait for whatever news he had to share. She needed to offer to sit and listen for a while, even if she had a long list of things to do. And she needed to remind him that the choice she made was God's best plan for her, just as much as it was for him.

The peace Joy had found at home vanished as soon as she entered the studio lot once again. She arrived early to do her consulting work, and today she had yet another small part in the episode. She tried to forget that she would be on people's television screens all over the country in not too many months, and she tried to pretend she was just doing it to spend time with her new friends, but it didn't work. Joy looked at the script, and the words danced before her eyes. The nerves in her neck felt taut, as if turning her head to the side would cause them to snap.

Next to her, Alicia nibbled on a carrot stick and smiled in self-satisfaction. Joy's *mem* was at home, preparing a Country Brunch, doubling the normal recipe that fed twenty people. The truth was, Joy would rather be there helping *Mem* cook than sitting here and studying lines.

Joy rubbed her forehead and her brows. "I don't understand how you do this. How you enjoy it."

"I love it. I enjoy stepping into a character, but it wasn't always that way. I used to feel like I was going to throw up as I waited for the director to call *action,* but then I just started picturing myself as Sandra Bullock."

"Sandra who?"

Laughter spilled from Alicia's lips. "Wow, it's so strange that you don't know who these people are. You don't know Sandra Bullock, honestly?"

Joy shrugged.

"What about Taylor Swift, Johnny Depp, or Brad Pitt?"

"I can't say I do, but they all have wonderful last names."

"Okay, then my tip won't work for you, but just act successful. Act like you know what you're doing, like you have confidence, and like you were made to be in this scene at this moment."

"Yes, I understand now. I simply have to act like you."

Surprise registered on Alicia's face. "What?"

"I've seen you study. I've watched you get

focused for a scene. You take this seriously. You pour yourself into your work, and it shows."

Alicia placed a hand over her heart. Tears filled her eyes. "I didn't know you've been watching me."

"Yes. I have, and even though you said you've learned a lot from me, I've learned a lot from you too. There's a Bible verse that says, 'And whatsoever ye do, do it heartily, as to the Lord, and not unto men.' You are new in your relationship with God, and the reasons behind your acting might change. But I believe by using the talents God's given you, you've been honoring Him. We always honor Him when we become the person He designed us to be. God designed you a certain way for a purpose."

"It's strange. God designed me to act and you to sew, and in His perfect plan He knew that's what would bring us together."

"It's strange and wonderful. It's hard to understand, and I suppose that's part of the mystery of it."

"What do you mean?"

"I used to believe I had one path in life. To live as a good Amish woman, develop my natural skills, and become a good wife and mother. But the path isn't as straightforward as it seems."

"So do you think this television thing is just a side path, and when our filming ends you'll end up back on the straight and narrow path?"

"No, I don't think of this as a side path. I think of it as the path God needed me to be on to make me humble, to lead me to depend on Him. I've lived in the Amish community my whole life, and I believe it's perfectly possible to live a good life without getting God involved too much, but I'm thankful that I didn't fall victim to that way of thinking. I may have lost my chance at a husband and children, but I have a relationship with God that is more —"

"Do you really think that?" Alicia interrupted. "That you've given up your chance of marriage and children because of this?"

"It's a fear, but . . ." Tears sprang to her eyes. She lowered her head. "I suppose I won't know . . ."

Alicia reached over and gave her a hug, whispering into her ear. "It's just like a good screenplay — you never know if there's a twist in the plot coming up that will hurl your characters in a new direction."

Joy nodded, but her friend's words didn't help. She didn't want a new plot twist. She wanted what she had always wanted, but now with this new relationship with God added to that. She just wasn't sure if it could happen. Deep down she knew God's path was the right one, no matter how much her heart ached for Matthew and the life they could have had.

"I just don't understand." Alicia's words broke off her thoughts. "Why did you do it, then? If you honestly think you're risking your future with Matthew, why did you stay? Was it the money?"

"No. It wasn't the money. Yes, we are using it to pay for my father's medical bills, but that was never it."

"Then what was it?"

Joy focused on Alicia's gaze.

"It was me, wasn't it? I told you how some of the most important people in my life have walked out on me. But you didn't. You stayed."

"You started asking questions about God. I saw something in your eyes. It was hope, I think."

"And you were afraid that if you walked away, I would harden my heart again?"

"Yes, I suppose that was it. Harden it not just to people but to God." Joy smoothed her skirt, as if trying to press out the wrinkles with her hands. "Deep down I believe Jesus wanted me to show you His heart, Alicia. I will no doubt fail you sometime, but He never will. He has never left your side, and He will never walk away."

The words of encouragement slipped from her lips with gentleness, but Alicia's eyes widened, and a shocking look of fear crossed her face. Tears filled her eyes, and her mouth dropped open.

"I . . . I've got to go." Without saying anything else, Alicia rose and hurried back toward the studio set.

Joy watched her go, unsure of what had just happened. She thought over her words. *"Jesus wanted me to show you His heart . . . He has never left your side, and He will never walk away."* She expected that to bring hope to her friend, not fear.

Lord, I don't know what's going on, but You do. Be with Alicia now. I've told her about Your love, but only You can show it to her. Show her in a way that she'll know it's from You.

Joy blew out a breath and imagined it carrying her prayer up to heaven like dandelion fluffs on the wind. She and Alicia had different lives, but there was one thing she knew. Alicia needed God just as much as she did.

Maybe Elizabeth was right — maybe she'd never see the influence she made on this side of heaven. But then again, maybe she would. Maybe God would grant her a glimpse of what He could do in the lives of those who dared to step out and seek God. It was what she hoped for most now. He'd shown up in her life, and He'd show up in Alicia's — if she dared to let Him.

Country Brunch for 20

18 slices white bread
1 pound bulk sausage
1 small onion, chopped
1 pound smoky link sausage
1 dozen eggs
1 quart milk
1 teaspoon salt
1/2 teaspoon black pepper
1 pound shredded cheddar cheese
3 cups crushed cornflakes
1/2 cup butter, melted

Cut bread slices in half. Arrange half the bread in bottom of well-greased, large casserole dish or roaster pan. In a skillet, fry bulk sausage with chopped onion until browned. Drain and sprinkle half of the bulk sausage crumbles over bread. Layer half the smoky links on top. Repeat layers of bread, sausage, and links. Beat eggs and milk together; add salt and pepper. Pour over layers. Top with shredded cheese. Cover and refrigerate overnight. Remove from refrigerator 30 minutes before baking. Combine melted butter with corn flakes and sprinkle over casserole. Cover tightly with foil and bake at 325 degrees for 1 hour. Makes 20 servings.

THIRTY-FOUR

People are lonely because they build
walls instead of bridges.

AMISH PROVERB

As the evening slipped into night, Alicia sat on her balcony overlooking the ocean. She'd eaten leftover Amish Apple Salad the ladies had brought to the lot. The salad was sweet and simple, just like her friend Joy. And as Alicia sat she couldn't help but consider Joy's words, her actions. Joy had come onto the set like a timid little mouse, and over the days and weeks she'd spoken up. She'd sacrificed her own hopes of happiness to stay by Alicia's side. No one had ever done that for Alicia before. It overwhelmed her, and not completely in a good way.

She knew Joy had meant to comfort her, but it brought no comfort knowing that Jesus had always been by her side. In the general sense, she knew God was all around her, and that — like Santa — He knew who was naughty and nice. But the idea of Him walking with her, being with her through *everything* . . . a shiver ran down her spine.

That meant He'd been there when she was an eighteen-year-old girl, going to the right parties to be noticed, sleeping with the influential men in Hollywood, and hoping for special favors. He was there when she clung to the toilet, causing herself to throw up her food so she'd be the right size on camera. He'd been there when she drank more and more through the years, trying to numb the pain of not being enough, and later the pain of sacrificing her child for her own fame.

And that's what haunted her the most, the idea that Jesus was by her side as she chose to end her child's life. Her boyfriend at the time, her manager, and her friends told her it was the only way. And when she'd gotten the call that she'd earned the role of a lifetime, she knew what she had to do. Near the time her child would have been born, she was filming at Universal Studios on a back lot. *Entertainment Tonight* had reported her big break as a rags-to-riches story, but even as she showed up in the pages of *People* and *USA Today,* she felt more rags than riches. What was Jesus thinking as she'd lain there, trying to ignore the procedure and pretend it wasn't happening? He'd hated her, she was sure. In her mind's eye she tried to picture Him. But instead of seeing a face of anger, an image of His tears came to mind.

Tears?

I wept because I wanted to give you what you were searching for. You thought you were looking for money and fame, but I knew the only thing that would fill that hole in your heart was Me.

The words came as a gentle whisper to her soul. Jesus was there, but He wasn't angry as she first thought. He was hurting. He hurt with her because He knew that only He could provide what she wanted most.

The tears came then, heavy and thick. They filled her eyes and the sobs stuck in her throat. She sank from the chair onto the concrete of the balcony, now covered with debris from last week's storm. The bits of leaves and branches dug into the soft skin of her knees. Her soul felt as if it were ripping apart too, and it was almost too much to bear. Because to realize that Jesus was there was to acknowledge what she had really done. Whom she'd really been writing the journal for.

Years ago her psychologist had told her to

395

write a journal to herself — as if she were her best friend. He said it was a way to record her life and thoughts and to view herself in a more positive light. But now she knew differently. This whole time she'd been writing to her son, trying to share the life she'd robbed from him.

Her son. All along she had a feeling it was a boy, but could she really trust that? The tears came afresh.

In her physical being, she could never share a sunset, the ocean breeze, or the taste of a freshly baked cinnamon roll with him because he was gone, ripped from her body by her own choice. A mother's job was to care and protect, but she'd done just the opposite. She'd sacrificed her child for her own fame. And when the realization of that hit her, she'd masked the ache with alcohol, with another role, another party, another shopping spree. If only she could go back to that young woman who'd been seeking so hard to be appreciated and loved.

In her mind's eye, Alicia saw Jesus there too. She saw Him sitting beside her on the porch step, shivering in the cold as her mom lay passed out on the couch inside. She saw Him standing next to her and protecting her heart from the bully's vicious words that she'd never amount to anything. He was there as she waited by the phone for an invitation to the dance, and as she made a resolve to become so famous that they'd all be trying to call her and to get on her good side.

But if Jesus had been there the whole time, then she hadn't needed any of that, had she?

If Jesus had loved her even then, she'd already had what she wanted most — to be known and loved — even before she stepped into Hollywood. If Jesus was real and had always been with her, as Joy had claimed, then she'd been rejoiced over and accepted even before she'd uttered her first word.

"What am I supposed to do with this now, now that I know? What?" The wind off the ocean picked up her words. The cool ocean breeze swirled them, carrying them into its grasp.

Tell them. The wind whipped back to her, brushing her hair across her forehead, as if a gentle hand was stroking it. *Tell them what I have done for you. Tell them how I've always been there, and I will always be.*

"But if I tell them about You, I'll have to tell them about *me,*" she whispered. "Who I was and what I've done. Then they will know . . . everything."

When you reveal your pain, you'll also

397

reveal Me as the healer. As you are healed, you'll be able to offer the same to others. Give as Joy gave to you — completely, selflessly. Give as I have given to you . . . with My life.

Even though these thoughts were in her mind, she knew they were from God. She would never speak such things to herself — require that of herself.

"Now? Do You want me to tell everyone *now*? Spill it all out? Or when? When will I have to tell?"

When your heart is healed, then you will speak out of humility, out of thankfulness. Not today. Not even tomorrow. Don't worry about the telling. Only put yourself into My arms and discover My love. The rest will come in time. Your true story will spill from a healed and tender heart.

Alicia breathed a heavy sigh of relief. She didn't need to head to the nearest television studio and talk about all God had done for her. She simply needed to love Jesus and focus on how Jesus was changing her, and the rest would come in time.

Waiting on Jesus was the message God had for her. And deep down she had a feeling it was a message God had for Joy too. Their Lord gave with an everlasting love, yet He didn't rush His gifts.

Would Joy ever trust that God would give

her the desires of her heart too? For the first time Alicia felt the urge to pray for her friend. It was a strange feeling to think her prayers would make a difference. She simply had to believe and trust that God would give Joy the rest of what He had for her — in His perfect time.

Amish Apple Salad

1 egg, beaten
1 tablespoon all-purpose flour
1/2 cup sugar
1/2 cup water
4 apples, peeled, cored, and diced
8 ounces whipped topping

In a small saucepan, cook beaten egg, flour, sugar, and water until thick. Remove from heat. Stir in apples. Add whipped topping. Pour into serving bowl. Makes 6 servings.

THIRTY-FIVE

We make a living by what we get,
a life by what we give.
AMISH PROVERB

When Joy glanced up, his back was to her, but she still recognized the tall, light-haired man with the broad shoulders. Her heart leapt. She considered turning and leaving the restaurant, but *Dat* had specifically asked for noodles from Yoder's for his dinner. He'd been unable to eat much lately, and that he was requesting something was a good thing. Besides, Matthew would be seated before she even got close, and she could pretend she'd never seen him. *If only my aching heart would let me forget.*

He leaned forward and said something to an older woman, but as he did, Joy realized it wasn't Matthew's voice. She furrowed her brow. It didn't make sense. She took a step forward to get a better look. Her arm bumped against a rack of cooking books, and a copy of *Simply Delicious Amish Cooking* tumbled to the floor. She bent to pick it up and then righted herself. Peering up, she looked directly into the man's face. It was Matthew's face . . . but not exactly. The man's eyes were brown, and they held a hint of humor — not the deep ache in Matthew's gaze the last few times she'd seen him. He was also wearing a beard.

How? Who?

The book slipped from her hand again, and the man bent to retrieve it.

"Here, Joy, let me get that for you."

She straightened and let him pick it up. She crossed her arms over her chest. "You know my name? I'm sorry, I don't know yours."

"William Slagel, but call me Will. I'm Matthew's brother." A smile broke out on his handsome face. "I'm sorry I didn't introduce myself. I'd recognize you anywhere from the way my brother described you." He placed a hand to his chest. "Like a Swiss maiden on an alpine hillside with creamy smooth skin, honey-brown hair, and eyes the color of topaz."

Laughter burst from Joy's lips. "He said that?"

"Not in those words, but something to

that effect. I have to say I'm glad we had a chance to meet."

She shuffled slightly and touched the hair at the nape of her neck. "You are? It seems you're the only one."

A waitress motioned to Will. "Your table is ready."

Instead of following her, Will raised a hand, motioning to the next people in line. "Go ahead and seat them. I'm waiting for my wife."

The waitress nodded and moved to the couple behind him.

"So are things going well, over at the set?"

She tilted her head and eyed him, unsure how to respond. Was he teasing her, mocking her, trying to get more information to pass on to his family? But as she looked into his gaze there was only genuine interest.

"The television show is fine. It's stereotypical, though they have *gut* intentions. But my friends . . ." She bit her lip.

He lifted one eyebrow and waited.

"I see a difference in the people I work with. I'm getting a lot of questions about God." Surprisingly, emotion built in her throat. "They are hurting people in need of Him." Joy shrugged. "I can honestly say I'm glad to be there."

He nodded, and then his eyes lifted, moving to the door. A woman entered, and she moved toward them. She was shorter than Joy with a round face and large brown eyes. She wasn't beautiful, but there was a humored expression on her face that made Joy want to know her better, as if she had a good joke right at the tip of her tongue that she couldn't wait to spill.

She stepped closer to her husband and touched his sleeve. "Sorry it took me so long, but Micah wanted to go to the park with your *mem,* and I had to find his shoes." She chuckled. "I finally found them in your *mem*'s breadbox on the counter. You can imagine how well that went over."

Will smiled and shook his head, and then he introduced Joy.

"Oh, Joy — *ja.*" She clasped her hands together. "I was hoping to meet you. I'm Naomi." She leaned forward and took Joy's hand, holding it in hers. "I can't believe another woman is crazy enough to want to be part of this family. You have to stay on your toes with these brothers. And wait until you meet their sisters." She shook her head.

"I'm so sorry, you must not understand. I won't be joining the family. There are . . . problems." She sighed. "I *am* the problem."

Instead of releasing Joy's hand, Naomi squeezed harder. "I know it seems that way, but I also know Matthew has been sulking around the house since we've arrived for the season. I've known him since he was a child, and I know —"

The waitress interrupted. "Your table is ready now. If you'll please come with me . . ."

At the same moment a group of construction workers entered, and the woman's words were lost in the commotion. She offered Joy one last smile before she followed her husband to the table.

"What do you know?" Joy wanted to call after her. Confusion muddled her mind. She believed she'd lost all hope of being loved by Matthew from the moment she'd accepted the job with the TV show. But Naomi's kind words hinted at something different. Was there truly a chance to believe? To hope? Was it possible that she hadn't lost Matthew for good?

Matthew stepped through sawdust that was cleaner than snow and bent down to pick up a curling, crinkled shaving. It was just slightly darker than Joy's hair. His heart ached at the memory of soft curls that slipped from her *kapp*.

He couldn't believe it was only a couple of weeks until Christmas. Before Joy started working with the television people, he'd planned on asking her to marry him on Christmas Day. Joy didn't know it, but it was a tradition in his family. His grandfather had asked his grandmother to marry him on Christmas. And his *dat* had done the same with his *mem.* But now everything had changed.

He'd found his way into the garage again, pretending that he was going to work on a Christmas present. The truth was he had everyone's presents made weeks ago. Lately, he'd been making recipe boxes. He'd also started work on a dining room table. Something inside told him that he had no use of it. He wouldn't be getting married anytime soon, wouldn't have a home to put it in, yet each time he worked on it he couldn't help but picture Joy sitting there — in the mornings reading her Bible, across from him sharing supper, holding a baby on her lap, coloring a picture with a chubby hand in hers.

Stop it. Just stop it.

The Joy he had in his mind was simply a figment of his imagination. He believed her to be like that when they first started courting, but he was wrong. The Joy in his mind wouldn't work alongside television producers who were exploiting the Amish. She wouldn't be an actress, allowing herself to be captured on film, all for the sake of outsiders' profit and fame.

Matthew grabbed a plank and tilted it to test the straightness with his eyes. He then ran the soft pad of his hand down its length, appreciating its smooth warmth. He knew the type of table he wanted to make. It was a simple design that had been well thought out and established centuries before his birth. A table to last a generation. Many generations.

Just as Matthew got all the planks lined up for a tabletop, the door to the kitchen opened. His sister-in-law, Naomi, poked her head out. "Matthew, you don't mind if Micah watches you for a little bit do you? He loves watching Will doing projects, and he says he wants to spend time with Uncle Matthew." She grinned her round-faced grin.

"Uh, it's really not a place for a little one —"

Micah's shouts of excitement blocked out Matthew's words as the three-year-old dashed into the workshop.

With a quick *"Danke,"* Naomi turned her attention to the commotion her other two children were making inside and shut the door. With the heavy rain outside, the boys

407

had been full of energy with no place to get it out.

Micah darted toward his workbench, and tension tightened Matthew's neck. A small hand reached for a long chisel. Matthew sucked in a breath.

"Hey now." Matthew rushed over. "Those aren't toys. *Ne* touching those."

The boy pulled back his hand, and he gazed up at Matthew with large, brown eyes. Then he looked back at the row of tools. Their lure drew him in.

"*Ne,* Micah. Those aren't safe." Matthew squatted down so they were eye level. He placed a hand on Micah's shoulder. "I'm sorry, buddy. I know these look fun, but they are expensive tools."

Micah tucked his hands behind him and clasped them together. "E'pensive. *Ne* touch!"

Matthew chuckled. Obviously Micah had heard that word before. "*Ja,* expensive, and I'm sure your *dat* wouldn't want to have to replace them."

Micah's eyes wandered over the workbench, and even though he nodded, Matthew wondered if the boy truly understood.

"I find something." Micah dashed to the other side of the shop where Matthew's woodpile was. But instead of moving toward the scrap pile, Micah hurried to the stack of pricey soft wood Matthew had been saving for carving projects. The young boy picked up two pieces of basswood and proceeded to pound them together. Matthew cringed and rushed over.

He knelt next to little Micah again. "Hey, buddy, I can find you some two-by-four blocks to pound, but this wood is soft stuff. You must not bang it around."

Matthew took the blocks from his nephew's hands. "You must treat it with tenderness."

"Just like a woman's heart." The voice came from behind him. It was Will. His older brother crossed his arms over his chest and lifted one eyebrow, waiting for a response. Matthew hadn't even heard him come in. A tremor moved through his shoulders and tightened his neck. Will had been home for a week, and Matthew had been avoiding him. Months ago, when Will came down for a short visit, all Matthew had talked about was Joy. Even before he approached Joy's father for permission to court her, Matthew had poured out his feelings, sharing how devout and beautiful she was. Now Matthew felt like a fool. She wasn't the woman he'd believed her to be, and everyone in town now knew how wrong his choice had been.

Will walked over, sat Micah on the ground, and dropped a pile of scrap blocks in front of him. The boy immediately picked some up and started stacking.

Matthew took in a deep breath. He could tell from the look on Will's face that he wanted to talk, and from the comment about a woman's heart he easily guessed what the topic of conversation would be.

"Naomi and I ran into someone yesterday."

"Let me guess — Joy."

"I heard so much about her from you that I could have picked her out anywhere. She's a really sweet girl, and even though she didn't say much about what the conflict is, I can tell she really cares about you and misses you."

Matthew searched his brother's eyes. "She said that?"

"*Ne,* but the misery in her eyes was pitiful, just pitiful. Made me tear up myself, and I'm not much of a softy. She got an order to go, and our eyes met one last time before she left Yoder's."

"Did she say anything?" Why did hope glimmer in Matthew's heart? What did he want her to say? To do? Wasn't it too late?

"It was too noisy in there, but as she

walked out with her order she waved. Outside, she rushed away and headed down the sidewalk, hunched over as if the world around her had ended."

My world as I knew it, as I wanted it, has ended. The thought came unbidden, and Matthew quickly pushed it away. Will's words were like sandpaper rubbing against his heart. "I'm sorry she's hurting. I really am, but if she hurts so much, why is she still keeping that job with the television show?"

"You don't know?"

"She said it was for her *dat*'s medical bills, and I understand that. But the church took up a collection too. That's how things are supposed to work. I'm sure if she just came to *Dat* and repented —"

"Repented?" Will scoffed. "Do you think she's sinning?"

"Does it matter what I think? What matters are the rules of the community. If everyone did their own thing there would be *ne* order, *ne* sustainability." Matthew had heard those words from his father a hundred times if he'd heard them once, and now he found himself repeating them. "Besides, nothing *gut* can come from spending so much time with *Englischers.* Joy is there because she wants to be there. She's decided they're more important than the *gut* of the community. That television show is more important to her than . . ."

He didn't need to say the rest. His brother no doubt saw the pain all over his face. Heat rose up his neck, and a noose of disgrace tightened around his throat. He'd waited all this time to choose a bride, and he'd chosen poorly. How could he ever trust his own decisions again?

"That's what bothers you most, isn't it? Not that she made a bad choice, but how it makes you look."

"Of course." Matthew squared his shoulders and looked away. "We were courting. She knew how I felt. And still she made the decision she did."

"A wrong decision, so you think."

"A wrong decision, *ja*. It's what most people think."

Tired of the blocks, Micah got up and scurried into the house. Matthew watched him go and wished for a moment he could remember what the carefree life of a child felt like.

He bent down and picked up the blocks, tossing them back into his scrap bin. "Is Micah always so busy? He reminds me of us as boys."

Instead of answering, Will moved to an

old rocking chair that was in desperate need of a new coat of paint and sat down.

"You know *Dat* and *Mem* didn't completely approve of Naomi before we got married. She was the youngest of her family and was spoiled in every way. She wasn't that great of a cook. She sometimes lost her temper a little too easily. She wasn't the type of young woman *Mem* had hoped for her oldest son."

Matthew had been a young teenager when his older brother had gotten married. He furrowed his brow, trying to remember them courting, but only a few images came to mind. "So what happened?"

"I told them I loved her and we were getting married. I pointed out her strong points. She loved God with her whole heart. She was kind and generous. She paid attention to hurting people and spent time listening to them. To her that meant more than making a nice meal and showing off her skills. That meant a lot to me too."

"*Ja,* but the things you mentioned are minor. Joy has alienated the whole community. I can count on one hand the people who don't think she's made a horrible mistake."

"But what do you think?"

"I understand her point. She's a caring,

compassionate person. But . . ." But what did he think? Had he really ever decided for himself?

They waited in silence for a while, and then Will stood and moved around the workshop, examining the tools, the wood, as if waiting for Matthew to continue. The thing was, Matthew didn't know what to say. What to do.

"She cares about people," Matthew finally said. "She cares more about that than she does of what people think of her."

"So do you really want to let her go?"

"Of course not."

"Then what are you afraid of?"

"What do you mean?"

"Something is holding you back. Is it our parents' opinion? Or is it something more?"

Matthew looked to his brother, unsure of how to answer. There was fear, but it all centered on his parents' disapproval, didn't it?

Then, almost afraid to think harder and discover the true answer, Matthew cleared his throat.

Will turned to him. *"Ja?"*

"So when it came to *Dat* and *Mem,* what did you say to make them change their mind about Naomi?"

"I didn't say much. Instead I asked what

things were like when they first got married. They told a few funny stories about *Mem*'s quick temper and about how *Dat* used to hide in the barn and take an extra-long time to do his chores. Both admitted that they grew up and changed over the years. Even after *Dat* became a minister, many people in the community didn't think he was up to the job.

"I think the best thing you can do is remind them marriage is often what God uses to help us grow in strength and character. Marriage isn't finding someone who seems perfect and expecting them to do everything right. It's finding someone you can grow up with. After all, you surely fall short in some areas of your life too."

Matthew ran his hand down his jaw. "Maybe you believe Joy was right — her standing up for what she truly believed, instead of what other people may think. And like always, you think you're right."

"You said it. Not me."

Matthew thought about that for a moment. Was Will right? Joy had taken the job for the money, for her father, but she stayed for a different reason . . . because she met people who needed to know God's love. He sighed. A woman like that might be frustrating to live with at times, but she'd be a good mother, a good example of love and compassion. A good example of sacrifice. She'd given up so much — not for herself, but for others.

"What if it's too late? What if I go to her and she won't forgive me?"

"I don't think that's the right question. The right question is, what if you don't go to her? What then? What are you throwing away?" Will sighed. "Joy is a beautiful young woman, and you told me she loves God, which is even more important. I guarantee that in a couple of months there will be something else happening in this community that everyone will get riled up about. Things like this tend to lose importance over time. But if you don't go to her . . ."

"I could lose her forever." Matthew's words were no more than a whisper.

"Could you live with yourself if that happened?"

"What do you think?" Matthew sighed and then picked up the last block his nephew had dropped. "It would be so much easier if I had gotten this right the first time."

Will chuckled. "*Ja,* but when you do get married, you'll be saying sorry more than you ever thought. It's a *gut* lesson to humble yourself, Matthew. A *gut* lesson."

THIRTY-SIX

Blessed is the person who is too busy to
worry in the daytime and too sleepy to
worry at night.

AMISH PROVERB

Matthew strode down toward Phillippi
Creek and made his way to the boat ramp.
He needed quiet — something his house
didn't have right now with the extra family
members and kids. He needed fresh air and
the ability to think. To pray.

After talking to Will, he wanted to go to
Joy. He wanted to ask her forgiveness. He
wanted to tell his parents she was the one
he chose, but something still held him back.
Deep down he knew his parents' disapproval
wasn't the whole reason. But what was his
real fear?

He tossed rocks into Phillippi Creek, and
an image of his aunt and uncle came into
his mind. He must have been only nine or

ten years old when he attended their wedding. Although Matthew had attended many weddings before, this was the first time he'd really paid attention. As he listened to the minister's sermon about loving a spouse for a lifetime, Matthew knew he wanted that. Who wouldn't?

He'd watched them during the reception. The way they talked and laughed and looked at each other with loving glances. Seeing their love had made him feel warm inside.

His aunt and uncle moved to an Amish community in Montana after their wedding. When he saw them again ten years later, they weren't the happy young couple he remembered. They had five children at the time, and although their family had expanded, their hearts had closed up. They interacted with each other but didn't talk. When they looked at each other, it was with more disdain than love. He'd told himself that his uncle just hadn't found the right woman. If he'd chosen wiser, things would have been better. And that's why Matthew had waited so long and looked so hard. Had he just used his parents' disapproval as an excuse?

The flapping of wings startled Matthew, and he looked downstream and spotted a white ibis. It had long, pink legs like a flamingo, but its feathers were pure white. The feathers on its tail were tipped in black as if they had been dipped in ink. A large pink beak curved from his face.

The bird walked along the shoreline, probing the moist mud for insects, and Matthew still had a hard time believing he lived in a place where birds like this were common. Not that he wanted to live here forever. No, he knew where he wanted to end up, and who he wanted to end up with. *Joy.*

He knew deep down that no one was perfect and no guarantee for a happy marriage existed. Opening himself up to another for love also meant opening himself up for rejection, pain. He had to face the facts. He could end up in a loveless marriage just like his uncle did. Yet . . . *what if I don't go to her?* Will's question from earlier came to mind. *What will I lose? What will I give up if I don't risk it?*

Wasn't it better to love a little and hurt a little than to love a lot and hurt a lot? His defenses told him so. Then again, running from possible rejection meant running from love too. As much as he tried to deny it, he did miss Joy. He did *love* Joy, but in the end, would fear win? At the moment he still wasn't sure.

The shuffleboards were strangely bare as Matthew walked past Pinecraft Park. Instead a group of men was circled around Amish Henry, who was reading out loud from a newspaper.

There must be some exciting news in the Budget *today,* Matthew thought, but when he looked closer it wasn't the *Budget* they were reading, but the *Sarasota-Herald Tribune.*

The *Tribune?* What type of story could be causing such a stir?

It took five minutes to walk to the post office and a few coins before Matthew had a paper in his hands. Sure enough, there was a headline right on the front page. He strode over to Big Olaf's and found a seat on one of the picnic benches outside.

Actress Rekindles Love on Sarasota Set

Alicia Lampard, best known for her Grammy-nominated performance in *The Lockup,* has found herself in the role of a lifetime. Lampard, who had been expected to divorce her producer-husband Rowan Grant after their five-year marriage fell into shambles last year, says divorce is no longer on the table. The sultry actress has been spotted in her husband's arms on Siesta Key Beach as of late. So what has brought about the change?

"I've found love in the most unexpected place. I'm playing an Amish woman for this new series. The role is different from anything I've done before. To play a peaceful person I've had to discover peace. I've had to look into myself and see how broken I was, and then I had to look to the one place where I could find wholeness, and that's God."

Lampard credits her spiritual awakening to the friendship of an Amish woman named Joy. "She answered every one of my questions — not that she has all the answers, but she was there for me and she listened. She did her best."

The Daybreak is a new series being filmed in Sarasota in a small community the locals call Pinecraft. Alicia's character's journey mirrors her own. "Sadie is a young Amish woman whose young husband died, and she feels trapped in a community that pushes for marriage and children. I accepted the role for a change of pace, but I know now that this part was an important part in my own life's plot. I don't know where I'd be if I hadn't opened up to a new friend who pointed me to God."

The Daybreak will air in the spring, and Lampard hopes viewers will tune in. "In the midst of our busy lives each of us needs to be reminded what hope and love are all about. Sometimes we don't realize what we're missing until we see it in someone else. My prayer is that others will see God in me, even as I struggle on this journey. Because it's truly the only love that will make a difference."

Matthew's heart swelled with both happiness and shame as he read those words. Shame as he realized he'd forced Joy to choose between him and working on the set. Pride that she'd chosen rightly.

Joy cared for him. He had no doubt about that. And yet she turned her back on that — on her chance for love — to do what she knew was right. To do what God had asked her to do. And lives were changed. This actress's life was changed, her husband's life was changed, and who knew how many other lives. He smiled at the thought of her strength, but then wondered what step to take next.

I have to go to her. I have to tell her . . . tell

her what? That he'd made a mistake? That he loved her? That he wanted to spend his life with her no matter what anyone thought? But even if he did, would she forgive him? Could she trust him? Matthew hoped she could.

He rose, left the paper on the table, and strode away. He guessed Joy was still at the set in the old warehouse. His heartbeat quickened just at the thought of seeing her, but he knew now wasn't the time to go to her. Not yet. His heart also ached when he realized the hurt he'd caused. He'd been trying to stick by the rules and gain the approval of others, and all it had caused was pain. His heartache, but mostly hers.

Before he went to Joy, Matthew needed to look closer at himself. He needed to turn to God in repentance. He needed time to consider how he could follow God better and be concerned about the rules of the community less, especially since his father was the bishop. He'd show his dad this story, and maybe it would be something for *Dat* to think about and pray about too. When *Dat* was a young bishop he hadn't gotten everything right, but he was teachable. Matthew just hoped it was still so.

Matthew also hoped she'd give him a second chance. He hoped he'd have months

— years — to show her how wrong he'd been, by loving her well.

THIRTY-SEVEN

No joy is complete unless it is shared.
AMISH PROVERB

Joy walked through the kitchen door and paused in her tracks. A woman stood in the middle of the kitchen, and strands of reddish blonde hair had slipped from the back of her *kapp.*

"Hope!"

Her sister turned, and Hope wore an expression of pure joy on her face. Joy rushed forward and gave her a hug.

"Can you believe it, Joy? Only two days until my wedding."

"And my wedding too," Lovina called, coming from the living room.

"I'm just glad you made it," Joy said, turning to Hope.

Hope shrugged. "We didn't expect Emma to come down with the chicken pox. We had to wait until she was well enough to travel."

"There are *ne* worries." *Mem,* Faith, and Grace walked out from the back room. "We have everything all ready. Having five daughters, one has to be ready for anything, *ja?*"

Joy looked from face to face, taking in the sight of them all together. "It's been a *gut* month for love. Did you read about Alicia and Rowan?"

"Ja." Grace folded her arms over her chest. "I wish you would have told me sooner. It's *ne* fun to read that type of exciting news in the paper."

Joy shrugged. "In Rowan's words, he looked up one day and saw that the changes in Alicia were real. And since then they've been inseparable. Even though I haven't seen it, one magazine captured a photo of them snuggling on the beach, like husband and wife should."

"I hope I find an inseparable love someday." Grace sighed. "But until then I'm happy to be attending a beautiful wedding, in a beautiful garden, with my beautiful sisters."

Two blue dresses were laid out on *Mem*'s bed. Hope's was a light blue, the color of the Florida sky. Lovina's was a darker, purplish blue. Joy sighed and fingered the cloth of her oldest sister's wedding dress.

She had thought she'd have a day like this soon, but now she knew that wasn't to be. She couldn't imagine loving anyone but Matthew Slagel, and because of her decisions she had no opportunity to be loved back.

Behind her someone cleared her throat. She looked up in surprise and turned. *Mem* stood there, and compassion filled her gaze.

"It'll be a beautiful day," *Mem* said softly. "*Danke,* Joy, for being so happy for your sisters despite your own pain."

Joy swallowed her emotions. She quickly turned her face to the bedroom window and watched the bird chattering on the tree branch, hoping *Mem* didn't see her tears.

Joy took one glance in the mirror before joining her sisters on the far side of the pie shop. Hope and Lovina both sat in folding chairs just inside the door, wearing their blue dresses, waiting for everyone to be seated outside so the wedding could begin.

If it wasn't for their matching smiles it would be hard to tell they were sisters — Lovina with her short, thinner frame and dark hair, and Hope, who was much taller with reddish blonde hair and a fuller face.

Hope pinched her cheeks to give herself more color. "Can you believe it? My wedding day!"

"*Our* wedding day." Lovina chuckled. "And *Mem* and *Dat* will have two fewer daughters."

"I'd like to think we're gaining sons rather than losing daughters." *Mem*'s sniffle sounded behind them. "Both Noah and Jonas are welcome additions to our family. Little Emma too." *Mem* sighed. "Just think, today I'm not only gaining two sons-in-law, but an adorable eight-year-old granddaughter!"

Two car doors slamming shut sounded, one after another. Hope's eyes widened. She winced. "Who's that? Did someone invite *Englischers*?"

"It's Rowan and Alicia." Lovina glanced at Hope and straightened in her seat. "I told Joy she could invite them."

"You told Joy?" Hope's mouth dropped open slightly. "But it's my wedding too."

Lovina jutted out her chin. "Oh, they're nice people. The more the merrier is what *Mem* always says."

The frown on Hope's face didn't fade. "They aren't going to film it, are they?" Hope turned to face Joy.

"Of course not." The words shot out of Joy's mouth, but then she bit down slightly on her lower lip. "I . . . I don't see why they would."

"Can you please check, Joy?" It was *Mem*'s voice, tight, concerned. "You know how some people view those cameras. I'd like for this to be a joyful day for your sisters."

"*Ja,* of course."

Rows of folding chairs had been set up in the garden behind Me, Myself and Pie. Families filed in together. Couples mingled with their neighbors and friends. Nearly everyone wore either Amish or Mennonite dress, which made finding Joy's friends easy.

She saw them seated in the last row of chairs, nearest the building. While everyone else chatted with each other, they sat still and straight. Alicia fanned herself with her hand, even though the weather wasn't hot. As good of an actress as she was, she was doing a poor job hiding her nerves.

"I'm so glad you've come." Joy eyed the scene. She saw Alicia's purse and a white and glittery gift bag that read For Your Wedding on the side. There wasn't a camera in sight.

Alicia stood and offered Joy a quick hug. "I'm so glad to see you." She tugged on her red, flowery dress with short sleeves. It hung below her knees, but the shoulders had large cutouts, showing most of her arms and her shoulders.

"I tried my best, but I don't fit in at all."

"And she bought pot holders," Rowan commented. "A dozen of them for each bride. Who buys pot holders for a gift?" Even though he teased, Rowan gazed at Alicia with adoration, and Joy's heart swelled.

"But they do love to cook, don't they, Joy?" Alicia asked, eyes wide.

"Yes, especially Lovina."

"Well, we won't keep you." Alicia patted her hand. "I'm sure you have duties."

"Yes, I'm the sister whose job it is to greet the guests." Joy tried smiling. "But I shouldn't have to worry too much. My father seems to think today everyone will forget how I've acted and where I've been working — just for the day, of course."

"Or rather used to work," Rowan said. "It's hard to believe yesterday was our last day on the set — just in time to head back to our home for Christmas." Her friend's face glowed as he said those words. "It'll be especially meaningful to celebrate Christ's birth with my wife this year."

A few minutes later, Joy stood at the corner of the building, welcoming guests. The chairs were filling quickly. Everyone from Pinecraft had shown up for this special event.

Joy smiled at an older Amish couple, and then the smile froze on her face. Behind them stood Matthew, head and shoulders above them, looking at her. She blinked, and a small gasp escaped her lips. It was almost like a dream seeing him there. Seeing the tenderness in his eyes. He stepped to her.

"It's a beautiful day, isn't it?" He slipped off his hat and brushed his hand through his hair.

"*Ja.* We couldn't have asked for better weather."

He leaned toward her, and for a moment she thought he was going to kiss her cheek. She froze.

"Can we talk later, at the reception?"

"*Ja.* Of course." Hope buoyed in her heart but then sank again when his parents made their way toward them. Matthew pulled back quickly and joined the other guests being seated.

It's never going to happen. Their opinion of me will always win.

As the bishop moved to the front garden area, Joy cleared her throat and clutched the single white rose in her hand closer to her chest.

"Nervous?" a man's voice spoke right behind her. Her heart leapt. She turned expecting to see Matthew, but it was his older brother, Will, who stood there.

"*Ne.* Happy, that's all."

"That's a *gut* response." Will sighed. "I just wish it were the truth. For an actress you don't hide your feelings well, but don't worry, Joy. I have a feeling this story will turn out well in the end." Then, with his small son tucked against his chest, he turned and found a seat in the back.

The wedding was beautiful. Both of her sisters made beautiful brides, and Joy was pleased that for the most part everyone seemed to accept her. She'd been afraid she'd feel ostracized at her own sisters' wedding.

More than once at the reception Matthew had asked to talk, but as soon as they tried to find a quiet place she'd get called away.

As the brides and grooms gathered for dinner, Joy made a point to go to Matthew and apologize once again. "I'm so sorry. It's such a busy day."

"Of course, Joy. I understand." He offered her a soft smile, but there was more in his eyes. "Don't worry. We can talk over the next couple of days. Maybe on Christmas?"

"*Ja,* I'd like that."

Near the end of the evening, Joy found herself sitting next to Elizabeth. The older woman's smile seemed as large as Florida itself, and her eyes were wide, full of life and full of hope. She seemed to be enjoying herself, watching all the families and couples, and then — seemingly out of nowhere — Elizabeth turned to Joy with some sage advice.

"The most important thing about marriage is forgiveness," she stated plainly. "It's the difference between having a poor marriage and a great one."

Joy smiled and looked to the table where both of her sisters sat, being served their dinner. "*Ja,* I'll have to tell my sisters that."

"Oh *ne.*" Elizabeth pointed her small, frail finger Joy's direction. "My advice isn't for them. It's for you."

Joy lifted the white rose to her nose and breathed it in. It had been in her hand all day and was starting to wilt, but the fragrance was still just as beautiful. "All right then. I'll tuck that in my mind for a later time."

"And tuck this away too," Elizabeth said with a smile. "The best time to practice forgiving is before one says *I do.*"

Joy nodded, wondering if the older woman

had forgotten that she and Matthew were no longer together. Either that or Elizabeth's spirit sensed something Joy didn't. It was almost too much to hope for.

THIRTY-EIGHT

*Sometimes we must patiently endure
before inheriting a promised blessing.*
AMISH PROVERB

The day after the wedding, Joy's family gathered around the dinner table, enjoying leftovers from the wedding. Tomorrow was Christmas, and like usual it would be a quiet and reverent time with only a few simple decorations that they'd set out in the morning. The weather was still warm, and snow was a distant reality, but they would have fun watching her new niece Emma opening the few presents they'd gotten her.

All day as Joy had helped to clean up the garden, she had told herself not to get her hopes up. The fact that Matthew wanted to talk to her didn't necessarily mean anything. For all she knew, he could be heading up to Indiana to his farm. And then what? Where would that leave her?

Her father scraped up the last of the food on his plate. Then there was a knock at the back door.

"Joy? Can you get that?" *Dat* asked.

She looked around the table. All eyes were on her. "Can't Grace get it?" Her eyes welled up with tears. She didn't know why she was crying. Perhaps because both hope and fear battled for first place inside her.

"Sweetheart, I think it's for you," *Mem* stated plainly.

Joy stood, not knowing what to do. She took one step to the door and then paused. "I . . . I really don't want to talk to anyone now." Still, she opened the door, urging her knees to hold her up.

Matthew stood there with his arms crossed over his chest. He was looking the other direction, toward the road, as if trying to decide whether he wanted to stay or go.

Joy went outside, closing the door and then the screen door silently. The moon and stars were bright overhead. Crickets chirped a lonely song. Matthew stood with his back to her, clearly deep in thought. Her chest swelled with emotion as she imagined walking up behind him, slipping her hands around his waist, and pulling herself close.

She took a step, and a loose board on the porch creaked. Matthew removed his hat and turned. Sweat ringed his shirt, and his damp hair clung to his forehead. He held his hat to his side with his left hand and extended his right hand to her.

She stood for a long moment and turned her attention to the sprinkler head dripping water onto the walkway and the small bird that pranced in the water as if wading through a pool. Her heartbeat quickened as she looked back to his hand. *This is good-bye.* Finally she turned her attention back to his gaze and waited for the words to come.

"Just because my *dat* is the bishop doesn't mean he's always right."

"Excuse me?" Joy's eyes widened. That wasn't what she expected to hear.

"Even some of the apostles messed up and got things wrong."

She opened her mouth and then closed it again, sure she wasn't hearing him right.

Pulling his hand back, Matthew took a small orange Bible from his jacket pocket and flipped through it, stopping near the back of the book.

"I've been praying about this a lot. I've been asking God to search my own heart and to show me the many ways I've messed up." He cleared his throat again. "I know God's book says we need to respect our

437

parents. I understand it's one of the Ten Commandments — "Honor thy father and thy mother." But does that mean we must do everything our parents say for the rest of their lives? Is there a difference between honoring them and obeying them? If our parents are ever in error with their thinking, is it all right to point it out?"

Joy clasped her hands in front of her and waited. She knew the questions weren't for her. Her throat tightened with emotion at seeing him, and she didn't dare hope that the words to come would bring him back to her. No, she couldn't hope that yet.

"I've been reading through Paul's letters, and last week I was reading the first chapter of Galatians. Paul had been traveling and preaching, telling people about Jesus, and after a while he decided to return to Jerusalem. Some of the apostles were still there, and after talking together they'd come to the conclusion that they all had the same ideas about Jesus. They were all sharing about Him — Peter and the others to Jews in Jerusalem, and Paul to the Gentiles in other countries. And Peter and his friends decided that what Paul was saying about Jesus was correct.

"The apostles gave Paul approval, yet Paul came across something that bothered him about Peter. Peter was fine eating with Gentiles, which God now allowed, but as soon as other Jewish Christians were around, he stopped and separated himself from them. This made Paul mad, and he confronted him. He basically told him he was wrong. This passage reminded me that even God's chosen men can be wrong at times. Even my *dat*."

Hope swelled in Joy's heart as Matthew closed the Bible and put it back into his pocket. "What are you saying?"

"I'm saying I think you did the right thing, helping with that show and all."

"What changed your mind?"

"Well, first I read an article in the *Sarasota-Herald Tribune* where Alicia talked about how you pointed her to God and what a difference He has made in her life. Later that day I was talking to my friend Abraham. I had to apologize to him for something I did — for the way I treated him — but that's another story. Anyway, he said he went to lunch at Yoder's one day and one of the cameramen from the show approached him, just to talk, I guess. This man — Steven was his name — said you made a huge impact on his life too."

"Me?"

"*Ja*. It seems he's been watching all the

Amish, you especially, and he was impressed by your tender and quiet love. He says he's working with Alicia a lot, and he can tell she's a different person now. She has a peace and love he's never seen before. And he's happy to see her and Rowan getting back together. Steven also told Abraham he's been separated from his wife for over a year, and she's been keeping his kids from him."

"Kids?" Joy gasped. "I didn't know he had kids."

"*Ja*. And now he and his wife are going to see if they can make things work. She's coming down to Florida so they can talk things through."

Tears filled Joy's eyes. She placed her hands over her mouth, holding in her soft cry.

Matthew reached over and touched her arm. His touch was tender. His caress was gentle. "I was so focused on sticking to the rules, Joy, that I missed the greatest rule of all — love God and love your neighbor. I know it wasn't easy for you to follow your compassion, but I want you to know I understand now. I really understand. I asked God to forgive me. I'm hoping you will too."

She wiped her tears with her fingertips and then wiped them on her apron. "Matthew, I . . . I don't know what to say."

"Say you still care for me even though I'm a fool."

She nodded. "There were times I was mad at myself for it, but, *ja,* I do. I really do."

"Gut." The word released with a heavy breath. "I was hoping you'd say that."

She rubbed her hands up and down her arms, trying to smooth away the goose bumps. The air was warm out, but even greater was the warmth growing inside her chest.

Matthew took a step toward her, and Joy considered suggesting they go somewhere else, somewhere more private to talk, but then she changed her mind. She didn't want to break the moment.

"Even when I wasn't around you, you didn't leave me," he said. "Your thoughts, your encouragement. I found myself in my workshop a lot."

"Why?"

"It made me feel close to you. I made forty-five recipe boxes in three weeks."

Joy's eyes widened, and laughter spilled out. "You did?"

"*Ja,* and a few gift shops in town are carrying them. They asked what else I can make."

"And will you take them to Lovina's pie

shop too?"

Matthew got a shy look on his face. "You don't think she'd be mad at me? I mean, all her competition is carrying them now."

"I think she'll understand. Lovina isn't one to hold a grudge, even if you did break her little sister's heart."

"I did?"

Joy looked down at her folded hands. "Well, we don't need to talk about that now. I'm just thankful we're talking again."

As Matthew stepped closer, he tipped his head down and gazed into her eyes. There was tenderness there, love. She released the breath she was holding. *He still loves me.*

"I was wrong, Joy. I listened to the wrong voices. I wish I could go back and make things right. I'm just hoping you'll give me a second chance. Will you forgive me?"

She bit her lip and turned away. She never expected to hear those words, and she wanted to savor the moment. Finally, she turned back to him, tears rimming her eyes. "Of course. But I have to know. You said you found yourself in your workshop because you thought of me there. Was that because I gave you the idea for the recipe boxes?"

"At first, but then it became more than that. As I worked with the wood, God used

442

it to speak to me."

"What do you mean?"

"Every piece of wood has a unique grain. Did you ever learn about tree circles in school?"

"*Ja,* of course."

"One day I was sanding down a tree circle to be made into a stool for my youngest nephew, Micah, and I started paying close attention to the rings. Some were so thin, I'd almost guess the tree was close to death — that was a hard year. Then other circles were thick, and I wondered how a tree could grow so much all at once. As I sanded, something inside told me that was like marriage."

"What do you mean?"

"I've seen many couples coming to talk to my *mem* and *dat.* I pretended I didn't know why they were there, but I could see it in their eyes — the pain, the questions, the weariness of it all. Times like that are like the thin rings of the tree. During the hard months and years, a tree doesn't appear to be growing. It might even look like it's dying. But then I've seen those couples stick it out and come to places of love and growth. That's one thing *gut* about being Amish. Divorce is unacceptable. I think *Englisch* couples give up too quickly, and they miss their best years to come."

She studied his face, his eyes, dreaming of spending every day for the rest of her life with him. "That's beautiful, Matthew."

"And I think that's part of our courtship too, Joy. I've been watching you from afar for a long time. I was impressed then, but I have to say I'm even more impressed now. You listened to God and did what was hard. And at first I didn't agree."

"Do you agree now?"

"I understand. Can we leave it at that?"

She offered him a shy grin. *"Ja."*

"I just hope I haven't hurt you too badly. If you forgive me, I'd like to continue to court you. I still have hopes that you'll someday be my wife."

Joy fought with worry deep inside. She could see from Matthew's eyes that he meant what he said, but she didn't want to hope too much. She wasn't sure she could take getting hurt again.

"And your parents?" It was the question that worried her the most. "What do they think?"

"I've already talked to them. They're beginning to understand."

She stood there quietly, trying to take in his words. He watched her for a moment before again reaching into his jacket pocket.

"I have something for you. I was going to wait until tomorrow, on Christmas, to give you this, but it couldn't wait." His hand held a small wooden disk, and he extended it to her. It was a tree circle, sanded down and stained so the natural colors of the rings came through.

"If someday you're willing to marry me, Joy, know that I will do my best to love you in the thin spaces as I do through the thick ones."

"Through thick or thin. I heard that at an *Englisch* wedding once."

"*Ja,* I've heard the phrase before too."

She sighed. "It means more to me now. Just like a tree, we will know hard years and plentiful ones. And being committed to both will carry us through. And yes, Matthew. I will marry you. I long to be your wife, almost as much as I long to draw close to God."

Matthew extended his hand, and Joy placed her hand in his. His skin felt warm, and her breaths quickened as he squeezed.

Then, without warning, Matthew pulled her into his arms, and placed upon her lips the softest kiss. It was a kiss of forgiveness, of love, and of hope. That was where she wanted to stay forever — with Matthew, in his arms. And now she knew for certain —

that was also exactly where he wanted her to be.

EPILOGUE

Christians never meet for the last time.
AMISH PROVERB

Alicia stood at the doorway of the warehouse, looking at the space that was nearly empty. All the props had been packed up and stored in Sarasota somewhere. They'd all worked hard. They'd done their best, and now it was up to the viewers. If the show got good ratings and the network approved a second season, then they'd be back. She liked the idea of that. She looked forward to working with Rowan on this very set. She always loved working with her husband, which is now what she called him again.

Alicia also especially looked forward to spending more time with Joy. She'd purchased a gift for her and dropped it off — a cell phone.

"You don't have to use it for anyone but me," Alicia had told her, "but I need to be able to talk to you, Joy. I need to be able to hear your voice and have someone speak some sense into me when all the Hollywood voices fill my head." Thankfully, Joy agreed.

Alicia heard a car park outside, and she knew it was there to take her to the airport. Rowan's assistant had arranged for her luggage to be picked up, and then her. He'd gone ahead to his next job, and she couldn't wait to join him in Canada, despite the cold there.

She'd said her good-byes to Joy last night, but still she hesitated. She'd discovered so much in Pinecraft. She'd discovered so much about herself and about friendship. Mostly, she'd discovered so much about God.

Finally, Alicia brushed a strand of hair back from her forehead and took a deep breath, heading out. She had nearly reached the car when she noticed someone hurrying her direction. It was an Amish woman. It was Joy!

Alicia moved in her direction. She laughed when she noticed Joy carried a big bundle in her arms.

Joy paused right before Alicia, panting. "I have something for you. I know you have to go, but I don't want you to go without this." Then, without hesitating, Joy pulled a large quilt from the bag.

Alicia gasped. It was one of the most colorful quilts she'd ever seen, with blues, purples, and reds designed in an intricate checkered pattern. She ran her fingers over the design, now understanding how much work had gone into this. "Oh, my goodness. It's so beautiful!"

"It's the one my Aunt Martha made."

"It's yours? The one you kept on your bed? Oh no, Joy, I can't keep it."

Joy shook her head, refusing to listen. She pushed the quilt into Alicia's hands. "It's mine, and I want to give it to you. I want you to remember me when you're gone. More than that, I want you to remember that God is stitching together every piece of your life." Joy chuckled. "Besides, in Canada, I think you're going to need it far more than I need it in Pinecraft."

Alicia didn't know what to say, and so she did the only thing she knew to do. She gently set the quilt on the backseat of the car and then pulled Joy into an embrace. And with her friend in her arms she said a silent prayer of thanksgiving and hope. Her future was different because of this friend, and Alicia hoped someday her story would bring hope to the lives of many others too.

Somehow she knew it would. God had

brought her this far, and He would see her through to the end.

READER'S GUIDE

1. What did you find unique about Pinecraft, Florida? What surprised you about the setting?
2. What are the specific themes in *Sewn with Joy*? What did you take away as a reader?
3. In what ways did you relate to Joy? Does she remind you of yourself or someone you know? If so, how?
4. Alicia's pain and struggles are revealed more as the book goes on. How do you feel about the struggles she faced? Do you think they are true to life?
5. *Sewn with Joy* gives glimpses of the characters from *Made with Love* and *Planted with Hope*. In what ways are the sisters different? How are they the same?
6. How well do you feel the Amish community is represented in this book? Did you learn anything new about the Amish?
7. Who is your favorite character in the novel? Why?

8. What do you appreciate about Joy and Matthew's relationship? Do you find it realistic? Why or why not?
9. What part of this novel most surprised you?
10. What did you learn about God's grace in this novel?
11. What recipe do you want to try?
12. What was your favorite Amish proverb in the book? Why?
13. Who would you recommend this book to?

LIST OF RECIPES

ABOUT THE AUTHORS

Tricia Goyer is an inspiring wife, mom of ten, and grandmother of two. A *USA Today* bestselling author, Tricia has published over 55 books and has written more than 500 articles. She's well known for her Big Sky and Seven Brides for Seven Bachelors Amish series. Tricia loves cooking, reading, homeschooling, and mentoring teenage mothers in her community.

Sherry Gore is the author of *Simply Delicious Amish Cooking* and *Me, Myself, and Pie* and is a weekly scribe for the national edition of the Amish newspaper, the *Budget*. Sherry's culinary adventures have been seen on *NBC Daytime, Today.com,* and *Mr. Food Test Kitchen.* Sherry is a resident of Sarasota, Florida, the vacation paradise of the Plain People. She has three children and is a member of a Beachy Amish Mennonite church.

The employees of Thorndike Press hope you have enjoyed this Large Print book. All our Thorndike, Wheeler, and Kennebec Large Print titles are designed for easy reading, and all our books are made to last. Other Thorndike Press Large Print books are available at your library, through selected bookstores, or directly from us.

For information about titles, please call:
(800) 223-1244

or visit our Web site at:
http://gale.cengage.com/thorndike

To share your comments, please write:
Publisher
Thorndike Press
10 Water St., Suite 310
Waterville, ME 04901